Handfast

SARA BROWNE SERIES BOOK 3

Tricia T. LaRochelle

FLAMING HEART PRESS

Manufactured in the United States of America

ISBN: 979-8-9861756-4-5 (ebook)

ISBN: 979-8-9861756-5-2 (print)

Published by Flaming Heart Press, United States of America

Distributed by Ingram Book Group

Cover design by 17 Studio Book Design

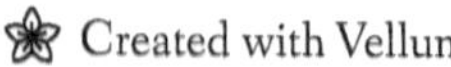 Created with Vellum

Praise for the SARA BROWNE SERIES

"LaRochelle's third installment in the Sara Browne series is a winning tale filled with vibrant characters, a compelling story-line, and a sweet sexy romance." —The Prairies Book Review

"Tricia LaRochelle understands what makes an effective romance story work. She doesn't just offer a girl-meets-boy setup. What she assembles is an interesting pair of characters with flaws that make them distinct, relatable, and utterly human. She handles Sara's traumatic past with sensitivity and keen attention to its emotional and psychological components, which makes Sara a convincing and fascinating case study in PTSD." —Readers' Favorite

"LaRochelle writes like a pro and delivers a profoundly entertaining romance story with genuinely flawed characters and a deftly handled plot with explosive moments. The prose is dazzling, the first-person narrative voice is expertly executed, and the dialogues sparkle from page to page." —The Book Commentary

I dedicate this book to all the brave women out there who face adversity and triumph against it and to my niece, Jess, who is one of the bravest people I know.

Handfast

Prologue

Excitement fizzed inside of me like champagne. Today was August twenty-fifth, one of the best days of the year. Why? Because on August twenty-fifth, three years ago, I had met Scott Williams at a tailgate party on campus. It was my first party, actually, and my first big step toward creating a semblance of a college social life.

Initially, I had forgotten the actual date, but Scott sure hadn't. In fact, he treated our anniversary as if it were a national holiday, bringing me flowers, writing me love notes, taking me out for fancy dinners, and always ready for plenty of lovemaking at the end of the evening. (Unless the dinner was going to be a feast, then we'd take care of that part beforehand.)

This year, he went a step beyond, *making* me dinner instead of paying for one (lasagna, which he knew was my favorite, with garlic bread and even a salad). For dessert, he had gone to a local bakery and picked up a chocolate cake with pink icing shaped like a heart, which he placed in the center of the table.

"Why don't you cut us a piece," he said, handing me a large knife after he had picked up the dinner dishes and placed a small plate and a clean fork in front of each of us. That's right, he did the dishes, too.

After smelling hints of vanilla and buttercream throughout dinner, I was dying to dig in. Only when I plunged the knife into the delectable-looking pink icing, the blade hit something hard. I wondered if it was a rat, a finger, or something disgusting you hear about on the news. (I was definitely a glass-half-empty kind of girl.)

Only, the obstruction wasn't a rat or a finger.

Scott's whole vibe screamed with excitement. His pupils dilated. "What in the hell did they put in our cake?" he said with what sounded like mock annoyance. I knew because he smiled as he said those words. *Smiled?* He was practically bouncing in his chair like a little boy who was about to get his favorite gift from Santa himself.

I poked my fingers gingerly into the cake and pulled out the last thing I had expected to find: a small white cardboard box.

Huh?

I looked up at Scott, his eyes dark and intense, his lips fidgety as though holding something back he was dying to say. Something important.

That was when my heart galloped like a horse running down a track. "What's this?"

As Scott handed me a damp washcloth, which he had cleverly pulled out of nowhere—and I wiped my hands and the small box clean—I thought about the first gift Scott had ever given me: a white gold pendant with two dainty hearts entwined, each bedazzled with tiny diamonds. "*Those hearts are you and me,*" he'd said.

Even though the contents of *this* smaller box could have been another necklace or even a bracelet, somehow, I didn't think so. Instead, the flush of blood rushing into Scott's cheeks and the anticipation surging from his eyes told me this was an even *specialer* gift.

I opened the box to find another smaller box clad in red velvet.

Scott took the box from my hand (his own hand trembling) and got down on one knee. He swallowed, his eyes brimming with emotion.

He opened the box, its tiny hinges creaking.

By now, my heart had gone from galloping to nearly stopping. Mainly because one rather large diamond stared up at me from the palm of Scott's hand, its stone glistening brilliantly against the sun beaming through the dining room window, two smaller stones flanking it, all wrapped in a silver-colored band. I'd never seen a ring more beautiful.

"It's a three-stone baguette diamond in platinum," he said with a shrug. "That's what the dude who sold it to me said."

It was stunning. And it also looked expensive, the stones larger than I was used to seeing. My hands flew to my mouth as my jaw dropped, my eyes wider than wide.

"I hope you didn't pay too much for it," I said, still in awe of the ring that looked like it belonged to a royal or a celebrity. My stomach did flip-flops but in a good way.

Scott made a tsking sound. "Don't be silly. You're worth every penny." He paused as though trying to gather his thoughts—or maybe remember the speech he had rehearsed in his head. "I've waited three years to say this to you." He took my hand, breathing labored, his cheeks now the color of a wild-caught Maine lobster.

I'd never seen Scott so nervous. I'd seen him upset, angry, worried, and shocked—heck, I'd even seen him depressed—but never nervous. Not *fun* nervous, anyway.

He sucked in a breath and began. "Before I met you, I had

no idea what being in love was like. I thought I knew, but I didn't have a clue. Being with you has taught me so much these past few years. Not only are you the most gorgeous creature I have ever laid eyes on ..." He smirked, his eyes dancing with erotic thoughts, something I saw whenever he was "in the mood," which was pretty much all the time. "And sexy as hell, but you are braver than anyone I've ever known." A shadow fell over his face. "On top of that, and even after all you have been through, you still have the biggest heart. Being with you makes me want to be a better person." He shook his head and exhaled. "I find myself imagining things I never thought I'd want."

"Like what?" The words tumbled out of my mouth like a five-year-old with no self-control.

The corners of his luscious lips twitched upward. "Well, for starters ... a house ... with kids ... a dog. The thought of *you* mothering my children someday makes me believe that dreams *can* come true." He looked down for a moment and shook his head again before pinning my gaze with his vibrant blue eyes. "I realize you're too good for me. And I also know that I don't deserve you, but fuck if that's going to stop me from asking you the most important question of my life." He inched closer, his irises locking me in place, his voice low and imploring. "After we graduate next spring, Sara Browne, will you do me the honor of being my wife?"

My eyes welling with tears, I leaned forward and fell into his big, burly arms, his musky scent welcoming and his lips tapping tiny kisses against my head and cheek. "Of course I will. I can't imagine anyone else as my husband or the father of my children. So, yes, yes, yes," I said, giddy and slightly dizzy from the emotions swirling through my head, my heart, and every cell of my body.

Holding me close, Scott stood, easing me upward. He

wiped his eyes free of mist, and then after releasing one very long breath, he pulled back and placed the ring on my left finger, the one designated for this particular piece of jewelry.

Once I had stopped crying and Scott's breathing had returned to normal, I gazed up at him, wondering how to reciprocate his powerful gesture.

As if Scott were reading my mind, he took my hand, his gaze roaming all over my body, his eyes glowing with mischief. He rubbed his jaw as three words escaped from his lips: "Dance for me?"

Back when I was at the boarding school, I'd spent most of my free time alone, especially on the weekends and some holidays (the ones Abigail couldn't make the trip for). My self-imposed isolation earned me the nickname "cave girl," which I never outlived. Not there, anyway.

To pass the time, I would often turn up the music on my wireless speakers and dance around my room—sometimes when I was cleaning or sometimes when I just felt like getting into a groove. No one could see me, so what did it matter? I was able to go nuts without fear of being mocked by my suitemates or my snobby roommate, Claire.

Years later, when I was cleaning and dancing in my dorm room, someone did notice: Scott. Interestingly enough, the song was quite sexy, and I was thinking about him as I danced around, straightening up and dusting. When the song ended, he pushed through the door—the one I had *thought* was closed —and said, "That was one of the sexiest things I've ever seen." The bulge in his pants agreed—although just bending down to pick up something from the floor would cause the same reaction from him. Scott was insatiable sexually, which I often told him. "Only with you," he'd say, which always brought a smile to my face and a lift to my heart.

For weeks, Scott went on about how "hot" my dance was and how much he'd like to see it again. And so, I researched new songs that I thought would be fun to work with and even choreographed a few dance moves to go along with them. I watched a movie or two involving women dancing, some in strip clubs (a girl could have fun), and surprised him every now and then with a *dance*. Sometimes, my dances were sensual or artistic, and other times they were just plain raunchy, which I knew would please Scott the most. In those cases, I'd finished with barely any clothes on. Every time I danced for him, we'd celebrate my performance by making love. It was sexy, it was fun, and it was something we shared just between us.

I had already been working on a few songs I hoped Scott would like. One stood out from the rest: Rihanna's "Diamonds." What could be more appropriate, I decided, the ring twinkling from my finger in support.

"I would love to dance for you," I said.

I changed into a tight pair of super-short shorts and a low-cut tank, no bra. Scott had already cleared the coffee table out of the way, along with anything else that could possibly provide an obstacle. He anchored his chair at the edge of the room where he sat, his hands resting on his thighs, anticipation vibrating off him like sound waves. Scott often drummed his palms to the beat, his body swaying just a bit to show me he was into the song. His eyes said he was into me.

With the gorgeous ring adorning my finger and his proposal still blooming in my heart, I felt artistic, sensual, *and* a bit raunchy. So I gave him all three. Following the rhythm, I twirled, I thrusted, and I bent over, looking at him between my bare legs. I rolled on the floor, losing myself in the feeling of my body, the music, and Scott's gaze.

He sat there, my captive audience of one, his eyes taking it all in, the swell in his pants ready to satisfy. As the song was nearing its end, I stood over Scott, my legs encasing his strong thighs, my bare feet kissing the imitation parquet flooring. I ran my hands seductively from my stomach up over my breasts as I flipped my hair back. Then I arched backward and used one foot to push off Scott's powerful chest as I performed a backward walkover (the one I had practiced a gazillion times) that ended in a forward split. By the time the song ended, Scott was practically drooling, which was what I was aiming for.

"You fucking turn me on like no one else," he said in a low-and-husky voice. "Get over here, woman, before I explode." He used his index finger to beckon.

As my encore, I crawled over to him and slowly rose up over his lap like a panther, my eyes undressing him, my mind intent on one thing: pleasing. As he lifted his hips, I yanked his gym shorts down, freeing him from restraint. Seconds later, his shirt was off and thrown to the side.

I slid my hands up and down his chiseled abdomen, enjoying the softness of his skin against the firmness of his muscles. Then I started at his neck and licked my way down to his impressive erection, which eagerly awaited.

Scott tipped his head back and ran his fingers through my hair while I devoured him. Every moan that escaped from his lips encouraged me to work harder. He moved my head back and lifted my chin, so he could connect with my lips. Our tongues swirled around each other, hungry for more, as I rose.

Scott wasted no time pulling my top off and inching down my shorts before I straddled his lap and guided him inside of me. While Scott licked and suckled my breasts, I moved my hips up and down until a torrent of sensations forced me to cry out. "Oh my God."

Scott gripped my hips, helping me move, his breathing

labored. "You feel so fucking good," he said before "Holy shit" shot from his mouth like a cannon.

A moment later, I climaxed, too, my body spasming with pleasure on a level that I'd grown to expect. My lungs strained to breathe, my muscles turning to hot lava.

It was the best proposal any girl could ever hope for.

Chapter One

The following spring ...

"Thank you, Provost Shipman, for that kind introduction. It is my honor to be here at Commonwealth University to deliver this year's commencement address."

The presenter was a CEO of a local nonprofit, Aliza something (I didn't catch her last name), who had graduated from the college eight years ago. Aliza's dark skin popped against her red skirt and matching blazer. She wore a crisp, white blouse underneath and a smile one could only describe as *winning*. Aliza spoke with pride about her years at Commonwealth University and how the institution had helped mold her into the successful and savvy businesswoman she was today.

Behind Aliza, the sky wore a vibrant blue for this special day in May. A few powder-white clouds drifted overhead like sailboats across a calm sea. An abundance of flowers, greenery, and potted trees cluttered the stage, offering color and lushness for the photogenic platform. An enormous flat-screen stood at the back, capturing every moment for the families and allowing presenters to appear larger than life. Thick metal poles hoisted large speakers amplifying every syllable.

As Aliza's speech continued, I thought about the past four years and what a blur they had been. They say "Time flies when you're having fun" and it had, even when it wasn't so fun. After the rape that nearly destroyed me, and after our psychotic art teacher kidnapped and almost murdered Amy and me, my life went back to normal, or as normal as one could expect for someone like me—a magnet for tragedy.

It took me a year to stop bracing for the next catastrophe at any given moment or to realize that some other creep wasn't lurking in the shadows, waiting to take me down. The rape—by my classmate, Rick Sweet, whom I had considered my friend at the time—would always be a part of me. Physically, I was fine. My internal wounds were another story. I was healing, but I would never be quite the same. Although, as time passed, the trauma began to shed my system like a bad case of chicken pox. I was left to rebuild ... again. At least I wasn't alone on my journey to recovery. I had the best boyfriend and best friend a girl could ever ask for: I had Scott and Amy.

Speaking of Amy, a small gust of wind pushed through, carrying an assortment of colognes and perfumes, along with one other, more distinctive smell. *Was someone smoking marijuana?* I chuckled to myself. It was probably Amy. She could be such a brat.

But really, my best friend was amazing. She'd gotten me through the rape, and when we were kidnapped and almost murdered, Amy became more than my friend. She became my sister. To this day, I still can't believe Dr. Adams had everyone fooled. He had been our favorite professor, one who'd taught art, no less. A creative man. With his impeccable credentials and non-threatening demeanor, he'd been many of our peers' favorite teacher. Several students were devastated when they heard the news that their caring teacher had really been a serial killer. He had flown under everyone's radar.

Scott, Amy, Luke (Amy's boyfriend), and I considered pressing charges against the school. How could they let this happen? But they had been so attentive, paying our medical bills, setting up counseling, and offering us full scholarships for our remaining terms, we chose not to. They also instituted self-defense classes on campus, tightened security, and added more rideshare programs with vetted drivers. We met with the administration on multiple occasions, offering our advice, which they used to make the campus safer, conducting additional background checks on all staff members. And from what Sheriff Murphy had informed us, this wasn't the first school Dr. Adams had taught at. It was just the first one where they caught him.

The counseling came in handy. And we needed a lot, even Scott and Luke, who had helped save us. Whether you were the victim or the one supporting the victim, a person couldn't possibly go through something as horrific as we had and *not* need mental help. Scott stopped seeing his guy, Dr. Cannon, last year, but I still sought advice from Dr. Zeller from time to time.

The four of us also discussed transferring out, but we didn't want to be separated—at least Amy and I didn't—and no one could agree on a school that had everything we all needed.

Since the college had already awarded Scott a soccer scholarship, he negotiated a master's program that kept him close while I finished my degree. I loved that he had a reason to stay, one that would only advance his education and his chance at finding a job he enjoyed. He had a passion for architecture, but he also had an interest in computer science. The extra years allowed him to explore both fields to the fullest.

And since Scott still had his apartment, I moved in, officially, anyway. (I was already there most of the time.) Sharing a home with Scott was a dream. Without a minefield of problems between us, I was able to see what *normal* life with my man was like. I was relieved to discover that my hottie of a boyfriend was fairly neat, helpful with chores, always ready for spontaneous fun, and supportive when I stumbled mentally.

Even though I made sure to visit my bonus mom, Abigail, in Vermont often, Scott and I had spent our summers in Charlottesville since Scott needed to remain local for soccer obligations. For those few months, Scott's only job was playing soccer, working construction (part-time) for a friend of his coach's (which only made his muscles toner and his skin tanner), and pleasing me. The general contractor liked Scott so much that he allowed him to work on refining a few blueprints and listened when he offered suggestions on design. Scott would return home on *those* nights, bursting to tell me all about it.

I worked at a small restaurant in town that hired special needs students, mainly because Gwen had asked me to, the girl who I had started tutoring freshman year. In my spare time, I continued to tutor Gwen and a few other students once a week to help strengthen their reading skills.

My little sister, Mel, was a toddler now, which meant she was full of mischief *and* energy.

Whenever I traveled home to Middlebury, I babysat, providing Abigail and Joel with some much-needed date nights. A few times, Scott, who doted on Mel, calling her his little Tasmanian devil or "Tazzie" for short, went with me. It seemed Amy's habit of nicknames was wearing off on him, too.

Aliza brought me back to the moment as she sighed from the stage, her eyes softening and her smile as bright as her red lipstick. "As I look out at all these young and very capable faces, I am inspired and hopeful for the future ... Your generation has dealt with some challenges, but it is those challenges that will make you strong as individuals. If you will indulge me, I'd like to share a story with you ..."

Although the speaker was inspiring, I had a hard time staying focused. This used to be my problem whenever my parents dragged me to church (which only happened on holidays, weddings, or funerals) or to any school function that involved speeches. As the presenters droned on, I'd always find something else on which to center my attention, like the woman sitting two pews up, donning a funny-looking hairdo in church, or a child who kept picking his nose and wiping it on the back of his father's blazer (that happened during Christmas Eve mass).

With nothing but caps and gowns as far as the eye could see—and without an adult here to force me to pay attention—I twirled the dazzling ring around my finger, reminiscing about Scott's proposal from last August and the dance that I had performed for him afterward. Even though I'd danced for him many times over the years, that one held special meaning.

Sex wasn't always easy for me. The first time Scott and I'd made love after the rape, it rejuvenated me. I'd broken through a barrier. And then it was sporadic for about six months, Scott treading lightly before we found our rhythm. Now we couldn't keep our hands off each other, making up for lost time.

From the stage, Aliza continued her speech. "My advice. Stay curious. Don't shy away from a challenge. And don't be afraid to fail. Some of my biggest blunders turned out to be my best lessons in life. Stay passionate about what you do. You have made it this far, and that is something to be proud of. Commonwealth University has rewarded your efforts. Now it's time for you to go out there and show the world what you're made of."

A round of applause erupted from the crowd—moms and

dads full of smiles, a few eyes shining with pride and tears. The air was electric, inspired with the hopes and dreams for our future.

"I believe it's that time when we get to acknowledge each and every one of you with your degrees and your accomplishments. And for that, I will defer to Provost Shipman. Thank you for giving me the opportunity to speak with you today." Aliza placed a hand over her heart. "It's been an honor."

Aliza seemed like a kind woman, and I immediately felt guilty for not listening. For a moment, it was as if my deceased mother were watching *and* scolding me from my shoulder. Although I had caught the finer points, I reassured myself *and her*, if she really was nearby spiritually. Regardless, I knew she'd be proud of this moment. And so would Daddy. *Love you, Mom and Dad.*

As I wiped a tear from the corner of my eye, Aliza stepped away from the platform as more applause filled the gap between one speaker and another.

Sporting a thick gray mustache, the likes of Mark Twain that concealed his upper lip, and donning a full head of matching gray hair, Provost Shipman cleared his throat from the stage. He looked so official in his black cap with gold tassel swinging off to the left and his gown sporting dark, thick stripes across each sleeve, a satin-and-velvet hood plunging down his back—definitely more tailored than what the students wore.

I didn't know the man personally but heard he was approachable with tough standards. After meeting Dr. Adams, I'd given up on getting to know the staff.

"Thank you, Aliza, for that inspiring speech." Provost Shipman slipped on a pair of glasses that made him look even more distinguished.

"I ask everyone for your patience while I read the names of your precious sons and daughters. I will do my best to avoid any embarrassing mistakes." He tapped the rim of his glasses. "I just upped my prescription, so let's hope these babies do their job."

Murmurs and laughter drifted over the heads of the crowd.

A few more announcements followed, and then it was time for the awarding of diplomas. Since my last name was Browne, I was on stage in no time. Scott stood and whistled, his hands clapping high above his head. Other people cheered, too, but all I could see was my handsome and very tall fiancé, who was practically jumping up and down.

When his time came, I was happy to return the favor with several two-finger whistles and plenty of "Yahoos."

* * *

Once the formalities were over and we'd thrown our caps, I found Scott as he was heading in my direction through the massive-sized crowd. His height and blond curly hair always made him easy to spot—my adorable flag—especially today, among the teary-eyed parents and screaming students. "Congratulations" came from everywhere, yelps and laughter filling the air like confetti.

"Congratulations, Babe," Scott said, whisking me up in his arms and spinning me around. His soft lips found my cheek, my mouth, and then my cheek again.

"Congratulations to you, too." I brought my mouth to his ear. "I got bored during all the speeches and started thinking about last August when you proposed to me."

Scott's dimple winked at me from the left corner of his mouth as he lowered my wedge sandals to the grassy field. "Oh, yeah?" He stared down at me, his smile encouraging.

"Uh-huh, and remember the dance I performed for you afterward?" Before he could answer, I pulled him closer and playfully bit his earlobe. I wasn't normally like this, but with all the excitement stirring around me, I was ripe and ready to be plucked. "Do you also remember the way I licked your—"

"Jesus, Babe. What are you trying to do to me?" Eyes wide, Scott half coughed, half cleared his throat, his cheeks ruddy. He spoke under his breath. "That kind of talk is gonna get both of us in trouble. It's probably not the best time for me to have a hard dick right now if that's okay with you." He kissed the top of my head, his smile widening. "But later, when we're alone, you can show me exactly what you're talking about. I'm always up for that."

"Yes, you are," I said, my mind filled with dirty thoughts. "This is your fault, you know."

Scott brought his lips to mine. "Oh, yeah? How's that exactly?"

I kissed him and then said, "You created a monster."

"Scott, over here." From about fifty feet away, Mrs. Williams came running over, waving her arms frantically, Scott's sister, Kelsey, on her heels.

"One of my proudest accomplishments. And you fuck like one, too, my little she-beast." Scott tapped my nose, clearly loving the teasing between us.

Shaking my head and wrinkling my nose, I pulled back and jabbed him in the ribs.

"Ouch."

And that was all we had time for before his mother ran up and thrust her arms around her Herculean son. "Congratulations, honey. We are so proud of you." She pulled back and then embraced me next. "And we are just as proud of you, too, Sara, dear."

Kelsey joined in the fray.

Scott's father wasn't coming, but he'd made a point to call Scott on FaceTime last night to congratulate him.

"I'm sorry, son. There are too many graduations going on around town, and I'm limited on staff at the dealership."

Since he'd made Scott's undergrad graduation, Scott cut him some slack.

"It's okay, Dad, I understand."

"We'll celebrate when you get home, son. Sound good?"

Scott's voice lifted. "I'll be ready. Hey, who the hell are the Steelers trading now? ..."

And that was where their conversation lost me. Of course, I relished watching them talk on the phone, mostly discussing sports teams and who was going to draft who. It was their tone that I enjoyed the most, loose and easy, devoid of years of tension and angst.

The father-son cease-fire had officially started when the kidnapping story involving me and Amy had hit the airways. In fact, Mr. Williams had arrived at Scott's apartment within hours. Apparently, he'd left right from work. Didn't even collect Scott's mother, who had shown up the next morning. We had just returned from having dinner with Abigail and Joel in town and were lounging at home in our flannels when a knock at the door had startled me. I thought it was Abigail at first, but at the time, I knew she was tired during dinner and eager to get back to her hotel room and rest. She was also *very* pregnant then, her feet swollen, right along with her belly. Joel had promised her a foot massage, which had sealed the deal. Once she knew I was safe and sound, all her energy had drained.

My second thought was the press. Had they found us? Since the hospital released me, we'd had Scott's place to ourselves. I was worried our fortress of solitude had reached its expiration date.

When Scott answered the door, however, we were both

surprised to discover Mr. Williams standing there in the cold February darkness.

"Dad, what are you doing here?" Scott's tone was edgy, his spine stiffening, and I was sure Mr. Williams had noticed it. I crept up behind my sweetheart and placed my hand on the small of his back, hoping he received my unspoken message: *I'm right here, Handsome.*

Scott sighed and pulled me closer, his arm draped over my shoulders, his head leaning sideways over mine.

Mr. Williams raised a palm in a peace offering sort of way. "I'm not here to fight with you, son. I just heard about what happened."

His gaze slid over to me next. "Were you really kidnapped? By a teacher?"

I nodded, Scott pulling me closer and kissing my head. I could feel his relief and the strain that whole experience had put on him.

"Who in the hell vets the staff here?" Mr. Williams threw a hand up, ready to release a dump-truck-sized load of complaints.

Now it was time for Scott to raise a palm. He shook his head. "Dad, we're too tired for this. She's home, she's safe, and right now, that feels pretty damn good."

Mr. Williams opened his mouth and then closed it. He tightened his lips and swallowed as though trying to rethink his approach. That was when I had stepped out of Scott's embrace and taken hold of his father's arm. "Mr. Williams, please come in. Let me tell you about what a hero your son is."

To my surprise, Mr. Williams sat at our dining room table and did nothing but listen. I knew this was atypical behavior, especially from what I'd seen up to that point. His previous visit had been a total disaster that ended in a pushing match between Scott and his dad, their tempers out of control.

Ten minutes later, Scott's father removed his coat, draped it over his chair, and listened some more, his brow bearing down, his eyes taking it all in. At one point, Scott brewed a pot of coffee, which they both enjoyed, and a cup of tea for me.

When I finished explaining the whole sordid mess—leaving nothing out about Scott confronting Dr. Adams and finding us in the woods (and making sure he knew it was Scott who had solved the case)—Scott's dad stood abruptly, which prompted Scott to do the same. I thought he was going to leave, which seemed like a strange thing to do, although I knew impulsive behavior in the Williams family ran like springtime sap through a maple tree. At least it did with father and son. Only he didn't leave. Instead, Mr. Williams approached Scott and paused for a second. Or maybe it was a few seconds because it felt like hours. All at once, Mr. Williams opened his arms wide and hugged Scott, patting his back for emphasis.

Tears rushed to my eyes, my heart brimming over with sentiment.

"You did what I would've done. We protect our own. That was very brave, son." He detached himself but kept a firm grip on Scott's shoulders. "You did me proud." He nodded once, his jaw tight with certainty, before he let go.

In my mind, Scott transformed into a ten-year-old boy, standing before a man he had once idolized. Most parents wore the badge of hero at one point in their children's lives—that was until that child grew up and learned otherwise. Scott had battled with his dad for years, and now it appeared that battle had come to an end.

I was so glad I had been there to witness it firsthand.

Scott swallowed, the muscles in his jaw flexing as though trying their best to hold back a monsoon of tears that so desperately wanted to overflow from his eyes. Scott rarely cried, but I sensed he was about to release decades of pent-up sorrow in that moment—if only he had allowed himself. Which he hadn't —not when his father was there. Regardless, it had been a huge first step for them both. Gargantuan.

As the graduation crowds milled about like a gaggle of human-sized geese—and just as loud as one—the memory brought a smile to my lips. I was happy for Scott and his family.

Speaking of families, where was mine?

I stood on a chair to get a better look, and then I saw them: Abigail, Joel, and Mel weaving through the crowd like thread through a needle.

I waved my arms over my head like an aircraft marshaller guiding airplanes to their hubs. "Abigail, Joel, over here," I screamed.

Abigail smiled and nudged Joel, who took Mel's hand as the three of them approached.

I jumped down.

Just as Mel crashed into my legs, Abigail pulled me in for a very long hug. "Congratulations. You did it. We are so proud of you." She smelled of lavender and motherly love.

Joel stood back and smiled, the way he always did when Abigail and I were reuniting or sentimental.

Even though Joel wasn't my natural father, and I'd only known him for a handful of years, he had done a good job of providing a stable home for Abigail, Mel, and me. During the summer months, when I stayed with them, he always made me feel welcome and part of the family. My babysitting skills didn't hurt matters.

When Abigail released me, I scooped Mel up in my arms, her hair a bouquet of bubblegum-scented shampoo and her breath a burst of fruit juice, which she'd probably just finished in the car, the evidence forming a faint pink ring around her lips. She wore a pair of red leggings with pink hearts all over them and a pink T-shirt with a large red heart at its center to match. What a cutie.

"Hi, Sawa," she said between those puffy cheeks I wanted to squeeze every time I saw them.

Mel hadn't quite formed her "r's" yet, or her "l's" for that matter, which made my nickname all the more precious.

"How's my baby sister?"

She furrowed her brow, her hazel eyes scolding. "I'm not a baby," she said with a forced frown until I tickled it away, and she yelped.

That got Scott's attention. He came over and tapped Mel on the nose. "Hey, Tazzie," he said, making her blush.

Yup, he could even make a three-year-old blush.

For the next several minutes, both Scott's family and mine greeted each other and discussed how happy they were about our accomplishments. The two moms talked about the upcoming nuptials, even though we hadn't set a date yet. If it were up to Scott, we'd be married tomorrow or yesterday (and probably by the justice of the peace), but I figured there was no hurry. I could enjoy being Scott's fiancée just a little bit longer. We had our whole lives to be together, and what a great feeling that was.

For about five minutes, I let that thought comfort me like a fresh glass of lemonade on a hot summer day. And then something strange happened. Amid all the positive vibes swirling around me like a magic spell, I developed a bad case of inexplicable shivers. An odd sensation prickled up my spine as I put Mel down to relieve my arms of strain. I'd only experienced this feeling a few times in my life, and I never liked it much. The last time was when Rachael, the girl who hated me for dating Scott, was gawking down at me from a second-story window in the library during my freshman year, her arrogant eyes shooting daggers. *Was someone watching me now?* In a busy place full of life and energy, my mind slowed, and my heart raced.

It couldn't be Rachael. She had transferred out two years ago, thank God. And then another haunting thought whittled away at my resolve. Was Rick here? Last I heard, he had moved out of state. According to his father, the senator, Rick had changed his ways.

As the people around me joked and chatted, and Mel ran around my legs, playing peekaboo with Scott, who crouched down, giving her his full attention, the heebie-jeebies continued to niggle at my nerves.

What is happening?

All at once, the reason for my discomfort emerged from the crowd. A big reason. For a moment, time stood still. What was I seeing? I blinked, and then I blinked again. It wasn't possible. My father died ten years ago. I knew this because I was there when it happened. So, what was he doing here now?

Chapter Two

The strange yet familiar man was tall, just like my dad —maybe six foot one—his shoulders broad, his sandy-colored hair, slightly long but clipped just above his collar, and his hairline starting to recede. The top of his off-white oxford was open an extra button, allowing the material to fan out, framing his oval face. His pale-blue eyes were just like the ones that stared back at me every time I gazed into a mirror.

As my father's lookalike stepped closer, a few gray hairs shimmered against the sun. He was older, yet he was the same. And then he looked at me, and my legs turned to cooked spaghetti, my head as light as helium. If my heart was beating, I was oblivious.

Scott stopped playing with Mel and rose. "Are you okay, Babe? You're as white as a ghost." He clutched my arm, giving it a gentle rattle. "What's wrong?"

A cacophony of voices whirled past my ears, colors blurring, the earth spinning. The only distinct thing was those eyes, so familiar, bolting me in place. It was a dream come true. *It isn't real.*

My breath hitched as I tried to figure out how in the logical world my father had come back from the grave. I took hold of Scott's arm to steady myself.

He examined me, his hands clamping down on both of my arms now. "You're scaring me," he said. At least I thought he did.

I couldn't speak. And even if I could, what would I say? *I think my father just came back from the dead?* I knew it wasn't *really* him, but the resemblance was remarkable. Was he a twin?

My father never spoke much about his family. All I knew was that they lived in Ireland. There was *one* instance when I was ten years old. I found him pacing the kitchen one Saturday afternoon in August. He kept rubbing his jaw and moving his head around as one would do when having a nonverbal conversation with themselves, his neck corded. I remembered this because I had cracked the window in our garage the day before when I was throwing my softball against the outer wall. For fear of punishment, I didn't tell anyone. Maybe they'd assume a fallen branch had done it, which was my reasoning at the time.

As he paced, I was sure he knew what I'd done. With my head hanging low, my eyes filled with remorse and an equal measure of tears, I entered the kitchen ready to bare my soul.

"I'm sorry about the window, Daddy." I remember laying it on pretty thick with my *sad-girl* act—my lower lip out so far you could trip over it. I *was* sad but even more terrified.

My parents weren't angry people, and they weren't overly strict, either. For the most part, we got along pretty well. Maybe that was why I hated disappointing them, and believe me, I remembered every time I'd done so. The letdown expression on my parents' faces, the words they didn't say but felt. Honesty was a biggie in our house, especially when something got damaged. Looking back, it wasn't a big deal, but back then, it felt like the world was ending.

When he saw me, my dad snapped out of his funk and said, "Window? What window?"

His blue eyes dismantled me, and I explained myself, knowing full well that since I hadn't told anyone about it, I would probably get a week or two added to my punishment, which usually involved doing extra chores and limited screen time—or none at all. For a ten-year-old, that was plenty—my parents' disappointed expressions being the worst of it.

"I can pay for it with my allowance." Considering I used to make five dollars a week to clean my room, fold the laundry, and help Daddy with whatever outdoor chores he needed, I knew it would take some time to settle my account.

As though I had disappeared, my father stared right through me. "Have you seen your mom?" He rubbed his chin again, the corners of his eyes wrinkled, right along with his brow, his shoulders higher than normal.

"She's in the basement doing laundry," I think I said, wondering if he had heard me correctly. "About the window—"

He waved me off. "Yeah, yeah. I'll order a new one."

I'll order a new one? This was *not* my dad's typical reaction. First of all, my parents weren't CEOs or rich by any stretch of the imagination, and money was often tight, my dad being a custodian and my mom, a teacher at the local high school. My mother's parents died when she was young, and she had to work her way through college, applying for every scholarship she said she could get. My dad's parents remained a mystery, mainly because we never spoke about them. Every time I tried, he'd just shut me down or change the subject.

Anyway, on that particular day, my dad plunked himself down at the kitchen table and released a heavy breath, one loaded with angst. "I have to go … meet someone. I'll be back soon." He stared off into space, his face unusually drawn.

"Who?" I asked, perplexed by his behavior. My dad and I complemented each other like burgers and fries. Most of the time, we were inseparable. "Can I go?" I had asked.

He didn't answer.

I moved closer and nudged his shoulder. "Daddy, I said, 'Can I go?'"

Once again, he snapped out of his somber mood and shook his head. "No. Sorry, munchkin, not this time."

"Why? Where are you going? I want to go with you!" I said, being the annoying ten-year-old that I was. "We can get ice cream at Rosie's diner afterward. Come on, Daddy. It will be fun."

My father leapt to his feet, his chair nearly toppling over backward. "I said, NO! Now go find your mother."

I jolted.

He wasn't angry about the window. In fact, I wasn't even sure he remembered me telling him about it, but the mere suggestion that I go with him had shot his temper through the roof like a rocket.

"Is something wrong at your job?" I tried to process what was happening.

"No. This has nothing to do with my job, Sara. Now go find your mother." He tightened his face and gave me a stare that said "Don't push me, kid." I could count on one hand the number of times I'd witnessed it.

Then he pointed toward the basement door. "Now!"

I assumed he *was* angry with me after all. Being ten, I had no idea. I dragged my feet toward the basement door with my tail between my legs. "Okay. Sorry, Daddy."

My dad ran a hand down his face. He released another distressed breath. "I'm sorry, munchkin. I'm not happy about seeing this person. I'm sure your mom would appreciate you helping her with the laundry," he said as he snatched his truck keys off a hook on the wall and left.

When I found my mother in the basement folding clothes, I pummeled her with questions like I was a pitching machine at a ballpark. "Daddy is upset. ... Do you know why? ... He left. ... He said he had to go meet someone. ... Do you know who it is? ... I wanted to go with him, but he wouldn't let me. ... Why not? ... It's Saturday. ... I could've sat in the car. ... He always lets me go. ..." And I was just getting started.

Finally, my mother dropped the shirt she was folding and raised a palm. "My goodness, Sara, enough with the questions." She stared at me for a few seconds as though contemplating what to say. Then, she sighed. "Your father has only one sibling. A brother. And he's in town. He contacted your dad last night and asked to meet with him."

His brother? My dad had a brother? I had an uncle?

That filled my head with a gumball-sized machine of more questions. "But—"

"Wait." She took my hand and led me over to the basement steps, where she encouraged me to sit, then took the spot next to me. "You're growing up, so I can tell you a little bit more, but you have to promise me." She pointed with an authoritarian finger. "Promise me that you won't ask me any more questions and that you won't talk to your father about it. Ever." She tilted her head, her eyes as serious as they got.

I knew she wasn't kidding around.

"If you *can't* do that, I won't be able to tell you anything. This is a sensitive subject for your dad, and I need you to keep quiet about it."

Hearing the words *sensitive subject* had me eager to know more. My family never had secrets, not big ones like this one. I would have promised the moon and the stars to find out more about my father's private life. Instead, I used my index finger to draw a large cross over my heart. "Cross my heart, Mommy." I recall thinking, *I can do this.* I'd never told Daddy that Mommy threw out his favorite old shoes that she said, "*Stunk to high heaven,*" and I'd never told Mommy that Daddy kept a stash of beer behind his table saw in the shed that he would enjoy after mowing the lawn or landscaping. Not only that, I liked that she thought I was old enough to handle serious issues. It made me feel grown up. Like a big girl.

"Your dad and his brother ... your uncle ... don't get along very well. And they haven't for years. I don't know exactly why, just that it's been going on for a long time. From what your father has told me, his brother and he are very different. He's not as"—she paused and looked up as though trying to find the right word—"responsible and, according to your dad, he's not to be trusted."

"Why is he meeting with him, then?"

My mother lifted her shoulders and let them drop. She wiped a few loose strands of her golden hair off her brow. "Honestly, I'm not sure. His phone call came out of nowhere. Your father didn't even know his brother was in the States."

It all seemed so strange to me.

"Your uncle has some bad habits, from what I understand."

Habits? That sent my mind in a whole new direction. Was he an alcoholic? Or a druggie? Did he have a gambling problem? My mother watched the questions rise in my throat.

"That's enough for now, Sara. I've already told you more than I intended to. And I am trusting you to keep this to yourself." She had stared directly into my eyes, dismantling every impulse to ask more.

In fact, I had never asked another question, not even what the man's name was, even though I really, *really* wanted to know.

Scott's voice pulled me back to the present. "Are you sick? Want me to get you some water?" He searched my face for an explanation, his eyes filled with worry, his hands remaining clamped on the upper portions of my arms. "Answer me, Babe."

"What's wong with Sawa." Mel stared up at me, innocent and curious, her hands holding onto my legs.

The two of them pinned me between them.

Their questions waited in the air just as Abigail took notice of my shocked face. "Sara, what's ..." Her eyes swiveled toward the familiar stranger, who I couldn't for the life of me stop staring at.

"Oh, hello, Aidan. I didn't see you there. We waited for you by the entrance for as long as we could, but we had to get a seat. I'm so glad you found us."

The man named Aidan just stood there, his gaze sliding from Abigail back to me, his eyes tentative.

Joel walked up and shook Aidan's hand. "Sorry, man. She was worried she wouldn't find a good seat."

Aidan nodded once. "Sure thing. I apologize for bein' tardy."

The lilt in his voice was unmistakable, his speech fluid, words running together.

Abigail regarded me as she took a breath and clasped her hands together. She was practically bouncing in her skin. "As you can see, we have a very special surprise for you, Sara." She pivoted her body toward Aidan, which prompted him to take a few steps closer.

"This is your uncle, all the way from Ireland. Isn't that cool?" She stared at me, her eyes brimming with excitement.

I wasn't sure what to do.

"Hi, Aidan" was all I could force out. My dad didn't like this man, and I had to be cautious. Why was he here? What did he want? At the same time, I had this strong desire to wrap my arms around him and never let go.

"Good to meet ya," Aidan said with a strained grin. "I see ya have your da's eyes."

His accent was heavy ... and his words rapid. I loved an Irish brogue. My dad had an accent, too, but it wasn't heavy. From what little I knew, he'd moved to the States when he was much younger. That must've been tough for a man with no connections. And brave. Anytime I asked him about it, he'd just say he wanted a new life. "*Plus, your mother was waiting for me to sweep her off her feet*," he'd add with a twinkle in his eyes and a wink, my mother smiling right along with him. "*She just didn't know it yet.*" He'd follow up those words by wrapping his arms around my mom's waist, right before they exchanged a few kisses and giggles.

Abigail's smile was fading, probably because I looked so shocked. She motioned with her hand. "Well, come on and meet your uncle, Sara." Her tone carried a why-are-you-just-standing-there influence. "Doesn't he look just like your dad?"

I nodded. *Yes, too much like him.*

Abigail smiled at Aidan. "I'm so sorry, Aidan. Could you give us a minute?"

Scott stood back as Abigail planted herself in front of me, blocking my view. "Is something wrong?" Her eyes strained with concern. "Is it difficult for you to see him because he looks so much like your dad? I hadn't even thought of that. I hoped enough time had passed."

Snap out of it. The man is just visiting. He's not going to rob you. Still, my dad's opinion carried a lot of clout with me. Although, I couldn't explain that to Abigail. Not here, and not right in front of Aidan.

I struggled to express what I was feeling. "I'm sorry. I was just so surprised to see him. As you said, he looks so much like my dad."

Keeping one ear inches from our conversation, Scott said, "So that's what's wrong?" He blew out a breath and wiped his brow. "Jesus. You really freaked me out for a minute." He leaned in closer and whispered, "You haven't met him before?"

I shook my head, then realized that the three of us must've looked like we were in some sort of football huddle.

"He does look a lot like all those pictures you showed me of your dad." Scott rubbed his jaw. "This is getting awkward. We need to do something here." He turned toward Aidan and stepped forward, shaking his hand. "It's nice to meet you, Aidan. I'm Sara's fiancé."

Every time Scott tossed the word *fiancé* into the air, he stood a little taller, his voice filled with pride.

"It's great that you were able to make Sara's graduation. Long trip from Ireland." Scott relaxed into the conversation like he always did when making small talk—open posture, engaging mannerisms—he was good at that.

Me, not so much.

"The trip wasn't so bad," Aidan said. "Just a hop across the pond."

I appreciated Scott giving me another second to get ahold of myself. I cleared my throat and stepped around Abigail. "Are you here on business? Or pleasure?" I wanted to reach out and shake his hand, too, just like everyone else, but I was afraid I might not let go. My feelings tangled up like a ball of Christmas lights.

"I came on business, but I remembered Robby had lived in Vermont and that ya now live with Abigail, so I looked her up." He gestured toward Abigail, his speech rushed.

Robby? Was that my dad's nickname? And Aidan knew I

lived with Abigail? I assumed he knew nothing about me. Or cared to.

"She told me about your grad." He tipped his head back and forth. "I had a small window and thought I'd come and meet ya in Virginia." The discomfort in his eyes was easing away, his Irish hospitality blossoming into his rosy cheeks and smile.

"That was so nice of you. I'm glad you were able to come." Good, I was sounding normal again. Although I couldn't quite fool my pattering heart. "How long are you here?"

"A week or two." He crossed his arms over his chest, but not in a closed manner, more of a making-himself-comfortable gesture. "I have some business in Georgia I need to attend to, and then I thought I'd come visit ya in Vermont." He uncrossed his arms. "I hope you'll be there."

"That would be great." I motioned toward Scott. "We're going to Scott's place for a graduation party. I'll be there for about a week, and then, I'll be heading back to Vermont."

"That's grand. Will work right with my schedule and all."

Demanding her own attention, Mel put two fingers in her mouth and began to speak, which did nothing to help her already challenging speech. "I thaw a bawoon. I thaw a big bawoon." She pointed with her whole hand toward a gigantic-sized hot-air balloon on the Great Lawn, which the school had rented as an attraction. They were offering tethered rides for people. Adult people. Not toddlers. It was all part of the gradu-ation celebration. They had also staged photo spots all over campus for families to enjoy, some with professional photogra-phers but most without. The school provided water stations and outdoor gift shops, along with what was called The Gauntlet—a twenty-foot walkway that graduates could walk through after graduation, lined with family members and staff from each department. They really went all out for the occasion. We had yet to walk The Gauntlet, although, in this moment, I felt like I was experiencing a different kind of gauntlet.

"I want a wide." Mel patted my legs, her fingers making wet marks on my graduation gown. "I want a wide." Then she gazed up at Abigail. "Mommy, I want a wide."

Abigail smirked. "I'm sorry, sweetie, you're too young for *that* ride."

Mel's cheeks fumed red. An argument ensued between mother and toddler.

"No, Mommy. It's for me. It's my turn."

"Melinda. Roberta. Saunders, I already told you. You are too young for that ride."

Something registered in Aidan's eyes when Abigail addressed Mel by her full name, which came from both my mother and my father.

"Is she named after—?"

"Yes," I said as my mother's words from the past weaved into my brain like a crochet hook. "*He's not as responsible as your dad. And, according to your dad, he's not to be trusted.*" And then I thought about his *habits*.

I wanted to know more about Aidan. Was he silly like my dad used to be? Funny faces and all? One time, my dad made funny faces during a funeral, no less, which caused me to giggle and my mother to roll her eyes. That earned us a "*shhh*" from the woman in the pew in front of us. Where did he get that silliness side from? I was dying to know.

I always felt like my dad and I *got* each other on a level that most people didn't. *Burgers and fries.* Which made sense considering our favorite fast-food restaurant was the A&W off Route 7, where they served your food on trays that hitched to the window of your vehicle, and where they used meat from the local butcher. Only in Vermont would you find a fast-food restaurant that served local, organic meat.

Thinking about him and my mom made my heart whimper. That icy road in Vermont had cheated us all out of a lifetime of memories. I loved Abigail and my new family, but something told me I'd love them just as much if Mom and Dad were still here.

Unable to give up on the balloon ride that she was way too young for, Mel crossed her short arms and pouted, her lower lip defiant. "Mommy's meanie. She won't wisten. It's my wide."

Still crouched down, Abigail ran her fingers through Mel's soft locks that matched her own shade of auburn. Honestly, the girl was the spitting image of her mother. Poor Joel, his features would have to show up on Mel sometime.

"If you stop fussing *right now*, I'll get you a balloon of your very own. Would you like that?"

Mel didn't answer, but I could tell her wheels were turning.

Even Aidan chuckled at that. "Strong-willed," he said, "just like your da was."

Tell me more, I thought, even though Mel wasn't technically related to my dad. I had this sudden urge to shake him like he was a tree, hoping all his stories about my dad would fall like apples around my feet. I'd scoop them up and savor each and every one of them. It had been so long. "Yes, my dad *was* strong-willed. And funny," I said with a smile, hoping Aidan would take the bait and pick up where I left off.

"Funny?" Aidan inched his head back and wrinkled his face at me. "Robby? Ya may be talkin' a load of blarney there, lass." He chuckled in an I-know-more-about-him-than-you-do sort of way. "My little brother was ..." He rubbed his jaw, his eyes more teasing than fun. "Way too serious for his own good. A bit of a melter. I couldn't get away with anythin' around him. We used to call him *peeler*, or what ya call a police officer. The boy needed to loosen a stitch." He shook his head and stared at the ground. "Made it tough to be around him." His face got all serious.

Really? You came all this way to talk crap about my father? His words burned through my veins like boiled molasses, and my smile faded. "That's not at all what I remember about *my* dad. He *was* funny. Very funny. And a good father."

Scott closed in on me, his hand finding my lower back. "It's okay, Babe. He was just—"

"I know what he was doing." I snapped my head in Scott's direction.

Aidan raised his gaze to meet mine, his tone leaning toward sarcastic. "Ha, and I see ya have his temper to boot."

Aidan's comment made Scott stop short, his defenses rising. I could feel it. He held his tongue, though, probably because he *and* I felt like we were staring at some version of my father. And I knew Scott respected that.

I chewed my lower lip. No one, not even his brother, was going to put my father down, especially not right in front of me.

I lowered my voice. "Maybe it wasn't such a good idea for you to come."

Everyone stared at me as though I was a bomb that was about to go off. Depending on what Aidan said next, maybe I was.

Chapter Three

"Can I take your order?" The tall waiter with coal-black hair stood next to me, a small electronic tablet in his hand, which he used to jot down my menu choices.

"I'll take the chicken marsala with mashed potatoes and a side salad with ranch dressing."

The dark-haired waiter tapped the screen. *Tap, tap, tap.* "And to drink?"

"An unsweetened iced tea, please." The waiter nodded and walked away.

"Mashed potatoes." From my left, Aidan nudged me with his elbow. "Is that your *Irish* comin' out, lass?"

"Ha, I guess so." I smirked.

His eyes became sorrowful. "Are we alright, then? I'd do well to keep my mouth shut. Didn't mean to be showin' my ass like I did. Sometimes I can be such an eejit."

This was about the third apology Aidan had given me. After I had gotten upset earlier, Aidan had immediately felt bad about it, which only made me feel worse for overreacting.

He explained that being my dad's big brother, he saw him one way, and, it appeared that as his daughter, I had seen him another. "Plus," he pointed out, "I only knew Robby for the younger years of his life—it's been donkey's years for me. Your mother *and you* saw the man he came to be."

His eyes timid, his chin low, Aidan personified remorse. I apologized back to him for being so sensitive, and that was when Abigail invited him to join us for dinner, the entire group taking one big sigh of relief.

The waiter returned and placed a glass of Irish whiskey in front of Aidan, the strong, woody aroma tickling my nose before he brought Scott and Joel a beer and Abigail a glass of red wine. Circling the table, the waiter placed a glass of white wine in front of Scott's mom and his sister, Kelsey, who had also joined us. Knowing the numbers in advance (except for the addition of Uncle Aidan), I had reserved a large table at a local Italian restaurant in town called Lorenzo's.

From the other side of me, Scott leaned forward and cleared his throat. "So what do you think of the States, Aidan? Have you been here before?"

I knew Aidan had been here before but waited to hear what he would say. *Always suspicious.*

Aidan lifted his glass and said, "Sláinte," then took a sip of his drink.

Confusion clouded Scott's eyes as he lifted his beer and said, "Cheers."

"Ya have yourselves a fine country. It's grand for sure." He took another sip as everyone stopped talking and listened. "I came to visit about twelve or so years ago."

So far, so good.

After the waiter returned with my iced tea, I took a quick sip. The chilled, caffeinated liquid refreshed my dry throat. "Didn't you visit with my dad when you were here before?"

Aidan's eyebrows shot up, his cheeks flushing. "I wasn't aware that ya knew of such things, lass. So Robby talked about me?"

By his body language alone, I couldn't tell if he was happy or alarmed. And after I deciphered what I presumed he just said, I hesitated to reply. No, my father hadn't talked about Aidan. Not one word. *"I have to go meet ... someone"* was all he'd said, and it was blatantly clear to me back then he wasn't happy about it. I wondered what went on between them that day. My dad didn't come home until after I had gone to bed. And the next day, he acted as though nothing had happened. Keeping my promise to my mother to stay quiet about it, I never pressed the issue.

"Um. You know, he died so long ago. I don't really remember." I took another sip of tea, hoping to hide behind my glass.

Always in tune with my feelings, Scott placed his arm across the back of my chair. "So, Aidan. How's the soccer in Ireland? ... Or I guess you call it football." And they were off and running.

Thank you, Scott.

* * *

The next day, Scott and I finished packing up our tiny apartment. We had been working on nothing else for over a week now. Hard to believe that two people could acquire so much stuff.

In the kitchen, I grabbed a roll of packing tape and secured our box of pots and pans. We planned to store them in Scott's parents' attic for when we got our own place. "I wonder what business Aidan has in Georgia." I wiped a hand across my brow, my palms wet from perspiration.

Scott was undoing a shelving system in the dining room

that we'd been using for kitchen stuff like larger pots and pans, cereal, and other pantry items. The kitchen cabinets were few and far between, enough to allow space for plates, glasses, mugs, and silverware, and that was it.

"I have no idea." He rose and stretched his back out before joining me in the kitchen. He scratched his temple. "I wasn't going to ask you this, but I get the feeling you don't like him much." He made a face. "What's weird is that you seem to like *everyone*, so I wondered if there is something about him you haven't told me." From all the bending over, my ponytail had fallen forward, which he brushed back as I straightened my spine, my muscles enjoying the stretch.

I set my packing tape down, took his hand loosely within mine, and thought about what he said. "It's not that I don't like him. I mean, how could I not like someone who looks just like my dad?"

"But?" Scott never missed a thing when it came to my feelings.

I scrunched my face a little, trying to figure myself out, especially before I saw Aidan again, which would happen in a couple of hours for lunch, along with Abigail, Joel, and Mel, before they left for home, and Aidan to the airport. He insisted on staying over to see us off. "I don't dislike him. I just don't know him. Plus, my dad didn't get along with him very well"—I shrugged—"I guess ... I really don't know much about it." And then I told Scott what my mother had told me when I was ten. Information that I had carried with me all these years.

"Hmm" was all Scott had to say ... at first. Then he rubbed his jaw in a thoughtful manner. "Well, he said he's here on business. Do you think he's here for another reason?"

I went into the dining room, Scott following in my shadow. "No idea. I wonder if he comes here often. And if he does, why hasn't he contacted me sooner?" I could be reading too much into this. Maybe he'd never been here, except for that one time twelve years ago. Maybe this trip was exactly what he'd said it was. I rested my head against Scott's chest, listening to his lungs and feeling the thump of his heartbeat. *My happy place.* "I just hope he's trustworthy. No one from Ireland came to my dad's funeral, you know."

Scott caressed my back as though sad for me. It had never occurred to me to be sad about the whole thing until now.

"And I've never heard *one word* from anyone all these years, not my grandparents, no one." *Are they still alive?* "After the accident, I was in a state of shock. Plus, I was young. And knowing that my dad didn't get along with his brother, I just assumed that *none* of them got along. Over the years, I stopped thinking about it."

Scott's lungs expanded, his voice gentle. "I wonder why they didn't get along. Aidan seemed like a decent guy to me. And he acted like he wanted to get to know you more. I think he's harmless. Try not to worry about it. We don't know what their family is like. I know families that hate each other. Maybe he regrets not reaching out sooner." He rubbed my back some more. "I've always felt bad you didn't have any blood relatives in your life. It would be cool if this worked out." He pulled back and peered deep into my eyes. "Right?"

I stared off into space, unsure. "Yeah, maybe."

Scott kissed me. "You look like a woman who could use a break."

I huffed out a breath. "Yeah. You could say that." I was tired of packing and trying to figure out what we could take and not take. At this point, I was ready to toss it all into the dumpster.

Within no time, Scott was nuzzling my neck, his hands roaming.

Oh, you mean that kind of break.

"You know, we never christened this place on the first day we moved in." I could see ideas forming behind his eyes.

I thought about Scott's move-in day and how angry we were with each other. He and Amy had gone at it the day before, and neither one of us was too happy about it. Letting that unpleasant thought wander out of my head, I slid my hands lower to grab Scott's butt. "Well, maybe we should give the place a proper farewell, then." It was just what I needed right now. A distraction from my thoughts about Aidan *and* the Browne family.

"You don't have to ask me twice." Scott's fingers worked the bottom edge of my tank top upward. As I raised my arms over my head, he slid my top off and let it drop on the dining room table next to us, the one we were donating to the landlord. One less thing to move. Two seconds later, my bra popped, the material loose and ready to fly off, which it did soon after. With my breasts in his hands, Scott spent a moment fondling them and kissing each one. "What are you in the mood for right now?"

Loaded question. Good thing I'd showered already.

I pulled back, moisture building between my legs. "Anything you are."

Scott's erection shoved up against my hip, ready to play.

"Lay back." He eased me back onto the table, where he worked the waist of my shorts down, right along with my panties, over my ankles, and onto the floor. "I'm hungry for you right now." His eyes glowed, his mouth ready to savor. "Can I have a taste?"

"Oh, yeah."

I laced my hands through his soft locks and lost my mind as Scott excited the most personal regions of my body. He knew what to do, and he did it well.

* * *

As I caught my breath, Scott lifted his head and smiled. "I fucking love the way you taste. You ready for more fun? Because I'm just getting started."

I sat up, my hair breaking free of my ponytail in several places and my cheeks hot, along with my insides. My whole body was vibrating with sexual energy. "The question is, are *you* ready for more? It's my turn." I hopped off the table with rubbery legs and backed away, giving Scott room to undress. "Oh, yeah? Where do you want me?"

"Right there." I pointed to where I had just been.

Naked, he sat gingerly on the table, his gaze questioning, and the legs of the table straining beneath his weight. "You think this table is going to hold me?"

I nudged him back. "Yeah, you'll be fine." He'd worked me up too much to stop now. Plus, something about feasting on my man where he had just feasted on me was a real turn on, in a carnal sort of way. Scott brought out the animal in me.

Before long, I had Scott moaning, his fingers lacing through *my* hair this time, his breathing labored.

"Holy shit" shot from his mouth when he climaxed, just like *Oh my God*, often came from mine. He puffed out a few breaths, then said, "That was amazing, Babe. You've certainly perfected the art of blow jobs. *Man*." He rubbed his eyes as though trying to gain mental focus.

As I lifted my head away to enjoy his dazed and dreamy eyes, a knock sounded at the door. All at once the sexual vibe in the room plummeted like a thermometer in a glass of ice-cold water. I was sure my heart had stopped. *Please don't be Abigail or Scott's mom.*

Scott sprang up and so did I, our eyes wide, our mouths open, both our heads facing the door of doom.

"Crap," I whispered. "Who do you think it is?" It wasn't as if either one of us had been quiet. And it wasn't as if the walls of this cheap apartment weren't made of paper. Heck, I could hear the radio stations coming from people's cars as they drove past on the road out front.

"No idea, but here." Scott jumped down and handed me my clothes before I dashed up the stairs and into our master bathroom.

For a few seconds, Scott ran the faucet in the half bath downstairs before his footfalls moved toward the door. I heard voices but couldn't make out who they belonged to. If it *were* his mother or mine, I would be humiliated. Scott's groans, the *holy shit*, and the compliment about my blow-job skills weren't exactly made in a low voice. As I dressed, brushed my teeth, washed my face, and fixed my hair, I wondered how long the person or persons had been standing there. *Did they wait for us to finish?*

By the time I had reached the top of the stairs, I had worked myself into a frenzy. That was until I heard "Big Guy" from my best friend's mouth below. I expelled a breath that had been paralyzed in my lungs and jogged down the steps.

Amy gazed up at me, a teasing smile stretched across her face. "I was just telling the big guy, I'm glad to see you two are keeping up with your fiancé duties." She laughed as Scott, holding his crumpled-up shirt in front of him, grimaced, fake coughed, and darted past me, up the stairs, and into our room, making sure to pat my butt along the way.

Amy stood there looking like the cat that had just swallowed the canary. "At least I waited for you two to finish. You can thank me later." She scrunched her bangs to blend in with her spiky hair as if none of it was any big deal.

Typical Amy.

Okay, I was still embarrassed, but considering I'd heard Amy on multiple occasions with Luke when I had lived next door to her in our dorm, I didn't tear myself up over it. In fact,

Amy was the first person I had told about my first time with Scott. The girl knew everything about me.

"Sorry about that, Amy. I'll just thank you now." I tried to giggle, still not entirely comfortable with the whole thing.

Amy waved me off. "I'm just fucking with you. I couldn't care less about that shit." She took some black lipstick from her tiny crossbody purse and applied it to her lips, giving them a smack.

I moved closer and gave her a hug. "It's so good to see you. I missed you yesterday. Congrats, by the way."

Amy chuckled as she said, "Same to you. My family kept me busy, or I would've come looking for you. They already headed home this morning." She fiddled with her macramé bracelet. "I gotta go soon, too." Her gaze slid to the floor, a sad smile creeping over her face.

Amy and I had been through a lot together. *A lot?* We'd been through a war. And, somehow, we'd come out the other end, sane and productive. I couldn't have made it without her, and she couldn't have made it without me. We were each other's lifeline when we needed it most.

She was leaving, and for the first time in four years, we didn't have the luxury of saying *See you in a few months*. This was it. We would be going our separate ways. Of course, we'd see each other and keep in touch, but it would never be the same, and I sensed she was thinking about that as much as I was.

I placed a loving hand on her shoulder, my eyes straining to hold back tears.

"I'm gonna miss being able to see you anytime I want." I removed my hand and stared earnestly.

Amy nodded slightly, her jaw tight. "Me, too, Al." She raised her gaze to meet mine. "I guess I can't really call you that anymore." Her voice dipped.

I furrowed my brow. "Al? Why not?" If I had to let go of Amy, I wasn't ready to let go of *everything* we'd shared between us.

Amy tipped her head back and forth in a halfhearted sort of way. "Well, when I met you, I thought to myself. 'This girl is totally out of her element. And this school is going to eat her alive.'" She nudged me with her elbow, her tone sentimental. "You proved me wrong. *Al*. You're no longer Alice in Wonderland, trying to find her way." She chewed on her lower lip, turning the edges of her front teeth black. "You know, sometimes I think about all the shit that went down freshman year." She shook her head and reflected. "And I still can't believe it actually happened."

I rattled my head right along with her. "Same."

She stared off, her eyes unfocused. "Sometimes it feels like it was so long ago, like it almost happened to someone else." She met my gaze again. "And other times, it feels like it just happened yesterday."

Our thoughts seemed to get lost in the air for a moment, as if we were both in another time and place.

Amy snapped out of her trance first. "I've always called you a dork, Sara, but I've also always considered you *my* dork." Her eyes glimmered with emotion, something I rarely witnessed.

I smiled as a tear ran down my cheek. "Well, I'm proud to be your dork, Amy, and don't call me Sara again." I wiped a hand across my cheek and thrust my shoulders back. "My name is *Al*, if you don't mind, reserved for my best friend and no one else."

We both fell into each other's arms and sobbed. Yup, Amy actually sobbed, which given the rareness of it, had me bawling about that, too. I was a hot mess.

I detached myself and, with a mouth wet with tears, said, "I'll miss you, Amy."

Her dark eyeliner smudged around her eyes. "Me, too."

Not wanting to let go of this moment, I clasped both of her shoulders. "Thank you for saving my life more than once."

A chuckle mixed in with a "humph" escaped her lips. "Well, *Al*, you definitely saved my ass ... for real." She pulled her cell from the back pocket of her jean shorts and sighed. "Hey, I gotta run. Sky is waiting for me at his place. He's gonna spend some time in Connecticut with me this summer. We've got a place lined up in the apartment building where my brother, Griffin, lives."

Please don't go. "You sure you can't stay for a cup of tea or a beer?" My heart begged for more time.

"Nah, I can't. It's a long drive, and Sky wants to get a jump on it."

"Do you think you two will get married someday?"

Luke and Amy were the opposites who had attracted, and in my eyes, the perfect match: The folk singer and the alt-rock star, Amy being the latter, of course.

Amy shrugged and fiddled with her bracelet some more. "No idea. I guess if he asked me, I'd consider it. I mean, the guy did risk life and limb to rescue me."

Another moment of silence filled the gap between us. It was as if we were standing on opposing sides of a doorway that neither one of us wanted to close. I knew we had to leave each other, but I wasn't ready to let go. Not yet.

We were bonded for life, and that would never change, regardless of our zip code.

Once again, it was Amy who broke the silence. "Well, have fun in Europe. Call me when you get back."

Scott and I had decided to take the summer off and travel through Europe. For one month, anyway. I had been employed every summer for as long as I could remember, even during most school years, with part-time work. Scott had worked for his dad since he was a kid, spending most of his summers playing soccer or working part-time as well. And since his dad no longer thought that Scott would turn into a deviant should he have a few minutes to himself, we decided we needed an adventure, a good one. We'd mapped out some countries to tour, a few bed-and-breakfasts and hotels to stay in, and decided to leave the rest to chance. When would we get an opportunity like this again? And when we returned home, we'd think about full-time employment, but now, we were ready to become wanderers, at least for a little while. We ordered our passports last fall in anticipation of this.

My throat thickened. "I will. And when we get back, I'll let you know as soon as we pick our wedding date. My maid of honor will be the first to know."

Amy leaned closer, her grin cunning. "You mean maid of dishonor."

We both cracked up.

Taking slow steps, Amy headed for the door, me in her shadow, when Scott came bounding down the stairs, a new shirt on and his mouth refreshed, judging by the minty scent floating from his lips.

"Leaving so soon?" He didn't hesitate to walk right up to Amy and pull her into a bear hug.

Amy didn't fight it, her arms wrapping around his thick torso.

"Yup, Big Guy. Time's a wastin'." Amy pulled back from Scott's embrace. "Take good care of our girl here. Don't let any psychos nab her in Paris." She wagged a finger. "Only if it's for a photo shoot and only if they're payin' big bucks."

Scott grinned. "Don't worry, Amy, I'll take good care of our girl." He reached out and tapped the end of my nose. "Tell Luke hey. And we'll all hang out when we get back."

A moment later, my best friend was gone. My eyes gushed with a new wave of tears. "I already miss her."

Scott's voice purred. "Awe, Babe. It's okay. You'll see her again soon." He pulled me into his arms, kissing my head and rubbing my back. He was like a big warm cushion for my sorrow. And I loved the swaying, which always followed.

That lasted about three minutes before he ended the hug and swiped a hand across his forehead in a "phew" gesture. "Thank God it was her at the door and not our parents." His eyes flashed with caution and amusement.

"Yeah, no kidding. If it had been either of our parents, I would have died."

The corners of Scott's lips tugged upward. "Maybe we better keep our lovemaking to the bedroom." He took my hand and led me toward the stairs. "Speaking of which, you ready for round two?" He kissed my hand as he walked backward for a few steps, his eyes hopeful. "You think that air mattress can survive us?"

I cracked up. This man could never get enough sex. Then again, neither could I. "Only one way to find out, Handsome."

Chapter Four

"What time are we meeting Aidan and your family again?" Scott asked as he stacked my boxes by the door.

I checked the time on my cell phone, which flashed 12:45 on the tiny screen. "Forty-five minutes. We should have just enough time to finish getting these boxes into our cars, and then I'll mop the floors," I said. I wanted to leave the place clean for the landlord, and I didn't want any extra fees tacked onto our final bill.

I gazed around the vacant apartment and sighed. So many memories lingered here, fun times (mostly) between Scott and me. Not to mention the dinner parties and hangouts we hosted with our close friends. There were football games, holiday parties, and, my favorite, charades. Voices and laughter echoed from the walls. We'd made a home here. Our first.

Now the place just looked sad, as though we were abandoning it. Of course, I always grew sentimental when it came to moving from one place to another. Except for when I had to leave the boarding school; I was more than happy to move on from that pretentious place.

"I got the heavy ones." Scott hoisted a couple of boxes up and started out the door, holding it open with his foot so I could follow him.

With all the extra work and heavy lifting over the past couple of weeks, the muscles in my back were complaining on a regular basis.

"I still can't believe we got rid of all that crap. How could we accumulate so much?" I jogged down the deck stairs behind Scott, my eyes zeroing in on the sweat seeping through the back of his gray T-shirt. He'd need a quick shower before we left. We both would.

"We must be packrats, Babe. We'll have to remember that when we get our own place." Scott stopped by my car and used the key fob to unlock the doors. Then he pushed the one for the trunk and headed toward it. "I'm not planning on hoeing out this much shit on a regular basis." Sweat dripped down his neck, making the ends of his blond locks curly and wet.

I set my boxes on the ground and opened the back door to my car. "Me, neither." After I finished loading my things, I let myself enjoy a five-second break, stretching my muscles out.

It had been cloudy all day with a chance of showers, the scent of ozone warning of a storm. I only hoped we'd get our cars packed before the sky opened fully. A stiff breeze pushed through, and I leaned into it, enjoying the coolness against my skin. Early May in Virginia meant the weather was not too hot but not exactly cool, either. Storms could pop up at any time, today being a good example.

With his arms liberated of boxes, Scott approached. "We'd better hurry." He glanced up at the sky. "Unless we want to get soaked." He leaned closer and planted a breathy kiss against my lips. "At least we don't have to worry about furnishing that lake house you found for us this summer."

We'd rented a fully furnished lake house from early July (when we planned to return from Europe) through late-August. (We were splurging on ourselves this summer.) Located off Lake Champlain, the house was an hour north of Middlebury, where Abigail lived.

I wiped my brow and nodded as we headed for the deck stairs to retrieve another load. "Yeah, me, too."

I made sure there were plenty of spare rooms in our vacation home for guests, hoping my family and Scott's would visit *and* often. I knew Abigail would. "I can bring my johnboat," Joel had offered, which I took as a good sign. Joel liked to fish, as my dad had, so we'd have a perfect place for him. I planned to join him. Amy promised to visit, too.

We decided that between the time we spent in Europe and our time at the lake house, we'd figure out where we wanted to live permanently. And that would determine where to apply for jobs. Maybe we'd choose a state south of Vermont. (I couldn't say I ever really liked those long winters.) Although, I didn't want to be too far away that we couldn't visit my family anytime we wanted. Along with our wedding, we had a lot of plans to make.

But for right now, we wanted just to *be*. No pressures, no obligations, just Scott and me, celebrating our accomplishments and each other.

* * *

The waiter had just delivered our check for lunch, which Joel took care of, when Abigail placed her hand over mine on the table. "I know I keep saying this, but we are all so proud of you, Sara." She leaned forward and peered over at Scott, seated on the other side of me. "And you, too, Scott. Really, what you've both achieved is amazing. And I know none of it was easy." Her eyes glossed over like they always did when she became nostalgic.

As though they were listening, Joel, Scott, and Aidan stared over at me.

"Thank you, Abigail." I glanced at all of my family members. "Thank you all so much for your support and for coming."

That prompted a few smiles from everyone except Mel, who was busy playing with her tablet.

While Scott chatted it up with Joel and Uncle Aidan, I gave Abigail a side hug. "You have always been there for me, Mom, and I want you to know how much I appreciate it. I know I didn't always make it easy for you."

She made a tsking sound, leaning the side of her head against mine for just a minute. "Given the circumstances, you did better than you think. And even though I wished your parents were still here, I'm glad I get to be your bonus mom." She took a refreshing breath as if to reset herself. "It was too bad Scott's family had to leave so quickly. I was hoping to spend more time with them. His mother is really sweet."

"She is. I guess they're putting together a big graduation party for us, so she had to get home and prepare."

Abigail nodded. "When you come home, we don't have a big celebration planned, but we'd like to have a cookout with close friends and family. I'll get some desserts from Sweet Heaven in town."

From across the table, Joel perked up. "And while you're home, I'll take you fishing."

Uncle Aidan turned toward Joel, who sat to his right. "You're a fisherman, are ya? We have that in common." He addressed me next. "Robby loved to fish as well. My pa has property right off the ocean, so we fished a lot. Ate what we caught."

Whenever he mentioned anything about my dad, I found myself glued to his every word.

"I remember. My dad brought me fishing with him a few times. He taught me how to bait a hook and cast a line."

Aidan sat up straighter. "I'm not surprised, lass. He'd leg it to the coast any chance he could." He motioned toward Joel. "Maybe we can catch a fish or two while I'm up visitin' ya in Vermont."

"Count me in." Joel smiled, interest piqued.

Having something in common, I wanted to get excited about this. And I pretended to be, not sure if my father would approve. "That would be great. And I'd like to hear more about your and my father's lives in Ireland." *And why he didn't trust you.*

He nodded once with gusto. "Grand. It's a date."

As we spilled out of the restaurant and into the parking lot, I said my goodbyes to everyone, still a tad conflicted about seeing my uncle again. It was such a surprise to meet him, and so out of the blue. Could I trust him yet? I wasn't sure. If it hadn't been for my mother's warning—or my father's distressed behavior all those years ago—I'd be thrilled about meeting Aidan.

Abigail stayed behind, waving right along with me as Aidan hopped into his airport transport and left. "It was nice that Aidan came to see you. He's the first relative I've met from your father's family. Like ever."

I faced my bonus mom. "I know. It was. I don't think he got along very well with my dad, though."

Abigail tilted her head, her smile fading and her eyebrows pushing together. "Really? Why not?"

"I don't know exactly. My mom told me once that my dad didn't trust Aidan."

Joel slid the back door of their minivan closed with a clunk. "Hon, our reason for living is all strapped in. She's watching a movie on her tablet. We better get going before she gets too restless. We've got a long drive ahead of us."

Abigail nodded and waved haphazardly at her hubby. "That's alarming. I wonder what happened between them."

"I was hoping maybe you knew." *Darn.*

She shook her head. "No, not a thing."

"Hon?" Joel climbed into the driver's seat, his tone edging toward impatient.

"You better go." I hugged Abigail and waved to Joel. "We can talk about this when I get home."

* * *

We woke up early the next morning and set out on our journey toward Scott's family home, my short conversation with Abigail fresh in my mind. Did the fact that Abigail knew nothing about my dad and uncle's stressed relationship mean anything? She was my mother's best friend. If it were important, wouldn't she have told Abigail? Or maybe she had, and Abigail had forgotten. It *was* twelve years ago.

"Did you see that Lambo fly past us?" Scott asked through the car's speakers. His shiny black pickup truck that came with an impressive set of wheels and a powerful engine (perks of having a father who owned a dealership) remained one car length in front of mine, driving north on Interstate 81.

I took my car and Scott took his. I could have had Joel drive *my* car to Vermont, which was where I was heading in just over a week. But Scott wasn't sure he'd be able to leave when I was ready to go (he wanted to help his dad with some computer issues at the dealership and projects around the house), so I thought it best to be prepared.

"Yes. Impressive. What do you have to do to get one of those?" The sleek red sports car seemed to own the road as it swerved around cars in a fluid motion.

"Win the lottery," Scott said with a chuckle. "We're coming up on a rest area. You need to use the bathroom?"

Scott knew my small bladder all too well.

"Nope. I'm not drinking much of anything until we get to your parents' place." The entire drive was only five and a half hours, and we'd already completed two of them. I liked that the distance was halfway to Vermont, sort of, so I didn't have to endure another eleven- or twelve-hour trip later. I hated those long trips in the car, and so did my lower back and hips. "Are you sure your parents don't mind me sleeping in your room? I can take the guest room." I'd stayed at Scott's place a few times over the years, but always in their guest room.

Scott exhaled through the speaker, and I imagined him shaking his head at his paranoid fiancée. "Babe, we're engaged. We've lived together for three years. My mother wanted you to stay in my room last summer. Don't worry about it. They're fine with it. They love you. She was just saying to me on the phone last night how happy she is that you're part of our family now."

I sighed. "Okay. But don't count on any wild sex while I'm there." I had my standards, and I wouldn't force *anyone* to listen to our groans of euphoria through the floorboards or the walls.

Scott laughed. "Now you're just being mean. How about silent, wild sex?"

I imagined his thoughts dancing with crazy ideas.

"I don't think that's possible. It's only a week. We can control ourselves, right?" I knew it was a loaded question.

Scott made a loud "Ha" sound. "With you? And it's more

like two weeks if you include your trip to Vermont. What do you think I'm made of … stone? Anytime I see that naked body of yours, my dick can't control himself." His voice carried humor along with a bit of teasing. "You expect me to sleep next to you and *not* touch you?"

Hence the need for a guest room.

I snickered. "Yes. I'll wear thick pj's if I have to. I'll stick a pillow or two between us. I'll make you take cold showers before bed."

Another "Ha" echoed through my car speakers. "Won't work. Have you met me? And have you taken a good look at yourself lately? Any man who could resist your big tits and tight ass, not to mention what you've got hidden between those long legs, couldn't be human. Tell you what. We can practice trying to be quiet. It'll be our secret challenge. I can do it if you can."

What was it about Scott that drove me out of my mind sexually? This conversation alone had me wanting to drive off to some remote area and have my way with him in the car.

"To start our challenge, I'll lick and fondle your tits to get you ready, and if you can keep quiet, then I'll slide my fingers into—"

"Okay. I'm gonna have to stop you right there, bucko." I rolled my window down to capture some fresh air for my heated cheeks and chest, not to mention every sexual organ in my body, which was aching to be touched.

"Bucko?" Scott tried to sound offended, but I knew better. He was enjoying every minute of this fun banter.

"If you don't stop, I'm not going to be able to drive anymore. You want to cause an accident?" I was smiling as I said this.

"Well, we could talk about sports if you want."

There was that teasing tone again. He knew I *hated* sports talk.

"There's all kinds of trading going on or about to happen in the league that I'd love to discuss with you." His voice carried a splash of witticism. "Or how about soccer? Although, not much happening there right now. Too early in the season ..."

"Talk about anything you want. As long as it doesn't involve sex."

"Hey, you still got that picnic blanket in the back of your car?" he asked, changing the subject.

"Yeah, but it's buried under my suitcases."

"Cool. Then I'll make a deal with you. I'll talk about whatever you want: movies, books, even relationship crap if you'll indulge me one last request."

Now it was my turn to pour on the sarcasm. "I can't imagine what that could be."

"When we get close to my parents' place, I want you to follow me to a piece of property they own but nobody ever goes to. It's only a few miles from the house. Fifty acres. It's actually two twenty-five-acre parcels. One for me and one for Kelse to build a house on someday if we want. Not that we have to live there. Anyway, I have other things in mind for today." The lilt in his voice was unmistakable.

"Dare I ask?"

"After I do the things I just mentioned to rev you up, I'll taste and savor you, so you can scream all you want. I know how you like to do that. And don't worry. No one will hear you, except a few deer, maybe, and some birds."

Taste and savor? Man. Can I make it that long?

"I bet you're thinking *right now* about what I'm going to do to you, aren't you? I know my little she-beast." Scott was trying to draw me in again. "My dick is hard just thinking about it. And when I've made you cum, and you're all relaxed and limp, I'll start over and—"

"Okaaaay. Moving on." I cleared my throat and rattled my head. "So did you like that movie we watched last night?"

"I can't remember anymore. You've consumed my mind with your—"

"*Slumberland*, right? And you said you'd talk about anything I wanted ... *remember?*"

A deflated answer rolled through the speakers. "Man, you're getting tough in your old age. Okay, uh, yeah, I guess the movie was okay."

"I really liked how different the story was ..."

* * *

When Scott stopped to get gas two hours later, I called Abigail to let her know we were almost there.

"I'm glad you called. A letter arrived for you while we were at graduation. It's from your family attorney, Mr. Webster. He's the man who took care of your estate."

That was unexpected. I had never received a letter from him before. Being my legal guardian and then adopted mother, Abigail must have, though. "Really? What is it about?"

"I don't know. I didn't open it. As I said, it's addressed to you."

Through the windshield, Scott stood holding a gas nozzle inserted into his gas tank, watching the pump tick away his money, people coming to and from the convenience store next door.

"Go ahead and open it. I don't mind."

The sound of paper rustling crackled through my car's speaker, and then a pause, probably as Abigail read whatever it was. "It says that you will receive a sizable inheritance from your father's estate."

A sizable inheritance? Estate? "I didn't know my father had an estate. Does it say anything else? Like what it is?"

"No, it just says he would like you to contact him and set up a meeting to go over the paperwork. When we sold your parents' house, and I worked on getting you the life insurance your parents had left for you, I must've missed this. It seems like they would have mentioned it. I just can't remember. I can call Mr. Webster tomorrow and ask him about it, though. After I get out of work. Although, I don't know if he'd tell me much since you're over eighteen now, and it doesn't include me. I think lawyers have the same confidentiality agreements that doctors do. I'd be happy to try."

"That's okay, Abigail. I'll be home early next week, and I'll set up a meeting with him. You can come with me if you want." I *was* curious, though.

"I'd have to get time off. There's a lot going on at the end of the school year."

After Scott returned the gas nozzle to the pump, he gave me a salute and hopped into his truck, telling me it was time to pull up and fill *my* tank since vehicles occupied all the other pumps.

"I've gotta run, Abigail. I'll call you tomorrow. I just wanted to let you know we're almost there."

With his truck parked off to the side, Scott inserted the nozzle into my tank, making a clunking sound, before gas ran from one source to another.

I sat in the driver's seat, processing my phone call with Abigail. I'd never heard anything about an inheritance before, other than what I had received from my parents already. And since it was coming from my father's side of the family, did Aidan also know about it? Was that why he was here? My father had been gone for ten years, so, once again, I wondered why Aidan hadn't contacted me sooner. His sudden visit didn't quite feel so innocent anymore.

"Tired, Babe?"

I startled, not realizing Scott was standing right next to me. "What? A little. Why?"

"I just asked you if you wanted anything from the store."

"No, thanks, I'm good. Sorry." I wiped a hand across my forehead.

Scott seemed to study me for a moment. "You okay?"

The gas pump clicked off to indicate that the tank was full. Two cars waited in line behind me.

"I'll tell you about it when we get there."

"Tell me about what? I literally just got off the phone with you before we stopped."

The person behind us beeped, an elderly woman judging by the reflection in my rearview mirror.

"Okay, fine. we're almost there, anyway." He patted the door where my window sat open. "Don't forget to follow me to the land." He wiggled his eyebrows at me before stepping away to return the nozzle to the gas pump and close up my tank.

We arrived at the property, where grassy meadows unfurled into rolling hills and a lush forest. The springtime sun blanketed the land in warmth, promoting rich shades of green and beige, wildflowers sprouting their yellow, red, and purple blooms, and the wind combing through the grass with its powerful fingers. It was something out of a painting or a movie.

"This is beautiful." My eyes took it all in, my nose enjoying the fragrance of wheat, pine pitch, and various floral notes.

"Yeah, well, it's about to get much better." Scott took my hand and led me and my trusty blanket into a cluster of pine trees, which blocked the sun and carpeted the ground with their soft, flat needles. No tall grass. And no exposure to onlookers, not that there were any, according to Scott. Not the human kind, anyway.

Within minutes, Scott had my clothes off, and my body sprawled out on the blanket, his fingers stroking my insides, his tongue having its way with my nipples. Everything he said he was going to do, he did. And then some.

I *was* enjoying myself, or trying to. But at the same time, I couldn't get the inheritance out of my mind. Was it money? Or some sort of family relic? *It couldn't be anything as large as a house or an old castle, right?* My father never mentioned owning anything over there, at least not to me. Abigail said "sizable." And who had been taking care of this, whatever it was, all these years? *Aidan?*

Scott stopped what he was doing, which at that moment was me, and sat back on his haunches. "You're not really into this, are you? I didn't mean to push this on you. I know you're tired. I just thought—"

"No, it's not that. I'm sorry, Handsome." I sat up and cupped his cheek in the palm of my hand. "When we were at the gas station, I called Abigail to tell her where we were ..."

As soon as I finished telling him my story, Scott started in with the questions, the same ones that had been rolling around in my head like a pinball machine. "You think he's here about the inheritance? And she couldn't tell you what you're receiving?" He rubbed his chin, staring off as though trying to process it all.

I shook my head. "She didn't know, and I'm not *sure* that's why he's here. Like I told you, he's never once reached out to me all these years. *You* seemed to think he's harmless. And I trust your judgment."

We sat there, lost in our own thoughts.

Finally, Scott ran a warm hand down my arm. "Can't you just call your lawyer from here and find out what the inheritance is? Maybe that will help you understand more about it."

"I could, but I'd need to get his number from Abigail. Plus, your parents planned this big party for you, and we're going to be pretty busy over the next few days. I'll just call him when I get back next week." I sighed. "I'll be okay until then."

Will I?

Scott tipped his head to the side and lowered his brow as though unconvinced. "Are you sure? I don't think *I* could wait that long." His gaze kept roaming over my nakedness as though he couldn't seem to stop himself. Poor guy was expecting a hot hookup, and I was ruining it, not that he would ever say so.

Scott never pressured me, other than a little teasing. He knew sex would always be a complex issue for me since the rape. Yet, his love and affection for me never waned.

I took hold of his erection, stiff as a two-by-four, and went to work. "Let's talk about this later. We have more important things to focus on right now."

And so we continued. We did things that made the birds blush, the frogs croak, and the rodents run for cover. Not really, but I wouldn't be surprised if they had. Each new round inspired another until my body lay spent, my mind swimming.

Drained and satisfied, I actually fell asleep in Scott's arms, the sounds of nature, my lullaby.

As I drifted off for a short nap, I realized that if we *did* plan to build a house anywhere near this spot, I would never forget this day and the land we had christened.

Chapter Five

That night, I stood in Scott's room, unpacking a few things to put in his dresser (he had cleaned out a drawer for me) or hang in his closet.

He came up behind me, wrapped his big burly arms around my waist, and gave me a backward bear hug, his nose nestled into the nape of my neck. "Man, you smell good. And thank you for that little detour earlier. I think I'm good for a day or two now."

I turned around, my eyes wide, my mouth trying *not* to hit the floor. "A day? That's all that bought me was a day?"

He pulled me closer and kissed me with lips that felt like soft pillows against mine, his breath always fresh and inviting. When he ended the kiss, his dimple gave me a wink. "Then again, maybe I *can't* wait that long." His voice got all throaty and full of intention.

God, I loved this man. And I would do pretty much anything for him—or with him, for that matter. But this was his parents' house, and I couldn't go there. Family impressions meant too much to me.

"How about a compromise?" I leveled my eyes with his.

Keeping his arms wrapped around me like Spanish ivy, he whispered. "What kind of compromise? And can we try it now?" His eyes glowed with newfound energy.

I was about to offer more trips to the land when the sound of footfalls thumped up the back staircase. *Is someone coming?*

"I'll tell you later. Someone's coming." I shoved him back, which he didn't like much, judging by the way his eyebrows bared down.

Scott pretended to be insulted, his slight grin giving him away. "Man, you really are getting grumpy in your old age."

"Old age?" This was the second time he'd said that. I feigned anger with a jab to his ribs.

"Ouch. Yeah, you're what, a month and a half from turning twenty-two? You'll be an old woman soon. I may have to turn you in for a younger model."

Not waiting for my next jab to his ribs, Scott grabbed me and started tickling, which he knew I hated, mostly because I was *very* ticklish.

I squealed and tried to get away, but it was fruitless against his strength and determination. "No, no, no. You better stop right—" Another squeal shot from my lungs, several giggles bouncing off his bedroom walls. "Stop it, you brat." I wiggled and twisted, trying to break free. My hands slapped against his arms and chest.

A knock sounded on the door, interrupting our playful moment. We both paused before Scott released me from his grip.

Good. I had to pee, and Scott wasn't helping matters.

"Come in." I smoothed my hair back and took a breath, feeling flustered and much like a half-made bed.

Mrs. Williams poked her head in as I steadied my breathing. "Just wanted to let you know that dinner is almost ready."

She stepped into the room fully. "Do you have everything you need?" She crossed in front of Scott's dresser and past all the soccer posters decorating his walls, stopping at the foot of his queen-sized bed. Then she motioned toward a Jack-and-Jill bathroom that Scott had shared with his sister, Kelsey, for years, her bedroom located on the other end. "There are fresh towels, washcloths, and hand towels in the linen closet. And Kelsey has shampoo and body wash in the shower that you are welcome to use."

"Thanks, Ma," Scott said.

I followed Scott's mom into the bathroom. "Yes, thank you, Mrs. Williams. I brought plenty of everything. It is so thoughtful of you to let me stay with you again."

Mrs. Williams turned to face me, her hands finding my upper arms, her smile as warm as a summer breeze. "How many times do I need to tell you, dear? Please call me Beth"— she made an exaggerated shrug—"or Mom or whatever." She raised her index finger into the air. "Just as long as it's not Mrs. Williams. That is way too formal for my future daughter-in-law."

I corrected myself. "Thank you, Beth."

She removed her other hand from my arm. "That's better." She walked toward the end of the bathroom that opened into Kelsey's room. "Kelsey should be here in the morning. She can't wait to see you both and celebrate. Take your time coming down. We'll eat dinner in half an hour. I made Scott's favorite: chicken parmesan. Hope you're hungry." And then she was gone.

* * *

The next day, the party was hopping. There must've been seventy-five to one hundred people attending.

A large concrete pool, with mosaic tilework and two portable fountains on both ends, provided a nice centerpiece to the backyard, which was vast. An outdoor cooking area, complete with stonework encasing a gas grill and fireplace (a TV resting on the mantel) and a floor covered in pavers, gave Scott's dad an open-air clubhouse to cook and chat with his friends and family. He wore a goofy apron tied around his waist with the words "Kiss the cook" adorning its front.

A line of oak trees stood guard along the perimeter of the expansive lawn, allowing space for children to run wild while their parents watched from bistro tables with a beer or a glass of wine in their hands. A few people stood off to the side mingling.

Beds of wildflowers (the ones Scott had told me he'd helped his mother plant years ago), so impressive and lush they belonged in a resort, carved through the property like a river, offering color and fragrance.

A band pumped music through the speakers next to a makeshift dance floor, a few couples already showing off their skills.

As if that wasn't enough, a ballooned archway stood at the entrance to the backyard, offering visitors a fun doorway to pass through into the Williams family paradise. And, of course, no gigantic pool would be complete without an attached hot tub, also clad with impressive stonework and even a waterfall that cascaded into the lagoon-blue water. It was like a hotel or a spa, and I stood in awe of it every time I came here.

No children were swimming today, a rule Beth had made clear during large gatherings. "I don't want to worry about any little ones drowning during the commotion," she'd said, and being the cautious person I was, I always agreed with her.

My nose led the way to the food area where various scents ranging from garlic to tangy marinara sauce crept out from under the lids of several extra-large chaffing dishes containing hot entrées and sides from a local Italian restaurant. Cold salads and rolls complemented the well-stocked buffet.

As I forged a path toward the paper plates, napkins, and plastic utensils, I wasn't sure what I wanted to savor first. I was practically drooling.

While I munched on my food, I hung out next to a large bulletin board. It was embellished with pictures of Scott throughout his years from babyhood through college, and even a few of the two of us that promised a bright future ahead.

I thought of Abigail. She was invited, of course, but Joel, being the principal of the local high school, had some obligations that wouldn't allow him the freedom in his schedule to attend. Especially so close to the end of the school year. I looked forward to our more intimate gathering next week. And then I thought about my soon-to-be inheritance. Scott was right. A week was a long time to wait to find out what it was. I wished I had known more about it before Aidan had shown up. He had to know about it. How could he not? And here I was, hoping his visit was full of good intentions. Maybe it was. I sure wanted to believe that.

I finished my food and threw my trash away.

"Hey, Sis." Kelsey slung her arm over one of my shoulders, making me jolt. "Sorry. Didn't mean to startle you. My little brother taking good care of you?"

"Yeah. He's been great." I gazed over at Scott in his tailored cotton shorts and button-down Hawaiian shirt, chatting and carrying on with Jason and some of their high school buddies. It made me smile to see him in his element, his hands flying around as he told one story or another. He'd worked hard to get here, and so had I. And what was even more special was the fact that we'd done this together, supporting each other every step of the way.

As if he could feel my heart reaching out to him, Scott stopped talking, the commotion around him continuing. He puckered his lips, sending me a message: *Love you, Babe,* as he blinked, his eyes soft and sweet.

I puckered my lips, too, and mouthed the same message back.

Jason nudged him, and Scott was back in the fray.

"Okay, so if you're done making googly eyes at my brother, I think we need to get you a drink, girl." Kelsey tugged me toward the outdoor bar, where a guy wearing a crisp white shirt and black pants stood pouring drinks for guests. He looked to be our age.

Kelsey whispered into my ear. "Have you checked out the hottie my mom hired for a bartender? His name is Tanner."

We both gazed over at the tall, thin man with dark, slicked-back hair and a handsome face, who seemed to notice as he poured a glass of white wine for one of Scott's aunts.

His cheeks flushed pink as Kelsey moved in on her prey, dragging me along beside her. "Hey, Tanner," she said in a feathery voice.

"Hey ..." He struggled to remember her name, which made his cheeks even pinker.

"Kelsey, you've forgotten already?" She batted her eyes at him.

Tanner snapped his fingers. "Kelsey, right. What can I get you?"

"Got any more sangria?"

Tanner examined the long table behind him, abundant with wines and liquors, several large, white coolers off to the side for beer, seltzers, and bottled waters. "Sure, do. Would you ladies like some?"

Kelsey turned to me. "I know you don't drink much, but have you ever tried sangria?"

"I don't think so," I said as Tanner regarded us both.

Kelsey's eyes lit up like the flash of a cell phone camera. "You're gonna love this. It's got fruit in it, and it's perfect on a hot day."

As the late-spring sun relented to the night sky, heading toward another time and another place, the horizon celebrated with a spectrum of colors ranging from salmon to royal purple, a few wispy clouds soaking it all in.

Once he had finished grilling a generous number of hamburgers and hot dogs for any children or adults who preferred them to the catered entrées, Mr. Williams built a fire in the stone fireplace.

I helped Kelsey and Beth put the food away, carrying a hefty tray of burgers and dogs into the house. "I'm surprised Mr. Williams grilled so much," I said to Beth as I located some aluminum foil and sealed the top of the tray.

Beth waved me off in a casual manner. "He just wanted a reason to fire up his grill and chat with his buddies." She stood upright and arched her back. Her hands braced just above her hips. "I'm gonna need a good massage after today," she said, then her gaze locked on mine. "And what have I told you about calling us Mr. and Mrs.? Just call him Theo like everyone else does."

Scott's father's official name was Theodore Scott Williams.

"Okay," I said, a bit sheepish to be reminded of this. "I'm sorry. I don't know why I keep doing that."

Beth slid my tray of grilled food into the oversized fridge and closed the door. "Don't you worry, sweetie. It's all good. Could you bring this pasta to the basement?" She handed me another rectangular container, also sealed in foil, the scent of garlic escaping from its lid.

"Sure." And off I went.

The Williams home had two jumbo-sized refrigerators: one in the custom kitchen, complete with marble countertops, ceiling-high white cabinets, a sizable island with darker granite, and a farmhouse sink large enough to bathe a small human—and one in the finished basement, which felt more like an apartment of its own. Honestly, I could get lost in this place.

When I returned to the first floor, we spent the better part of an hour storing food in smaller containers and washing dishes while the men folded up portable tables and chairs and straightened up the back. Tanner, the caterers, and the band stuck around until ten before they picked up their equipment and left, Tanner making sure to collect Kelsey's phone number first. From then on, satellite radio kept the backyard rich with music.

A few people stuck around who weren't quite ready to leave, along with Scott's Aunt Freda and Uncle Melvin, who stayed over to avoid the long drive home at night. There was certainly plenty of room for everyone. The men continued to visit, while others took refuge in the house or at various bistro tables. People helped themselves to more drinks, water for the drivers.

Slowly, people drifted away or went to bed, Scott's dad lowering the music to an acceptable level.

I hung out with Scott until close to midnight, when he declared that he *had* to go to bed. "My dad scheduled us for an 8:00 a.m. tee time," he said. "And I'm fucking beat."

His eyes red and glossed over from the beers and drinks he'd consumed earlier, he bent down for a kiss, his lips tasting like one would imagine lips would taste after a day of partying and decadent food. Scott could eat dirt and taste great, so I wasn't complaining. I'd had a few drinks myself, dragging Scott onto the dance floor more than once. I especially loved the ballads that allowed us to push our bodies against one another and keep them there for the three- or four-minute song.

"My mom and Kelse are taking you for a spa day, right?" he said, running a hand down his tired face, his eyelids droopy.

"Yeah. I'm looking forward to it. Your mom was just saying how much she needs a massage." I knew she'd scheduled us for manicures and pedicures, but I wasn't sure about the rest.

"Want to head up with me?" he asked before a yawn stretched his lips wide.

"Um." I wasn't really tired, more wired from the day, and needed to wind down a bit before I suspected my mind would succumb to sleep.

"She can hang with us." Kelsey waved me over from a cushioned outdoor loveseat in front of the fire, her feet resting on a matching ottoman. "Get over here, girl."

Scott rubbed my back. "What do you want to do?" He yawned again.

In all honesty, I hadn't had much of a chance to get to know Kelsey over the years. Most of the time, Scott and I were away at college. Not that I hadn't seen Kelsey, I had. I just hadn't spent any *real* time with her. Although tonight, she was sitting with her best friend Joanna, or JoJo, as I heard people refer to her.

She had offered me an invitation that I didn't want to decline.

"Yeah, I'll hang out for a little bit longer." I wrapped my arms around my man and kissed his chest. "You get some rest, Handsome. I'll be up soon. And I'll try not to wake you."

Scott planted a soft kiss on my lips and unraveled himself from my arms. "If I don't wake up, have a good time tomorrow.

I'll see you at the end of the day." He took a few steps backward. "Can't wait to hear all about it."

"Night, Kelse. Night JoJo," Scott called out.

Kelsey's friend sat forward in her seat, her eyes intent. "Night, Fluke, and since when do you call me *JoJo*?" She brushed a swath of long brown hair back from one shoulder, the gesture reminding me of a supermodel with poised elegance. And JoJo was certainly attractive enough to be one with big brown eyes and plump lips, a sleek body that would complement most any outfit, which today was a pair of short shorts and a snug tank that exposed a few inches of her toned abs.

When Scott didn't respond, JoJo stood, her hand finding her hip, her eyes impatient. "Well?" She stood there staring Scott down.

What is this all about?

Scott exhaled and rubbed his eyes, another yawn breaking free of his lips. "Sorry, Rudder. *Night*." He turned and disappeared into the house as JoJo returned to her seat.

Even though I had no idea what JoJo and Scott were talking about, specifically, I assumed JoJo was one of Scott's many conquests from the past. The nickname was a mystery.

She and Kelsey resumed their conversation, mostly about Tanner, a glass of red wine in each of their hands.

"Come on, girlfriend." Kelsey patted the seat next to her.

I sat on the loveseat next to Kelsey on her left, a place that brought me better exposure to the fire's heat, although the flames were dying down for the night, the air growing cooler. JoJo had her own chair positioned on Kelsey's right.

"Looking forward to our mani-pedis tomorrow." Kelsey held one hand out and examined her fingernails. "My nails are trash."

"I'll fix ya up," JoJo said with a confident smile. She took another sip of her red wine.

I'll fix ya up? Did JoJo work there?

Kelsey turned to me. "JoJo owns the salon we're going to tomorrow. We're gonna get the star treatment." She smiled at JoJo. "Right, babe?"

JoJo pursed her lips and tilted her head. "You know better than to ask me that, girl. I gotcha."

Okay, so JoJo is rich? Is everyone rich here?

"That's great that you own a salon, JoJo. I can't wait for tomorrow." I sat back to relax when JoJo sized me up, the way women often did who felt threatened in one way or another, her brow tensing just a bit.

I'd grown used to this *look* from many of Scott's previous girlfriends, so I chose to ignore it.

The three of us stared at the orange and red embers that fought to stay alive, a few pops releasing any last-minute pockets of steam.

Kelsey yawned and then looked at my hands as though she had just realized something important. "What? No drink?"

I waved her off. "Nah, I'm good. I might go to bed soon."

Kelsey sat up and placed her wine on the small table between her and JoJo. "Nope. This is your celebration. You need a drink." She pulled her cell phone from the back pocket of her jean shorts. "It's only midnight."

I really didn't want another drink, but I sensed I had no choice in the matter.

Kelsey placed her hand on my leg. "Tell you what? I'll make you a tea and Baileys. Decaffeinated. Will that work?" She stared at me, her eyes unwavering.

Man, these guys could drink. I was a lightweight by comparison. Still, I didn't want to sound lame, so I said, "Sure. A tea and Bailey's would be great, but *I* can make it." I went to get up, but she took hold of my arm.

"I got this. Be back in a few." She dashed into the house,

leaving JoJo and me to our own devices.

After we stopped giggling about Kelsey's obvious determination, we reclined as best we could and focused on the fire again.

"The Williams's are nice people, aren't they?" JoJo took a sip of her wine, then held the glass on her lap, her voice soft.

"Yes, really nice. And that party was amazing. They went all out."

JoJo took another sip of wine and set her glass on the same table where Kelsey's remained. "Only the best for the Williams children." A soft giggle bubbled from her lips. "I've known Kelse and Fluke since we were in grade school. My dad used to work for Theo until he started his own KIA dealership five years ago. Theo was a big help to him."

After I caught that somewhat strange look from JoJo a few minutes ago, I worried we wouldn't get along, but she seemed okay.

"Wow. That's really cool. So your dad owns a dealership, too?" I stretched my legs out on the cushioned ottoman, my muscles taking a much-needed break.

"He couldn't have done it without Theo. And Fluke worked for my dad for free to help him get started." She took her wine back and enjoyed another sip, the glass nearly empty.

"Why do you call Scott, Fluke?" It seemed like such an unusual name. "And what did you want him to call you again?"

JoJo smirked. "Rudder." She finished her wine and set the empty glass down. "I'm sure he told you. He and I used to date." She reclined and returned her gaze to the fire, her feet finding the edge of the ottoman I shared, her toes perfectly manicured in a color that matched the wine she was drinking.

I was right. Why did everyone have to date Scott before me? Maybe it was casual? I sure hoped so.

Trying not to sound alarmed or jealous, I said, "No, he

hasn't mentioned it, but I'm sure he will at some point. So who are Fluke and Rudder?"

She giggled again. "During Scott's senior year, I made him watch *Finding Dory* with me. A bunch of us saw it, actually." Her gaze found me. "Have you seen it?"

I sat forward, my eyes locating Kelsey through the kitchen window, working away on my hot beverage. "Yeah, I did see it with my suitemate, Amy. We streamed it. Cute movie and funny." At least it wasn't some sexy movie. I tried to remember Fluke and Rudder with no success. "I don't recall those characters, though."

JoJo's cocoa-brown eyes warmed, her smile widening. "They were the sea lions that occupied the same rock in the ocean."

The light bulb went off in my head. "Oh, yeah. I do remember them. They were hilarious." Somehow this realization comforted me. This wasn't romantic, it was just silly, and maybe that's what their relationship was, too. Maybe Scott and JoJo were more friends than anything else. I took that idea and ran with it as if I were in a forty-yard dash.

"Everyone said that Scott and I were inseparable, so they started calling us Fluke and Rudder." She tipped her head in a reflective sort of way. "I don't know if you remember, but Fluke was the big one played by Idris Elba. Big muscular guy. Sound familiar?"

Considering it was so long ago, I was surprised JoJo bothered to mention it. Plus, she knew Scott and I were engaged. Was *she* jealous? I wasn't sure. I'd been through all that nonsense with Scott's old flames, and I wasn't about to go there again.

As far as I was concerned, Scott and I were rock-solid, and no one was ever going to come between us again. Not even a family friend who Scott had failed to tell me about.

Chapter Six

Her words slurring just a tad, JoJo settled into our conversation like a cat would settle onto a windowsill warmed by the sun.

"I hope you don't mind talking about this." Her gaze washed over my face, probably searching for any cracks or bouts of jealousy. "It's all past history."

Good. Glad you understand that. If she were mean like Mindy and Charlene—Scott's old flames who tried to intimidate me during my freshman year—I would have just gotten up and left, but she wasn't. Just reflective in an almost regretful sort of way. Still, if she became nasty, I was outta here, tea or no tea.

I did my best to represent *my* role as Scott's fiancée. "No, it's okay." And then I did something I wanted to kick myself for: I asked her a question. "How long did you two date?"

JoJo exhaled. "Well, let's see. We started dating, sort of, his freshman year. I was a junior." Her eyes were unfocused as though deep in thought. "We dated off and on for years. I guess you could say we were high school sweethearts."

Oh, please. She was really pouring it on. What was the point of this?

JoJo refocused her eyes. "I'm sorry, Sara. I shouldn't have ..." The way she chewed on her lower lip, her eyes tentative, I sensed she had more to say ... again.

Did I want to take my poison now or later? I let my big mouth answer for me.

"It's okay. Is there something else?" *Why do you always have to be the people pleaser?*

She shrugged as if it was nothing. "I guess I can tell you. You're getting married, so it's not a big deal, right?"

"Right," I said with conviction.

"Fluke and I talked about getting married a couple of times. We were each other's first, you know?"

Her words burrowed under my skin like a tick, and I wasn't sure I could take much more. How had I gotten myself locked into this ridiculous conversation?

"We would celebrate the end of every school year by putting our kayaks in the Bethlehem River. Scott would always bring a bottle of champagne for a toast, and we'd float on the river and talk about our year and what we hoped to do for the summer." A delicate giggle floated from her mouth, followed by a hiccup. "We were just kids, really, no real goals in mind. Mainly we'd talk about what concerts we wanted to see or places we wanted to visit on vacation."

Why are you telling me this?

Her gentle tone, the warm reflection in her eyes—she was treating me like I was an old friend, even though this was the first time we had spoken.

And then she hiccuped again, followed by a giggle, her hand covering her mouth.

Okay, I get it. She was drunk.

Part of me wanted to get up and leave, yet another part of

me was curious about what *else* she had to say. Scott had never mentioned any of this to me, so it couldn't have been as important to him as it was to her.

"In fact. At first, Fluke was going to go to college closer to home. Penn State. Same place I went. I suspect that if he had, we might be the ones ..." She slapped her hands on her thighs and wiggled her head slightly. "But then again, maybe not." She waved a hand out. "I've had too much wine. I'm blabbering. Just ignore me. That was all in the past." She stifled another hiccup that came out sounding more like a squeak.

I wasn't sure what she expected me to say. *Oh, that's great. I'm so glad you two were each other's firsts and that you almost went to college together and got married.*

"I'm really happy for you two." This time, her voice shook a little, just enough to let me know that it pained her to say so. She still loved Scott; I was sure of it.

Please don't start crying. I wasn't sure how to handle that.

She regretted losing him. I felt like telling her to stand in line. I should have been upset, and I was a little bit, but mainly because Scott hadn't forewarned me about her. Knowing him, he had probably put it behind him years ago. Clearly, she hadn't.

Saving me from an awkward reply, Kelsey appeared, a steamy hot cup of tea in her hand. "Okay, I made sure to put plenty of Baileys in for you." As she lowered the cup to my welcoming hands, the scent of Irish cream engulfed my nostrils.

"Thank you, Kelsey." I took a timid sip, hoping to avoid burning my tongue.

When JoJo hiccuped again, Kelsey cracked up.

"Hold your breath. Then, drink more wine." Kelsey made herself comfortable and placed a full bottle of red wine on the table between her and JoJo. "So, what were you two talking about?"

* * *

I drank my tea with Baileys, happy to have Kelsey back, who talked with JoJo about a few friends they had been in touch with recently, along with a new engagement that had apparently come out of nowhere. Not mine, thank God. Kelsey also commented that Tanner hadn't texted her yet.

"I'm sure you'll hear from him soon," I said. "He probably thinks it's too late to text you."

Five more minutes of muffled hiccups and JoJo's breathing steadied. As she drank more wine, her speech slurred even more, making me hope she wasn't driving.

I waited a reasonable amount of time and then made my apologies. "I just can't keep my eyes open any longer. Thank you guys for the company." I even went as far as saying, "It was nice meeting you JoJo," but I was lying.

Even though she was drunk or close to it, it was odd of her to blather on about Scott like she had. She told me way too much. Things that were hard to forget: first sexual experience, high school sweethearts, marriage, and more. Part of me couldn't help but imagine this striking woman with long, sleek brown hair, and modelesque features standing next to Scott at their junior *and* senior proms or at their high school summer parties, holidays, and New Year's Eves. "*We were each other's first*," she'd said. How old were they? I'd always wondered who Scott's first sexual experience was, and now I knew. I had hoped it was some random woman who came into his life for one night and flew away like a bird migrating south. No such luck. It was someone he knew. Someone *they all* knew. A friend of the family. They were a couple. An item, one that warranted a nickname.

I'd only seen JoJo a handful of times over the years, mostly in passing. If she'd acted one way or another toward Scott, I hadn't noticed.

I entered the kitchen, all the lights off, save for the light under the microwave and two decorative nightlights on both ends of the spacious room. I trudged up the back staircase nearest to Scott's room on the second floor.

I had never been with another man before Scott or after. Heck, I hadn't even kissed anyone before him.

As I crept the door open to Scott's room, his heavy breathing reached my ears. What a comforting sound, I thought to myself.

After the way Rachael, Mindy, and Charlene acted during my freshman year, we chose not to discuss old flames. Since I didn't have any, it wouldn't have been fair, anyway. "*All those girls were just sex,*" Scott had reassured me. "*No one compares to you. You feed my body and my soul.*"

I let that memory settle in my heart meditatively as the light of the moon filtered through the blinds, guiding me across the room and over to the dresser, where I pulled out an over-sized T-shirt before I tiptoed into the Jack-and-Jill bath. Outside the small bathroom window, Kelsey and JoJo laughed and chatted. I wondered if JoJo told Kelsey about our conversation. If she had, what did Kelsey think? Did she wish her best friend and her brother were still together? Not that it mattered, but I hoped not.

I brushed my teeth and washed my face before I shut off the bathroom light and made my way over to our bed, realizing something else about my conversation with JoJo: Scott and I had been through more trauma than most couples endured in a lifetime. If the last few years had taught me anything, it *was* not to jump off my internal cliff every time things didn't go well. The ring on my finger told me Scott was committed to this relationship. Whatever was going on with JoJo had nothing to do with me.

Careful not to wake Scott, I crawled into bed and snuggled up next to my man, his body warm and familiar. I inhaled his scent as the clock flashed 1:03 a.m. from his nightstand. If he didn't have to get up so early for his father-son golf day, I would have woken him and told him all about my JoJo talk. But I decided I didn't need to do that. Our relationship was beyond petty differences, especially ones from the past.

I allowed that to be my last thought as my eyes grew heavy, my mind drifting off to never-never land.

I crept by the garage window, worrying that Daddy would be angry with me for breaking it. Somehow the window transformed into the windshield of our truck, a gaping hole punched through its center, blood dripping from the broken glass like fangs from a giant vampire.

A voice sounded off in the distance, angry and loud. He knew. My feet pushed forward, even though I didn't want them to, my body edging closer to something I didn't want to see. Around the corner, two men stood in opposition, fists tight at their sides, the air around them dark and swirling, both of them braced for battle. Lightning cracked next to me. These men looked alike. Brothers. I knew them, but I didn't know them at the same time. And then they started fighting, my feet pulling my body toward the conflict like a magnet. No, stop. I don't want to go there. Blood flew from their noses. Heads cracked against the ground. Stop. One of them looked at me, his eyes bloodshot and strained with worry. It was my father, but he was different, not the same man I remembered. His red eyes pierced through me. "Get out of here! You can't trust him! I said, go!"

I sprang up in bed and gasped. My breath hitched, my heart thrumming in my ears. I was soaking wet, and my mouth was parched. It had been years since I'd had a nightmare of this magnitude. What did it mean? Using the calming exercises Dr. Zeller had taught me, I drew inward, talking myself off the invisible ledge. *It's just a dream. You're okay. Nothing is wrong. Breathe in, one, two, three ... breathe out ...* Before long, I was better.

A new sun defined the layout of Scott's room, but he wasn't with me. And then I remembered the golf outing.

It was nine already, so I pulled my rattled self out of bed and took a shower, the warm water a welcome respite.

You're okay. It isn't real. I continued to coach myself. I couldn't help but wonder why I had dreamt this. Was my dad trying to warn me, or was my brain sifting through the events of the recent past and spitting out garbage the way it often liked to do?

* * *

Voices reached my ears as I descended the back staircase that opened into the kitchen. Beth and Kelsey were cooking and chatting as they bebopped around the room, Kelsey making herself some toast and Beth cooking scrambled eggs, the scent of bacon wafting from the oven. Scott's Aunt Freda had just gone out the back door toward the patio, a mug of coffee in her hand.

"Good morning." Beth smiled, her ashen hair cut just above her shoulders, still slightly wet from her shower, a few curls popping out as the outer layers had dried. Her hair reminded me so much of Scott, as did her eyes, which were a striking shade of blue. Somehow, that always made me feel more at ease around her. I wanted to tell her about my dream but realized that would be weird. I'd tell Scott later. One more thing we could discuss and analyze, JoJo being the other.

"Good morning." I sniffed the air, trying to shake off my anxiety flu. "Smells incredible in here. Can I help?" My gaze traveled over the many granite countertops cluttered with plastic containers full of baked goods, bags of chips, and leftover paper goods from the party, the frames of a few empty chafing dishes stacked off to the side.

"Go ahead and make yourself a cup of tea. The water in the electric tea kettle is already hot. And there are a few boxes of tea there for you to choose from." Beth stirred her eggs on the large gas stove, scents of garlic and onion making my mouth water, speckles of diced ham providing color. "You remember where the coffee mugs are, right?" She pulled a tray of cooked bacon from the oven, amplifying its strong aroma.

"I do." I made my way there, passing Kelsey, who was chewing on a piece of toast and sipping from her coffee at the breakfast nook table. "Morning, Kelse." I smiled, feeling a tad awkward around her from my recent conversation with her best friend.

"Morning, Sis. Tanner texted me this morning. We're getting together later." She took another bite of toast, her teeth making a crunching sound.

"That's great. He seemed nice. And cute. So, how late did you and JoJo stay up?" I opened the cupboard next to the built-in microwave and chose the largest mug I could find.

Kelsey swallowed her latest bite. "We didn't stay up much later than you did." She smirked. "JoJo kept cracking me up the more she drank. Oh, and she got the hiccups again. I figured by then, it was time for bed."

If only she'd cracked me up the same way she had Kelsey.

"I made her stay in the guest room. No way was she driving home."

She's here?

The thought of more JoJo time dampened my already disquieted mood, but I decided not to let JoJo or that dream ruin my *girl's day*, something Beth had planned when she'd learned that the men would be golfing. It wasn't every day that I got to spend time alone with the women in Scott's family, so I was looking forward to it.

From the stove, Beth called out, "After our manis and pedis, I'm taking you girls to lunch at my favorite restaurant, and then I figured I could show Sara some of our favorite boutiques in town, Kelse."

Kelsey kept her eyes fixed on her phone, saying, "Cool, Ma. Can't wait."

I expected JoJo to appear at any moment, but as we ate breakfast and chatted about the day, she never did materialize.

"Isn't JoJo joining us for breakfast?" I finished my last bite of eggs and wiped my mouth with my napkin.

Kelsey nursed her second cup of coffee, her eyes starting to show clarity. "She left earlier."

One less worry for me. Not that I was worried, per se. Waking with a start like I did, I wasn't in the mood for more unnerving conversations about *my* fiancé.

"She had to open her salon. We'll see her again soon."

Oh, yeah. Great.

"It's unbelievable that she owns a salon. Didn't she just graduate from college?"

Kelsey set her mug down on the table, stretching her arms over her head and releasing a yawn. "JoJo was in my grade. So she got her degree four years ago. But I get your point: it's still impressive. Her dad's helped her out a lot. And we all send business her way as much as possible. She's also got a prime location. That helps."

Beth smiled as she cradled a glass of orange juice in her

hands. "We are so proud of Joanna. She and Kelsey have been best friends since grade school." Her eyes lowered, her smile fading. "When her mother died when she was in middle school, Joanna practically lived here until she was in high school."

The more I learned, the less I wanted to know. I'd lost my parents when I was young, and it appeared, JoJo had endured that same horrible tragedy. I was glad I hadn't said anything derogatory last night. "That's awful. How did she die?"

"Breast cancer. It came on fast and took her much too soon. Poor Joanna. She didn't have any siblings, either. She became like a second daughter to me."

Lost her parents when she was in middle school. She and I had more in common than I realized, aside from Scott, that was.

Beth put her glass of orange juice down and placed her hand over mine, the coolness of her palm traveling up my arm. She blinked. "I know you know how that feels. And I'm so sorry for you both."

"Thank you, Mrs. ... Beth." I stood, collected my dishes, along with Beth's and Kelsey's, and made my way to the dishwasher. All at once, the warning from my nightmare screamed inside my head, *"Get out of here! You can't trust him! I said, go!"* At the same time, Kelsey knocked her mug over on the table with a loud clunk.

I practically jumped out of my skin. The plates in my hand shifted and shook as I slowly placed them on the counter, my hands trembling. *Calm down. It was just a dream.*

"Are you alright over there?" Beth said, gazing over her shoulder at me.

"Yeah, they just slipped. I've got it now." At least she couldn't see my hands, which refused to stop shaking.

Beth turned to Kelsey. "Good thing you finished your

coffee," she said as Kelsey grabbed her mug and set it upright, a few droplets left on the table. "You almost got my phone."

After I finished loading the dishwasher, I took a stabilizing breath. "Thank you for breakfast. I'm going to go get ready. What time do we need to leave?" The clock on the microwave flashed 9:55 a.m. already.

Beth and Kelsey stood.

"It's about twenty minutes away," Beth said. "We should leave in fifteen."

I darted up the stairs. That gave me just enough time to slide into my favorite pale-yellow spaghetti-strap sundress, the one Scott loved the best—probably because it allowed the most cleavage—and apply a meticulous amount of makeup. To accent my outfit, I chose my tan, block-heeled sandals, the ones that laced up my calves and Scott said were "*sexy as hell.*" I let my hair fall, long and wavy, down my back, hoping to look my best.

I told myself in the mirror that this wasn't about rivalry. It was about standing my ground. And I was determined to look fabulous while doing it.

Lush with jungle-like greenery and tropical pictures that adorned the walls, wicker furniture—and a floral rug centering the room—JoJo's salon personified rest and relaxation. Flanking the reception desk, two waterfalls cascaded down the walls, the sound designed to relax and unwind.

Beyond the waterfalls sat several tables in a uniform fashion, some with women working on nails for their female customers. And taking up space at the back of the salon, two rows of oversized recliners ran along the walls facing each other.

Soft music emanated from hidden speakers, the scent of sandalwood reminding me of Amy.

When we arrived, my guard was way up, but it didn't stay that way for long.

Much less talkative and a little paler complexioned, JoJo wasn't as perky as she was the night before. Not only that, she rarely made eye contact with me.

I could tell she was embarrassed. Regardless, that didn't make what she said any less *honest*.

Validating my wardrobe choices, JoJo complimented my dress and my shoes with gusto. "You look hot, girl," she said, Beth and Kelsey nodding.

The nail salon was fine. My toes were soon shiny and French, Beth's and Kelsey's much more colorful. I chose to pass on the manicure but hung close by to chat.

During our time there, JoJo and Kelsey talked mostly about Tanner and a few other things while I tried to make conversation with Beth about graduation and our trip abroad. Thankfully, JoJo didn't bring up Scott again, and I was thrilled. The only thing she said in reference to last night was how drunk she was, which told me she might or might not have even remembered our conversation. Although, her sheepish demeanor suggested she did.

It didn't matter, anyway. I had more important things on my mind, like that horrible dream and what it could possibly mean. If anything at all.

While the logical side of my brain knew that I'd had many nightmares over the years and none of them had ever turned out to be true, the other side worried that my father was trying to tell me something. I thought about the vision or whatever it was I'd had in Dr. Adams's house. To this day, I wasn't quite sure if it was a dream or a message from beyond. That one instance was the exception to my rule. Was this?

Aidan didn't strike me as a violent man or mean, only a bit socially awkward and slightly unkempt. And Scott didn't pick up on that vibe, either. Even my dad was scary in my dream, and I *knew* that wasn't true. It was all so messed up.

I continued to ruminate over it, my thoughts tripping over themselves as they sprinted around my brain.

At lunch with the ladies, I tried my best to be active in our conversations, but the dream had taken the wind out of my sails. The uncertainty of it was unsettling.

In these moments, I wished I had a will like iron. I wished I was Amy, who would shrug it off and not worry about it. "It was a dream, move on," she'd say. The trouble was, I wasn't like Amy. My will was more tissue paper than iron. I'd lost too much in my life, experienced too much heartache to ever take the good times for granted. Or the people. *And that mysterious inheritance.*

All at once, Kelsey and Beth's eyes fell upon me, their voices subdued. Had they asked me something? My cheeks flared.

Beth touched my forearm. "Are you feeling okay? You've been so quiet."

I exhaled, trying to stop obsessing. "I'm sorry. I guess I'm just a little tired from graduation and all the moving stuff, plus the drive here." I rubbed my eyes for emphasis.

"We don't need to shop after this. We can head home, and you can take a nap. It's perfectly understandable. It's been a busy couple of weeks for you and Scott."

Kelsey nodded in support of her mother's offer.

"No, that's okay. I was looking forward to spending some time with you both." I sat up straighter in my seat. I hated how my mind had a way of gnawing on a problem like a dog with a piece of rawhide. "I'll order an unsweetened tea and perk up. I promise." I smiled. "So, Kelsey, what are you going to wear on your date? Where did you say you are going?"

* * *

Confident I had turned my somber mood around and had actually behaved like a human being, I followed Beth and Kelsey into the house, carrying my bags filled with two new pairs of pastel-colored cotton shorts, a floral sundress with flared skirt and spaghetti straps, and a wide-brimmed straw summer hat.

"Thank you so much for today. It was fun. And lunch was delicious." The grilled chicken sandwich with pesto and cheddar still lingered on my tongue. *Yum.*

"You are very welcome, dear." Beth's tone was as warm as an electric blanket around my heart. I loved that about her.

"Crushing on that sundress, Sis. I may have to go back and get one for myself."

"It would look great on you, Kelse, and I noticed they had a lot of different colors and styles."

The three of us headed up the front staircase, where I peeled off at the top for Scott's room to drop off my things. I was hoping that maybe Scott and I could go for a walk or talk somewhere private. I wanted to discuss that dream and what it could mean. JoJo, the less important topic, was another I'd have to address.

Hoots and hollers, along with kerplunk splashes, told me the men were living it up in the pool, music vibrating from the outdoor speakers. Once I had changed into my bikini and put on a coverup, I slipped on my flip-flops and made my way outside, my new sun hat perched on the top of my head.

Donning funny-looking tan lines across their foreheads designed specifically by baseball caps, Scott, Jason, Mr.

Williams, and a few other middle-aged men I had seen at the graduation party but didn't know, were carrying on in the pool. Beer cans lined the pool's edge, a few left on the patio table.

Wearing my new sun hat, I opened the sliding glass door and stepped out into the bright sunlight, just as Scott did a back flip off the diving board making an enormous splash and soaking the pavers several feet in my direction. I thought my heart was going to stop, fearing he could hurt himself.

"Dude, that was awesome," Jason called out from the hot tub, his beer raised in Scott's honor.

A moment later, Scott's head burst through the surface, water gliding off his muscular body like translucent fingers. He flipped his wet hair back and wiped the excess water from his face.

I clapped and pumped one hand in the air. "Nice one, Scott. Woo-hoo."

When my words reached Scott's ears, he turned and swam to the edge where I was standing. Then he jumped up and grabbed me, pulling my body, my coverup—hat included—into the water. Even my flip-flops went in. Good thing I didn't have my cell phone. One second, I was a spectator, and the next, I was a sopping mess. I sprang up, clutched my hat which floated on the surface, threw it onto the pavers, and gasped from the shock.

"You're in for it now," Scott's dad yelled from the hot tub, a beer attached to his hand. A few other people laughed. The men I didn't know.

"You jerk." I shivered, my body adjusting to the abrupt temperature change. "I hope you didn't ruin my hat. I just bought it."

Scott took my flip-flops as they started to sink and threw them onto the pavers to dry.

While blinking back water from my eyes, I swam for the

shallow end, but Scott wasn't having it. He caught up to me and dunked my head under, making me wonder what had gotten into him but figuring it was probably a twelve-pack or more. I hated being forced underwater. It always made me panic. When I bobbed back to the surface, I, once again, tried to get closer to where I could find stable footing. This time, Scott snatched me and pulled me into his body, planting several kisses all over my face with his wet lips, the alcohol on his breath lethal should it make contact with a spark.

"Cut it out. I haven't even taken off my coverup." I pushed him away and splashed water into his face with abandon. Then I raced for the stairs.

Scott just watched me with red eyes and an enormous grin stretched across his face. "What? I thought you looked hot." His eyes twinkled with mischief. "Well you always look hot to me." Then he burped. "Come on." He waved me over. "Get back in here."

Since there was no chance of talking to him about my bad dream or JoJo in his condition, I shoved the issue aside. In some ways, it was a relief.

A Foo Fighters song blared from the speakers as Jason chatted it up with Scott's dad in the hot tub, a few other people doing the same in the shallow end. Everyone had a beer, except Scott, who was swimming toward a can waiting for him not ten feet away. Once he had possession of his beer, Scott focused on me again.

"Hurry up, woman." He chuckled. "You're taking too long. I need my she-beast."

Did you just say that?

The men in the pool didn't respond, but I could feel their wheels turning: *What does she-beast mean?*

I hoped *and prayed* that Scott wasn't so drunk that he'd tell them.

I peeled my soaking-wet coverup off and wrung it out before draping it over a vacant patio chair to dry. "You're such a brat. Give me a minute. I haven't even put on sunscreen yet." I examined my sun hat for damage, then placed it on the patio table to dry as well.

After patting my skin dry with a beach towel, I applied my sunscreen, all while Scott kept taunting me with "Hurry up" and "You're taking too long" from the pool. He also kept splashing water in my direction, a few more burps bounding from his lips.

As payback, I waited a few extra minutes.

When I finally headed for the steps, Kelsey and Beth emerged from the house to join in the fun.

It turned out to be a great afternoon, filled with swimming, laughter, and celebration. I even had a few glasses of sangria, which loosened me up just enough that I could enjoy my silly and slightly drunk fiancé. Jason's girlfriend, Heather, came at one point, which prompted Scott and Jason to start a chicken fight game, where I sat on Scott's shoulders, and Heather sat on Jason's. Whoever knocked the other one into the water first was deemed the winner. Scott and I won two out of three.

That night, after we enjoyed a boatload of leftovers from the party the day before, Scott made his way to bed. Heather drove Jason home, Theo's friends hitching a ride with the only other middle-aged man who had switched to water, and Theo disappeared around the same time that Scott had.

Soon after, Kelsey left for her date with Tanner, which I helped her get ready for, and then Beth offered up a movie. "Chick flick, horror, suspense, or romance?" she asked as she streamed through the selections on her enormous TV, surround sound included.

"How about suspense." Even though it was only nine

o'clock, I was kind of tired and wanted something with action to keep me awake.

Before long, we sat nestled on the cushiony recliner couch, popcorn in our hands, and watched *Bullet Train*, a movie Beth had wanted to see that starred Brad Pitt, her favorite Hollywood crush.

As the sangria wore off and I had a chance to rehydrate my cells with several glasses of water, I thought about my Uncle Aidan again.

Maybe the dream about him was just my nerves creeping up like they always did, the warning from my mother echoing in my subconscious. She told me about him twelve years ago. A lot had changed for me in twelve years. Had it also changed for him? If it weren't for that unexpected inheritance, I'd be less worried.

I also thought about JoJo and her comments regarding Scott. Not that I was worried about her. Scott and I had gone *way* past that stuff. On the other hand, I was a little bothered that Scott hadn't told me about it first. It wasn't a huge deal, but maybe he could have prepared me for a moment like that. I knew his feelings for me were real, but I also had to believe that, on some level, he had feelings for her, too. At one time, anyway. Real feelings. Maybe it wasn't love, but *something* had gone on. It didn't help matters that she was a close friend of the family. Or that she was his first. And she clearly wasn't over him. *Argh.*

I couldn't do anything about it tonight. And with that thought in mind, I sighed and lost myself in the movie and the company of my future mother-in-law.

Chapter Seven

I awoke to the sound of water running in the shower, the spot next to me vacant for the second morning in a row. Once again, I had slept until nine, which wasn't a big deal, but I didn't want to get up too late.

I sat up, stretched, and went through my clothes, looking for something to wear. From all the swimming yesterday, my hair resembled a blonde Elvira Mistress of the Dark.

I regretted not showering the night before but didn't want to wake Scott at the time.

I knocked lightly on the bathroom door to hear a woman's voice say, "I'll be out in a minute," the shower turning off.

"Oh, sorry, Kelsey. No hurry."

A few minutes later, she unlocked my door and opened it a couple of inches, the scent of lemongrass and ginger riding on a wave of steamy air sneaking through the crack.

"It's all yours, Sis," she said as the door on the other side of the bathroom opened and then closed.

* * *

Feeling more presentable and less Elvira-ish and wearing a sleeveless T-shirt and a pair of coral-colored cotton shorts I had purchased yesterday, I jogged down the back staircase and into the sound of voices and pans clanking.

"Hey, Babe." Scott rose from the breakfast nook table and approached, landing a coffee-infused kiss on my lips. "Did you sleep well? I tried not to wake you when I got up." He smiled, his hair slightly wet and his skin coated with the light scent of musk.

Loving that smell, I inhaled and smiled. "I did. Your bed is so comfortable. What time did you get up?"

Scott rubbed my back, keeping his body close in a snuggly sort of way. "I only got down here about forty-five minutes ago. I slept late, too." He cracked a smile as he leaned in and nudged me with his shoulder. "Too many beers." He poked my waist gently with his finger. "Sorry, I threw you in the pool, by the way."

I made a humph sound, my lips trying hard *not* to smile. "Don't worry. I'll get even someday."

"I have no doubt." He chuckled. "My mom said you guys watched a movie last night. Not cool of me to pass out on you." He took my hand and led me to the breakfast table where eggs, hash browns, leftover bacon, toast, and pastries waited.

I waved him off. "It's fine. You were tired."

And I was starved.

Everyone said good morning, except for Beth, who told me to help myself to the buffet she had put together in the center of the long table. "I hope I didn't keep you up too late."

"Not at all." I smiled down at Beth, who had taken her last bite of eggs. "It was fun. I love watching movies. And it was a good one."

Beth perked up. "Any movie is good that has Brad Pitt in

it." Her eyes shined with the same mischief that Scott's often did. Honestly, those two were so much alike.

Scott's dad blew out his lips in disgust. "Brad Pitt. What a pussy." He stuffed a few hash browns into his mouth and continued to read from his trade magazine.

Beth chuckled. "Worried about a little competition, are you, Theo?"

"Yeah, Dad." Kelsey smirked as she examined her phone and nibbled on her danish.

Theo lifted his gaze from his magazine. "The chances of you meeting ole' Brad won't keep me up at night, dear." He beamed an exaggerated smile that also reminded me of Scott.

Scott was really a mixture of them both. So was Kelsey, with her wavy blonde hair and her bluish-gray eyes that resembled Scott's father's more than her mother's.

Beth raised her chin; her lips pursed in defiance. "Well, you better hope not." She took a sip of her coffee. "Scott, would you mind running a couple of packages to the post office for me? I have some graduation gifts for Danielle that I want to send to Uncle Frank."

Scott pulled out a chair for me, then got me a plate from the island and some silverware. "Sure, no problem, Ma."

I looked at Kelsey. "So, Kelsey, how was your date?"

"Fun. I'm going to see him again tomorrow. I'll tell you more about it later."

I spent the next several minutes enjoying breakfast while Scott and his family talked about the party and the golf excursion before Beth got up to wash the breakfast pans. Kelsey remained lost in her phone as the men switched their conversation over to sports.

Theo finished off his coffee and stood. "I gotta run. Interviewing a new receptionist and a new salesperson today." He took his plate and silverware to the sink to rinse and then to the dishwasher. He leaned in for a kiss from Beth and then disappeared into the foyer.

Beth leaned back. "Tell Peg I hope Jimmy's knee is better." And then she said to no one in particular, "I sure hope he doesn't need surgery."

I hoped so, too, even though I had no idea who Jimmy was.

While sipping his coffee, Scott rubbed my back as I finished my breakfast. "Wanna take a ride with me to the post office?"

I wiped my mouth. "Sure."

We had a lot to discuss.

* * *

Riding down the road, I relished the mid-May sun warming my side of the truck, inviting me to roll my window down and put on my sunglasses, the fresh air a welcome passenger.

Scott reached out and ran a hand across the nape of my neck. "My mother was saying you guys had a good time yesterday." He let that statement linger, so I answered him.

"Yeah, we did. It was a lot of fun." I gazed down at my toes, my conversation with JoJo springing back to life in my mind.

"I think JoJo still has her eye on you, though," I said it in jest, hoping he didn't think I was too upset about it. Only a smidge.

"Not really." Scott cleared his throat, his hand remaining on my neck, his fingers providing a gentle massage.

Then Scott removed his hand and pulled his truck into a grocery store parking lot. He sat sideways in his seat. "My mom also said you got quiet a few times. And then Kelsey told me it was probably because JoJo had said some shit to you when she was here for the graduation party. I guess JoJo was worried that she'd made you mad. What the hell happened after I went to bed, anyway?"

"Well ..."

"Okay, now I'm starting to worry. I'm sorry I drank so much yesterday and threw you in—"

"It's fine. I'm not worried about that, or JoJo, for that matter. She just rambled on about when you two were high school sweethearts. She'd had a few glasses of wine by then."

That was when Scott ran a hand down his face. I could tell it was all starting to register.

"That was a long time ago." His face tightened. "And it was only *two* years of high school. We hung out over the years but, most of the time, just as friends."

"I know, but she said you were each other's first. And you had all these traditions like taking kayaks out on some river at the end of the school year." I let my shoulders rise and fall. "She said you two were together so much that you even had a nickname as a couple." I waved him off. "I'm not worried about JoJo, Scott. It would have been nice to know all this beforehand, though." I made one last comment. "Did you two really talk about marriage at one point? She said you did."

Scott rubbed his nose. "I can't believe she told you all that. She must've been shitfaced. Let me clarify a few things. We were both drunk for our first time. She was sixteen, and I was fourteen, almost fifteen. I barely remember it. Second, we did date off and on during her last two years of high school, but we were never exclusive afterward. And when she went away to college, we never dated after that. Not really. We hooked up every now and then, and we hung out a lot, but mostly because she was Kelsey's best friend. JoJo was always around. Especially after her mother died. The nickname was not my idea. Half the time, I can't even remember who the characters are or what our nicknames are supposed to be. The kayak, we did one year." He raised his index finger for emphasis. "After that, we invited people like Kelsey, Jason, and Heather to join. And if we talked about marriage, I don't remember it."

"It's fine." I took his hand in mine. "I'm not worried. She caught me off guard. I do think she regrets losing you. That part was rather obvious. Maybe if you had gone to the same school, you'd be with her now." *Where did that come from?*

Scott was shaking his head before I even finished speaking. "We wouldn't have, Babe. First of all, I didn't want anyone tying me down in college. Until I met you, I *never* wanted any of that bullshit. Let me repeat, JoJo is *Kelsey's* best friend. She is two years older than I am. Do you know how many times I've berated myself for sleeping with her at all? I felt like I was sleeping with my stepsister. Yes, she is nice. And, yes, she's good-looking, but I never felt that connection to her other than friendship. After her mother died, I treated her with extra care. Treaded lightly around her. And maybe I should have been clearer with her back then about my intentions. Apparently, not making waves didn't work so well if she still feels these things."

"I get it, but I'm not sure she does—"

"Sara." Scott's tone meant business, and so did his tight jaw. "If I could go back and change what happened between us, I would. And any love I feel for her is more platonic than anything. JoJo is the kind of person who gets down when things aren't going her way. She really struggled with her mother's cancer and her death. She gets depressed. It sounds like that's what's happening now. She's attractive and needs to put herself out there. Once she meets the right guy, this stuff won't even matter to her." He took my hand and kissed it. "When I met you, my whole world turned upside down. I couldn't get you out of my mind. When she dated other guys, I was happy for her."

I knew he'd clear things up. Or I hoped he would.

"No way could I ever feel that way about you. When that douchebag fucked up our relationship freshman year, and that shit went down with Professor Crazy, I went out of my mind thinking that I'd lost you. And if I ever lost you again, just lock me up in a rubber room and throw away the key. I would never get over you." He lifted my hand to his cheek and held it there. "I've been with you for four years, and I still can't get my fill. I've always said you are the most gorgeous creature I've ever laid eyes on."

The bulge in his shorts seemed to agree.

"You are everything I've ever wanted in a woman and more. I can't believe I'm the lucky bastard who gets to marry you. I never belonged to JoJo, but *you've* owned my heart from the moment we met. She doesn't hold a candle to you. No woman does. You are the best this life has to offer."

Scott filled every cell in my body with his love and commitment. He pulled me closer for a passionate kiss that had my insides gearing up for more. His tongue twirled around mine as our mouths made their own magic.

When he sat back, he repositioned himself in the driver's seat and started the engine, which roared to life. "On the way back from the post office, we need to make a detour to that property I showed you the other day." As he turned his head my way, his dimple brought a hint of fun-loving character to his smile. "This is a perfect time for me to show you how much I love you."

I rolled my eyes. "Like you ever need a reason to have sex." I giggled.

"You know it, Babe, but this time, I'm gonna *really* show you."

What haven't you done with me and to me already? I faced forward, my pulse racing, my inner thighs starting to twitch. "I don't know how that's possible, but I do like the sound of it. Hey, there's something else I want to talk to you about ..."

* * *

Scott pulled the truck to a stop right where we had parked the last time we had visited this beautiful place with rolling hills and nature at its finest. "It was just a dream, Babe. A disturbing dream, no doubt, but you do have them from time to time. It's been a while since your last one. And with all this stuff going on about your uncle, I'm not surprised. I wish I'd been there to help you through it."

"It's okay. You were golfing. I guess learning about that inheritance has me worried he's only here for that. I want to get to know him, but I don't want to get duped. I've had enough of that in my life."

"Yes, you have. That's why I think you should try to get in touch with your lawyer and find out what the inheritance actually is."

"Yeah, I guess I could call Abigail for his number."

"You should. Why don't you call her now and ask her for it?"

He had a point. What was I waiting for? And then I realized the time. "She's at work right now." I sent her a text instead: "Hey, Abigail, can you give me a call when you get a chance? No rush. I want to get Mr. Webster's phone number from you."

I set my phone in the passenger cup holder.

Scott wiggled his eyebrows at me. "Hey, I think I have a moving blanket behind my seat." He wasted no time finding it before leading me to the same location within the pines where our special spot awaited.

With our clothes still on, we lay on our sides facing each other, neither one of us speaking.

Scott ran his fingers down my cheek, hooking a few strands of my hair behind my ear. "What would you like from me? This moment is all about you. I'll do whatever you want and for as long as you want."

Even though a dam of moisture had broken free between my legs, my nipples hardening at the sound of his promising words, what I really needed was something else. "Hold me?" Somehow that trumped anything else on my list.

Scott scooted his body closer, wrapping his strong arms around me, and pulled me tight against his chest. "Of course I can do that." He peppered the top of my head with a few delicate kisses. "We can lay here for as long as you want. And we don't have to make love if you don't want to, either. Like I said, it's all about you right now." He craned his neck to see me. "I've wasted enough time in relationships that were all about me. Truth be told, I was a selfish prick. Not with you, though. I would never pull that with you. You are my world now, and don't you ever forget it."

Soon he was lying on his back with my upper body draped over his chest like a throw blanket, my ear planted against his ribcage, listening to the sound of his heart and lungs, a few birds chirping in the distance. He strummed my back with his fingers.

The wind traveled through, rustling the grass in the meadow and the leaves on the trees. We were all part of the same ecosystem. All part of the same plan. Life was like a giant spider web, tethering all the living creatures together in one way or another.

And for Scott and me, our bond would never die.

Chapter Eight

The week came and went, each day stretching a minute or two longer and the temperature inching up the thermometer, making its slow stroll toward summer. As I traveled north on Interstate 91, the ground rose up and grew into the Green Mountains, the terrain exploding with greenery, the grass thick and ready for toes to sink into, or picnics to host for another season.

I had spent just over a week at Scott's parents' place and was driving to Vermont to do the same with *my* family. I was excited to see Abigail again and my little sister, Mel. In fact, I told Abigail I'd watch Mel all week for her.

It felt so good to have a sibling, even if she wasn't by blood.

I'd tried my lawyer, Mr. Webster, twice now and left messages for him to call me. "His mother fell two weeks ago and broke her hip, so he's been trying to move her into his place and get her scheduled for surgery. Normally, he's really good about getting back to his clients," his receptionist, Mrs. Clarke, had informed me. She apologized profusely before assuring me she'd let him know I had called. Again.

The mystery about the inheritance remained ... *mysterious.* Uncle Aidan was coming for a visit in a few days, and I wasn't sure how I felt about that. Not that I could stop him. I had no way to contact him to cancel.

I really wanted to learn more about my dad's familial history. And the fact that Aidan looked so much like my father had me yearning for his attention, even though I wasn't sure I was directing my feelings in the right place. He was part of my bloodline, yet I knew nothing about him or the Brownes in Ireland.

Something occurred to me that I hadn't remembered in a very long time. It was how, every now and then, dad would sit at the window and stare out, a glass of Irish whiskey in his hand and a faraway look in his eyes. When he did this, my mother let him be, giving him whatever space he needed and urging me to do the same.

Was he thinking about them at the time? Did he miss his mother or father? I couldn't imagine having parents on this earth and *not* seeing them. What could they have done to make him stay away? If only I could have read his mind, I would have known the answer.

"Promise me you'll stop for gas soon." Scott's voice interrupted my thoughts, reprimanding me through my car's speakers. We'd been chatting for miles.

"I will, *Dad.*" I stared at my gas gauge, which had just dipped below a quarter of a tank. "Stop worrying. It says I can still go like a hundred miles."

Scott's huff sounded like static over the line. "Don't push your luck, Babe. If you see a station, stop. Once you get over the Vermont border, there are a lot less places to find gas from the interstate. You're not in Pennsylvania anymore. And I don't need to be driving five-plus hours to rescue you."

Wow, he *did* sound like my father or what I imagined my

father would say to me at this moment. I rolled my eyes, which, thankfully, Scott couldn't see. "Okay, okay. There's an exit in five miles and a sign that showed several gas stations nearby. I'll find one, okay?"

"You better." He paused, the sound of a door opening and then closing.

I tried to imagine his movements. "Are you in your room?"

"Uh-huh. I just got back from stopping by the dealership. That new software my dad got is a pain in the ass, but I think I can help him figure it out. I plan on working on it tomorrow." The sound of his bed springs told me he was lying down. "I miss you, Babe. I hate it when you're away from me." He exhaled in a yawn-ish sort of way.

"I miss you, too. It's only a week, though, right?"

"Only a week, huh? It's more like nine days. How do you expect me to survive?" He hissed out another breath.

"I know. I hate it, too. I wish you could have come with me. Maybe you can finish up with your dad early?" I knew Scott had his work cut out for him, helping him update a website and the dealership's operating system. Not to mention some house projects that Theo had waited for Scott to tackle, so I anticipated his answer.

"I wish I could. He wants me to stay an additional week, but I reminded him we're leaving for Europe on the thirtieth, the day after my birthday."

"Yes! I can't wait to spoil you. For our graduation cookout, Abigail invited Joel's two brothers and their wives, plus Abigail's brother may even be able to make it if his current business trip finishes up in time. She ordered some desserts from a local bakery that I love. She's got drinks and music all lined up. And for your *birthday*, Abigail made reservations at a really nice restaurant in town. And then we fly out on our adventure the next morning."

Scott's voice lifted a decibel. "Cool. Sounds good. And then when we get back, we'll celebrate *your* birthday. You excited? Do you think you'll let me take you to a bar this year? You *do* have bars in Middlebury, right?" His sarcasm was hard to miss.

Before I could answer, he kept talking.

"Or maybe we can go to Burlington since we'll be renting that lake house up there. I *know* there are bars there. I think I told you my cousin used to go to the University of Vermont."

"You did. There are a few restaurants in Middlebury that have bars. I really don't need to go to the bars in Burlington. That's a college crowd."

Scott chuckled. "What is it with you and bars? And you're what, a week past graduation, and you're already snubbing the college crowd?"

I knew he was kidding, but he wasn't totally wrong. I wasn't snubbing college bars per se, but I'd never been particularly comfortable with large crowds, especially ones cramped with drunk people, which was why I had opted for a quiet weekend at home in Vermont with Scott and my family to celebrate my twenty-first last year. I didn't like it at the Kappa house, and after what happened with Rick during my freshman year, I became even more uncomfortable with it.

"Babe, you there? I'm just joking around. We can go wherever you want. It's *your* birthday. And maybe Abigail and Joel can join. Get a sitter for Tazzie. It'll be cool."

For *Scott's* twenty-first birthday, I held a small party at the apartment. Scott's best friend, Jason, his college buddy, Willy, and a few of his teammates came to town (since the school year had already ended). Heather had helped me set it up. The night after, he hit a few bars with the same crowd, staggering home in the middle of the night. And the following weekend, his mother and sister came to take him out to dinner.

What stuck out the most about his twenty-first was how his

dad had barely acknowledged the occasion. I think he sent a text that Scott scoffed at. My heart frowned at the memory.

Scott's voice changed, something new brewing in his thoughts, I could tell. "So I know your rule about having sex in my parents' house. And that was hot what you did earlier, by the way."

I thought about what I *did* at our special spot before I left town, my cheeks flushing and my heart pumping with sexual memories.

"How do you feel about phone sex? Is that acceptable? I promise I'll be quiet." He took a long breath. "A week is a long time without you sleeping next to me." His voice got all pouty. "You can't expect me to go without *any* love from my she-beast."

I wiped a hand across my forehead, the window going down. Man, Scott could get my insides rumbling.

And then I thought about my answer. Maybe my no-sex rule could use some adjusting. "I guess I can accommodate that."

"Ooooh. Right now?" I could feel his eagerness thrusting through the speakers.

I shook my head. "No, not right now. You just thanked me for earlier. Plus, I'm driving, silly. And I know you don't want me driving off the road, do you?"

"Of course not."

He sounded about as happy as Eeyore from *Winnie the Pooh*.

"But after everyone goes to bed tonight. I'll call you, and then we can have some fun. And we can do that as many nights as you want."

"Now you're speaking my language. But I have another problem. What am I supposed to do about my hard dick right now? Can you help me out? The man who loves you more than anyone in this world." He was actually begging. "Please. Just breathe heavy. That's all I need."

I giggled. Not the reaction he was looking for, I was sure. Being the overcautious person I was (and would always be), I wasn't psyched about distracting myself on the road. Especially with sexual stuff that could really take my focus away. Even breathing heavy, knowing what he was doing on the other end, was risky for me.

"I'm afraid you'll have to handle that one on your own, Handsome. But just think about how much I want to wrap my lips around that big—"

Stopping my words in their tracks, a call came in on the car's display, a number I recognized but wasn't particularly thrilled about: Senator Sweet.

Senator Sweet, the father of Rick Sweet, the man who had raped me freshman year, and the man who I had negotiated Scott's release from prison with for nearly killing his son, admitted that when he was a young boy, someone had raped his mother. I'd hoped he'd taken what Rick had done to me seriously. From what I learned over the years, he had done just that. In fact, Senator Sweet sent me updates once a year confirming Rick was on the right path: going to counseling, volunteering for victims of sexual violence, and donating his time and money to women's shelters. All good stuff.

Has it been a year already?

"Where did you go?" Scott was already breathing heavy.

"I'm sorry, Handsome, but can I call you back? I've got another call coming in."

"What?" Scott sounded so exasperated. "Who? Can't you call them back?" He acted like nothing else could be more important in the world than *his* sexual needs.

The truth was, I didn't want to postpone the senator. These calls only took a few minutes, and I wanted to get it over with. A small part of me also wanted to make sure all was still right in Rick's warped world, not that I was worried. *Much.*

"You'll be okay for a few minutes. I'll call you back as soon as I can." Before he could argue, I ended the call and switched over.

"Hello, Senator."

A high-spirited voice answered. "Hello, Sara. How are you doing? I hear you just graduated from CU."

It irked me that the man knew so much about me. Then again, he *was* a senator, who could find out pretty much anything he wanted.

"Yes, I did, and so did Scott. He did the graduate program."

"Fantastic. Then congratulations are in order. And I understand you are also engaged. Will you move back to Vermont after the wedding or to Pennsylvania, where Scott lives?"

Again, the man knew too much. It was weird.

"We haven't figured that part out yet." I cleared my throat. "What can I do for you?" I put on my cruise control and waited, passing the exit with all the gas stations. I assured myself that the town of White River had plenty of them, which was only an hour away.

"Just wanted to let you know that Ricky is still doing quite well. He's actually getting married, too."

The way he boosted his voice, I wondered if he expected me to be happy for him. I'd made a lot of personal improvements over the past few years, my attitude toward Rick being one of them. As time forged on and the senator's phone calls reinforced that Rick was doing well and stable, I worked on something that challenged me to my limits: forgiveness. For that, I relied on Dr. Zeller's assistance since Scott could barely speak Rick's name without anger burning in his eyes.

Considering the doctors had to wire Rick's jaw shut, I often wondered if he still suffered from his injuries, not that I would ever ask.

"Oh? Who is he marrying?" Normally, I would have said *"Who's the lucky girl?"* But that wasn't happening. If anything, I wanted to warn the person.

"She's a lawyer who takes on domestic violence cases. Honest woman. She'll be a good spouse for Ricky. Keep him in line." He sort of chuckled as he said this.

I held my tongue, letting Dr. Zeller coach me from the past. *"Harboring resentment and hatred for another person can keep you tied to them in an unhealthy way. And it can prevent you from moving forward. When you release feelings of resentment or vengeance, you are freeing yourself from that person. You are not saying what he did was right. And you are not saying what he did was okay. You are accepting that it happened, but you are releasing the emotional attachments from the guilt and the blame."*

As I processed this, an awkward silence dangled in the air between the senator and me like one of those pungent tree air fresheners dangling from a rearview mirror. What was I supposed to say? I couldn't find the words.

The senator cleared his throat. "Anyway, Ricky has been working really hard on righting some wrongs."

Wrongs? That was the understatement of the year.

"He wanted me to ask if you would be willing to meet with him. He wants to apologiz—"

"No way. I'm sorry, Senator, but I can't do that." My stomach churned at the thought as I white-knuckled the steering wheel.

"Yes, I understand. You see, Ricky recently admitted to me that he was abused by a distant relative when he was young. A woman who has since died. She played some mind games on him and exposed him to things he was way too young to handle."

Good. Of course I didn't mean that. *But good.* Dr. Zeller repeated herself in my head. "*When you release feelings of resentment or vengeance, you are freeing yourself from that person.*"

I'm trying, Dr. Zeller, I'm trying.

"Ricky said it really messed him up for a long time, and he lashed out. It was through counseling over this past year that it resurfaced. He really is a changed man."

I spoke through gritted teeth. "I'm sorry to hear that. And I'm glad he's getting help for it." I *was* sorry, like I would be sorry for anyone abused in that manner. "But I can't meet with him. It's too much." My lower lip started to tremble, my gut urging me to end this call.

The senator exhaled. "I understand." He sounded so disappointed.

He had no justifiable right to those feelings. I could forgive Rick. I could even move past it all, and I had, but meeting with him one-on-one was a bridge too far, as in the Seven Mile Bridge to Key West too far.

"You can choose the location. And I would never ask you to meet with him alone. I would be there, and I would even suggest that Scott attend as well." He paused. "As long as he can control himself."

Omg. Did you really just say that? I grit my teeth. "Control himself? Listen, I am glad you are all getting on as a family, and I hope Rick and his bride will be happy, but you have no right to ask this of me. In fact, I'd prefer it if you didn't call me anymore."

"No, please. I didn't mean to—"

"Lose my number, Senator." I ended the call and then screamed at the top of my lungs. *Argh.* He had a lot of nerve posing a question like that one. It wasn't as if his son had broken my heart or been rude. He'd abused me in a way that nearly sent me to a place I might never have returned: insanity. If it hadn't been for Amy ... and Scott. I shook my head. *Deep breaths. He's not in control anymore. You are. It's over. You've moved on. He's not a threat.* I kept repeating those things until my heart rate returned to normal, and I could breathe again, my stomach finally settling like a kettle of boiling water pulled off the stove.

As the adrenaline dissipated from my body, I tried Scott, but he didn't answer.

I'd told him I would call him right back and several minutes had passed. Maybe he had fallen asleep? Or, given the time, was having dinner?

Feeling frustrated by the audacity of the Sweet family, I stewed for another ten minutes, and then I called Dr. Zeller.

* * *

At Abigail's house that night, after everyone had gone to bed, I stretched out on my mattress, pj's on, and tried Scott again. I knew he wanted phone sex, but after what had happened on my drive to Vermont, I wasn't really in the mood.

Once I reached her, Dr. Zeller told me I'd *"handled the situation very well, given the circumstances"* and confirmed that Senator Sweet had overstepped his boundaries in asking me to do something so difficult. Most of the time, when I tried to call Dr. Zeller on the fly, I'd have to leave her a message, so I was lucky she was available.

We talked it through, and then we hung up with me feeling a little bit better about it all. I'd held my ground, and I was proud of that.

I still hadn't told Scott about it, but I was about to.

A groggy voice answered the phone. "Hi, Babe. I saw you called earlier. My dad dragged me out to the driving range and bought me dinner and a beer afterward."

It was nice to hear that Scott and his father were spending so much time together. No more missed birthdays. No more fighting.

"We just got back half an hour ago." He yawned. "I guess I dozed off." Rustling in the background implied Scott was sitting up, probably against his headboard like I was. "I waited ten minutes for you to call me back earlier until my dad came into my room and dragged me out. And, of course, I forgot my phone. Anyway, must've been an important call."

His question stood between us like a traffic guard seeking an answer.

"Was it that long? I'm sorry." My voice dipped.

"No worries, Babe. It's all good." And then his tone changed. "Are you ready for some ... fun?"

"Uh. Maybe. But first, I need to tell you about the phone call I received when I had to hang up with you earlier ..."

I had no longer finished speaking when Scott exploded. "What the fuck? Who does he think he is, asking you to do that? That whole family is mental. I hope you told him to fuck off."

"Sort of. He told me that Rick had been abused when he was younger, and that he's changed—"

"Who gives a shit?" Scott was screaming now. "You aren't seriously considering this, are you?"

"No, I was just trying to explain—"

"He comes anywhere near you, and I'll fucking end his life. I'm serious, Sara. That son of a bitch won't know what hit him." He huffed and growled like an angry rottweiler over the miles between us. "You know, sometimes, you are too goddamn forgiving, you know that? Jesus Christ. How can you even consider this?"

"I'm not. The senator has been calling me for years. You know this. Why are you freaking out on me right now?" My heart was beating out of my chest, my palms and pits all sweaty.

"Why do you let him call you at all? I've never understood that. It's messed up." His anger and frustration blared through the phone like a foghorn.

I wasn't expecting to have to defend myself. And I was getting flustered. His words lashed at me, opening wounds I thought had sealed. "Because I ... It's not like he wanted me to meet with him alone. He even suggested you come." *Why did I just say that?* What was coming out of my mouth? I had no intention of meeting with Rick.

All of a sudden, his tone changed again. "Yeah, that sounds great, honey. And after that, we can go have lunch with Professor Psychopath at the jail. Sound like a plan?" His sickly-sweet voice revved my anger like a motorcycle about to burn rubber.

"I don't appreciate your sarcasm. I called you to tell you about something that happened to me, and all you can do is think about yourself. Why does everything always have to be about *you*? Dr. Zeller said I handled the situation very well."

"When did you speak to her? Did you call her before you tried to call me?"

What was happening? How had this conversation gone so far off the rails? I pulled the phone away from my ear and stared at it, my mind perplexed. At least we weren't on Facetime. That would have been worse.

"Sara! SARA!"

I returned the phone to my ear, my teeth grinding together like a wood chipper. "I already told you I called you first. What difference does that make?"

Scott's voice fell, his volume low and alarming. "I'm telling you right now. You are *not* going to meet with him. Absolutely not. And if you think you should, we need to seriously think about a new counselor. If I'm in the same room with him, I won't be responsible for what happens."

His words sent a tremor down my spine, every part of my body quaking with fear. It reminded me so much of freshman year. All those horrible memories of Scott and me fighting, the mistrust. The things we had said to each other battered my heart like a strong surf against a mound of jagged rocks.

"I am sorry I told you about this—"

"You need to listen—"

"No, *you* listen!" I leapt to my feet and screamed so loud that Abigail showed up at my door, her eyes filled with worry.

With the door open a crack, she mouthed the words, *Are you okay?*

I put my hand up for her to wait and closed the door gently, sparing her from this unpleasant conversation. "You have no right to say those things. No. Right!" I paced the room, one hand flailing. "I have no intention of meeting with him, which I told the senator before he even finished asking me. I have worked so hard to get past all the ugliness that happened during freshman year, and I refuse to let you pull me back there. Without even hearing me out, you started assuming things that weren't true. You've insulted my intelligence and who I am as a person. I love you, Scott, but for the first time in three years, I can't bear talking to you for another second." I was trembling from head to toe. "You just turned a bad conversation between Senator Sweet and me into a traumatic event, and I am beyond angry with you about it." Tears started to flow. He had stripped me down to my core, like an apple that had been eaten and then tossed away in the trash.

"I'm sorr—"

"Save it. And after I told the senator that there was *no way* I was *ever* going to meet with his deranged son, I'll tell you the same thing that I told him: 'Lose my number.'" I punched the red End button with my finger, and then slammed my phone down onto my mattress.

Abigail crept my bedroom door back open. "What's going on?"

Before I could answer, I rushed past her and into the bathroom, where I emptied the contents of my stomach into the toilet bowl, sweat dripping off my forehead. All those years of healing, forgiving, and moving on. Scott had just thrown a dagger into my wheels of progress and right into my heart.

Chapter Nine

I cried in Abigail's arms for what felt like an hour, her comforting voice doing its best to soothe my frayed nerves.

"He was just scared for you. This is Scott we're talking about. He adores you. You two will work it out." She brushed my hair away from my face and continued to supply me with tissues.

"I know. But that was how he used to act every time something made him angry." I pulled away from the warmth of her supportive shoulder, my voice unsteady. "I thought we'd moved past all this stuff. I wasn't going to meet with him, Mom. *I wasn't.*"

"Shhhh. It's okay. I know you weren't." She ushered me back into her arms. "It's going to be okay. You're both bound to have setbacks. It's only natural. The senator was out of line. To put you in that position. It was wrong."

I was glad Abigail wasn't willing to turn on Scott, but part of me wanted to hear how awful he'd been, the little girl in me who just wanted to be right.

"Has he tried to call you back? Scott, not the senator." Abigail released her hold on me and wiped the excess tears from my cheeks, the ones I hadn't gotten to yet.

"I turned my phone off so he can't." I kind of half-giggled, half-hiccuped. "I told him to 'Lose my number.'" In retrospect, it was a childish thing to do. I understood this, but I was still too angry to care. Caring could be dealt with tomorrow.

* * *

I had just stopped sniffling and finally fallen asleep when a tapping noise sounded from my window. I opened my eyes and stared at my clock: 4:06 a.m. *Did I really hear something, or did I imagine it?* I waited.

Tap, tap, tap. There it was again.

Was it a branch?

I had to look. With my pulse racing like a greyhound, I tiptoed closer to the window, held my breath, and pulled the blind back a few inches to peer out.

The tall, dark figure standing there had me frozen with fear. *Bigfoot?*

"Sara. It's me. Can you let me in?"

Once I realized it was Scott and not an ape-like creature— and I could breathe again—I motioned with my hands and mouthed the words, *Go to the front door.*

He came all the way from Pennsylvania to see me? Given the time, he must've left right after our phone call. *That's over five hours on the road.* While part of me was flattered, another part of me wondered if he was here to put me in my place. I hoped I was wrong. Either way, I was standing my ground. No one was going to bully me into submission.

My answer came the moment I unlocked the front door. Scott wrapped his muscular arms around my shoulders. "I'm so fucking sorry. Please forgive me." He released his hold, his red eyes in full view. "I should never have talked to you that way. If you want to meet with Rick, I'll support you. I'll do whatever you want me to. It's okay. I can control myself. I don't know what the fuck was the matter with me. I tried to call you right back, but your phone went to voice mail. I was just surprised. The whole thing freaked me out a little. I know this kind of thing can be part of your recovery and—"

"I already told you; I'm not meeting with him. *Ever.*"

"Thank God." Scott let out a raspy breath, his shoulders releasing. He hugged me again. "I mean, it's okay if you do, but I'm glad you're not. He doesn't deserve your forgiveness."

With gentle hands, I pushed Scott back and stared with earnest. "But I *do* forgive him. I don't excuse what he did, but I don't want to spend my life tied to him by anger or any other emotion. And if he *was* abused, then it sort of makes sense why he was a messed-up jerk." I firmed my voice and fixed my eyes. This was a defining moment for us, and I needed Scott to understand. "I'll say it again: I'm not excusing him. What I'm doing is releasing *me*. And I have so much to be happy about that I don't want to waste another second worrying about him. He's not important enough in my life to come between us unless *you* let him. I'm not going to give him that much power, and I hope you won't, either." I placed a hand on his upper arm, the muscle beneath smooth and hard as a rock. "What just happened was not about him. You get that, right?"

Scott offered a reluctant nod; one shrouded in remorse. "I do. I know I didn't handle it well." He half-smirked. "If it's any comfort, I didn't punch any holes in the wall—didn't even want to—and I changed my attitude the minute you called me out for it." His hand found my shoulder, his tender squeeze supportive. "In my defense, if you hadn't hung up on me and turned your phone off, you would have known that." His left dimple did its best to lighten the mood.

He had a point. I had shut him down without giving him a chance to recant. "You're right. That was *my* bad. I'm sorry I did that."

He exhaled and rubbed his eyes. "No worries, Babe. I deserved it." He stretched his back out. "I'm not sure my back did, though. I'm helping my dad expand the pump house. That drive didn't help matters. I need a massage."

The glimmer in his eyes told me he wanted more. *What's new?* I thought as my heart grinned.

Just then, Abigail peered around the corner. "Everything okay out here?"

Both our heads turned in her direction.

"Yeah, Mom. Everything is fine."

"Sorry, Abigail, I didn't mean to wake you," Scott said, his eyes shameful.

She waved him off. "It's fine. I was heading to the bathroom, anyway." Then she made a quick exit.

I slid my arm around Scott's waist and smiled up at him as he leaned into me.

I'd learned in life that nothing was ever black-and-white. Somehow, we all seemed to fall within various shades of gray. We stumbled, we even fell, but we also picked ourselves back up and continued on. And sometimes, we were even stronger for it. Scott and I were a living testament to that.

* * *

Lying in Scott's arms, I awoke to a quiet house. We'd made love last night, despite my misgivings about it. "You have this thing about making love in a house with parents, but what do you think the parents are doing? If parents felt the same way about it as you do, no one would be having sex" was Scott's logic. I could tell he'd been thinking a lot about it.

And he was right. Maybe we couldn't have wild-and-crazy sex, but we could connect, which is what we did, quietly and carefully. Plus, I had locked the door.

All at once, something else occurred to me. *Where is Mel?* Uh-oh. I was supposed to watch her. I jumped out of bed, Scott groaning as his mind started to rouse.

"Where are you going?"

"It's eleven o'clock. I'm supposed to watch Mel." I jumped out of bed and dashed into the kitchen. A note on the fridge told me the answer, setting my mind at ease. Abigail had brought Mel to daycare to allow us time to sleep late. She was bringing her back between 11:30 and 12:00 to be with me, depending on how quickly she could get here. Since it was eleven already, that didn't leave us much time.

"I figured you two could use the extra rest," she also wrote, adding, "there are plenty of eggs and deli ham in the fridge."

Scott dragged his feet around the corner, rubbing his eyes awake.

"Sorry to wake you, but I've gotta watch Mel this afternoon. Abigail is bringing her back on her lunch break. I feel so bad I slept late."

Scott ran a hand through his hair. "You can blame me for that one." He looked away. "I seem to be on a roll lately."

"No. It's all good. Hey, I'll make us an *egga muffin* (something my parents used to make often and came with its own special name). Why don't you go take a shower? Abigail and Mel should be here soon."

Scott turned to walk away but stopped where the hallway met the kitchen. "I know this is a stupid question, but ... we're okay, right?" He tilted his head to one side, his eyes searching.

After last night, how can you ask me that?

I went to him and placed my hands on his chiseled abdomen. "We're totally fine. Better than fine. I understand why you got upset." I wagged a finger, making sure to keep my voice playful. "But don't do it again. Next time—if there *is* a next time—hear me out first."

Scott tapped several kisses on my forehead before he found my lips. "You got it, boss. No more freaking out on you."

I giggled a little. "That crack about Professor Psychopath *was* kind of funny"—I jabbed him in the gut, which felt more like concrete—"if I wasn't so mad at you." I shoved him away. "Now go take a shower."

Scott grinned. "Okay, okay. And I need to text my mom. She's probably wondering where the hell I am. My dad, too. I left so late that they were already in bed. Are you sure you want me to go back tonight?" He blinked with those sad eyes, the ones that reminded me of Puss and Boots in the movie *Shrek*.

"Well, you need to finish helping your dad, right? It's important, and then we get to spend the rest of the summer together. Europe first and then the lake house. It's going to be awesome." I inhaled an excited breath just thinking about it.

Scott's face lit up. "*Yeah*, it is. I'm pretty hyped."

"Uncle Aidan is supposed to arrive in a few days, and I'm kind of nervous about it. I'm going to call the lawyer again. I may just take a run over to his office. I'd like to find out what the inheritance is before Aidan gets here."

Scott palmed the back of his neck. As he let his hand drop, I could see his wheels turning. "You know, there's no reason why we can't extend our visit in Ireland a little bit and visit the area where your dad lived. If things go well with Aidan, you can tell him about it. If whatever it is that you're inheriting is still here, you may need to make a trip there, anyway, to get it. We can always skip Scotland if we have to."

I liked that idea. "Okay, let me see what I can find out first." When we had planned this trip, I wasn't sure what to do about visiting my father's family. Given the secrecy surrounding the Browne clan, I had decided I wasn't going to contact them, but since Aidan had shown up at my graduation, I was more conflicted than ever. Part of me was thrilled about getting to know them, the other part, wary.

What I really wanted to know was what had caused the rift between my father and Aidan. How far did it extend? What about their parents? Were they involved? There was so much I didn't know. My dad died when I was only twelve. Maybe he thought I was too young to handle adult issues. All I knew was that he and Aidan were the only siblings. I had to believe that Daddy would have opened up to me about it at some point. The only person I had left to ask was Uncle Aidan. He was the key to the Browne family secrets. *But is he willing to reveal them?*

* * *

That afternoon, after Scott left for home, I took Mel to Mr. Webster's office. His receptionist, Mrs. Clarke, had been with him for over twenty years now, her short, curly hair more gray than brown, her skin wrinkled, and her glasses a tad thicker than when I had last seen her. She always wore some sort of button-down floral top and dress pants, her smile always welcoming, except today, when a distinct line forged between her brows.

"I'm so sorry Mr. Webster has been hard to reach. His mother is really having a tough time. Poor dear. She's pushing ninety and is ... *was* still very active. You know, at that age, a hip injury can be the death of you." She paused as though deep in thought. "But he did call to check in this morning, and I reminded him that you had been calling." She looked up at the heavens and sighed. "With him gone so much, I've had to reschedule all his meetings. Everything is in disarray. I've got clients calling me left and right."

I could tell that Mrs. Clarke was one of those people who didn't handle curveballs all that well. She liked organization and order. I could relate.

"That's okay. And I'm so sorry about his mother. I hope she recovers soon. Do you mind if I ask what I'm inheriting?"

She shook her head and flailed her hands in a flustered sort of way. "I'm so sorry, dear. He didn't say. But I will be sure to ask him when I speak to him next." Her gaze found Mel who was standing at my legs, two fingers placed in her mouth like a whistle. The tension on Mrs. Clarke's face eased for a moment. "What a cute little girl. Is she yours?"

"No, she's my little sister, Mel."

I bent over to catch Mel's attention. "Can you say hi to Mrs. Clarke?"

With her fingers stuffed in her mouth, Mel said, "Hewoh," drool gathered around her youthful lips.

Mrs. Clarke seemed to melt at that. "I have three grandkids, all girls. They're so precious when they're that young, aren't they?"

I placed my hand on Mel's head, her hair as soft as silk. "Yes, they are. Well, thank you, Mrs. Clarke. I'm in town for the next two weeks. Do you still have my cell number?"

"Yes, dear, I've got it, and I hope to have more information for you real soon." She picked up the phone's receiver. "You two have a nice afternoon now."

* * *

The next day, Mrs. Clarke called to tell me that Mr. Webster's mother had taken a turn for the worse. "She had a stroke. I'm afraid he won't be back in the office this week, but he wanted me to tell you that you will be inheriting a parcel of land in Lahinch, Ireland." And then she spelled it out for me so I could write it down. "It's land that your father owned and will be bequeathed to you. Apparently, there was a stipulation about you graduating from college first. Am I correct that you just graduated? He seemed to think that you had."

"Yes. I did just graduate. Did Mr. Webster say how much land?"

"Yes, I believe it's ninety acres. Mr. Webster promises to be back in the office next week to pull all the paperwork together. Apparently, it's not on the computer; otherwise, I would have tried to find it myself. He was in a hurry and couldn't go into the details. But congratulations on the land. How exciting."

"Yes, thank you." I ended the call, not sure whether to jump for joy or worry. It seemed even more likely that this was the reason Uncle Aidan had decided to show up—at my graduation—after all these years. Did he want the land? That had to be it. Did everyone in that family want it back? Not knowing anything about the Brownes, I was at a loss. For all I knew, the family had sent Uncle Aidan as their spokesperson.

Then what was he doing in Georgia?

I called Scott right away.

"Wow. That's cool, Babe. Ninety acres? Have you looked up that area on your laptop?"

"I'm doing it right now." My fingers tapped away on the keyboard, inviting images of this remote area of Ireland, gorgeous terrain and coastline flashing before my eyes. "It's beautiful there. Do you think I'm gonna have a fight on my hands with Uncle Aidan or my dad's family? That must be why he's here."

"It could be. But you don't know that for sure. He didn't mention it at the graduation, did he?"

"No, but when would he have had the chance? It was too hectic. And he planned to come here afterward, so he knew he'd have another opportunity."

"Maybe he's willing to buy it from you. That wouldn't be so bad. *If* he gave you a fair price for it. Do you have any plat drawings or a map of the land?"

"I wish I did. My lawyer is dealing with some family health issues, but he told his receptionist that he'll pull all the paperwork together when he gets back in the office next week."

"Okay, then. Try not to stress over it. I'll be there soon, and we can figure this out together. Talk to Abigail and Joel about it, too, so when Aidan comes, you're prepared."

"I will."

At that point, Mel tugged on my arm. "Come on, Sawa. Wet's go pway cars."

I nodded and smiled at her. "One second, Mel. I'm almost done."

After she stomped her foot, she gave me *the look*, the one that said "You're no fun," as she walked away, her feelings hurt.

Yesterday, I didn't spend much, if any, quality time with my little sister—Scott being here in the morning and then taking her with me to the lawyer's office in the afternoon—so I didn't want to waste another day distracted. That wasn't fair to Mel.

"Listen, I'll call you later. Love you."

Taking my duties seriously as Mel's older sister, I devoted the rest of my day to running around after a toddler and playing cars in the sand. We even had a picnic in the park.

I spoke to Abigail and Joel that night about the land. At first, they were excited for me, but they also seemed to get why it could be worrisome. "It's good that Aidan will be here in a few days so you can ask him about it. And when you go to

Europe, you should visit there to see the land you're gonna own," Abigail said.

I agreed. "I just hope I don't encounter a clan of Brownes who are ready to fight me for it with pitchforks and guns." Somehow, my glass-half-empty perspective always had a way of blistering my optimism like a chigger bite.

Abigail angled her head and smiled with those motherly eyes of hers. "I doubt that will happen. Wait and see, and then decide what to do." She got a thoughtful look in her eyes. "I'm surprised I didn't know about it. Seems like someone should have told me." She made a flabbergasted raspberry with her lips and shook her head. "Then again, maybe they did, and I forgot. I doubt I'd forget something so important, though. Either way, try not to stress over it. This is a good thing."

She was right, and before I lost myself in another round of obsessive-compulsive thinking, I focused on Mel instead.

As the week passed, we watched shows that were beyond silly, played hide and seek, and used the sandbox Joel had built for her last year to the fullest. Most importantly, I got to bond with my baby sis, who was tenacious, outspoken, and loving. When I stubbed my toe walking through the living room, she sat me down and used tissues and tape (which I helped her with) to bandage me up, even though I hadn't broken the skin. And then she finished me off with a kiss to my "boo-boo," as she put it. Her favorite movie was *Brave* by Disney, no big surprise, and her favorite book was *Love You Forever*, which always prompted a series of questions about life and growing old.

After I asked Abigail if it was okay, I brought Mel to the cemetery with me on Thursday to help me plant flowers at my parents' gravesite, where I explained who they were as best I could.

"How come you have diffewent parents than me," she asked me.

I said that her mother had become *my* mother when I didn't have one anymore. When she became sad about it, I explained that I was lucky to have two mommies who loved me: one in heaven and one here on earth. "And I never had a little sister before, so I also get to have you," I said with a smile and a hug.

Later, I cuddled in bed with her when she was having trouble falling asleep. "I share my mommy with you, Sawa," she said before she dozed off.

My heart melted.

Back in my room, I caught up with Scott on the phone. Once we had rehashed the land issue for the umpteenth time and what it could mean, he asked how his *Tazzie* was doing.

"I took her to my parents' grave to plant flowers with me today. She was very curious about them and how she and I were related."

"I bet," Scott said, "that must've been a tough thing to talk about. Hey, you went to the cemetery without me?" He sounded so disappointed.

Over the past few summers, I had brought Scott with me to do the planting and the weeding. Each time, we'd talk about my parents and what they were like. The silliness of my dad, the nurturing hand of my mother. And each time, Scott gave me his full attention, asking thoughtful questions about what we all liked to do as a family. I told him about our vacations to Maine, hikes during the summer months, leaf peeping in the fall, and traditions we enjoyed, like making ornaments for our Christmas tree, all of it. When we finished, and I was loading my gardening tools into the back of my Subaru SUV, Scott would always stay behind for a minute or two, his hand resting on the granite monument, his lips moving.

"What did you say?" I had asked every time he returned to the car.

With a smug expression, he'd often reply with something

like, "It's between your parents and me. Maybe I'll tell you someday," and then he'd finished it off with a teasing phrase like, "if you're nice to me."

I thought about that as Scott continued to speak over the phone.

"I'd like to go there when we get back from Europe. We can weed the flowers and clean off the stone," he said.

An idea came to mind. "Maybe, but only if you share with me what you always say to my parents when I'm not with you."

Scott released a heavy breath. I could almost see the smugness returning to his smile. "I told you. That's between your parents and me. I promise I'll tell you someday, but only if you're nice to me."

"I'm always nice to you," I said with a humorous huff.

"I mean *really* nice to me. Like right now, what are you wearing, and how can I get you to take it off?"

Chapter Ten

On Friday, Uncle Aidan showed up. He was early. Every time I gazed into those pale-blue, almost glacial, eyes, I was starstruck. So much of my father existed in this man. In his DNA ... and in mine.

Abigail and I shopped for food, wandering the grocery store aisles, trying to decide what to make for him.

"How about shepherd's pie," she finally suggested.

"That works. Sounds like something he'd like." I wasn't sure why I said that. Other than Aidan's comment about me ordering potatoes at my graduation dinner, I had no idea what he liked. But seasoned ground beef, veggies, and mashed potatoes—to which Abigail always added rosemary and garlic—sounded safe enough. "And I'll make a fresh salad to go with it."

Back at the house, we went to work creating a meal for our Irish guest while I pondered when to bring up the land. Once Abigail slid the casserole into the oven and I had finished constructing my salad, we worked together on a cheesecake that included Irish cream from a recipe I found online.

Meanwhile, Joel shared a beer with Aidan out on the back

deck, their voices filtering through the kitchen window. I wished Scott was here. He was so good at small talk *and* helping me feel brave.

Just as Abigail set the cheesecake on the counter to await a spot in the oven, I pushed through the screen door and into the late-afternoon air. A blanket of clouds crowded the Vermont sky, a few dark rims threatening rain. Patches of blue sky poked through every now and then, telling me it wasn't quite imminent. Not yet, anyway.

"Would either of you like another beer?" I asked, ready to join their conversation.

"That reminds me. I bought some Irish whiskey," Joel said in a perky voice. "Bushmills."

Aidan smiled, his eyes sparking with interest. "I could take a wee bit." He used his index finger and thumb to measure the amount.

Joel jumped up. "Great. I'll get us some fresh beers and the whiskey while Sara keeps you company."

I sat across from Uncle Aidan. "So, how was your trip to ...? Georgia, was it?"

Aidan nodded. "Grand. Straight out. Got a lot accomplished." The sun glinted off his slightly overgrown hair that wasn't quite blond but wasn't quite brown, either.

"What do you do again?" I rested my hands on the patio table and relaxed back in my seat, the bar underneath providing a place to rest my feet.

"I'm what do ya call ..." He contemplated for a moment. "A jack-of-all-trades. Is that how ya say it? I do a little bit of this and a little bit of that."

"Yes, that is what we call it." Since he hadn't really answered me, I pressed on. "What type of business were you conducting in Georgia?"

Aidan took one final sip from his dark-colored beer. "Well,

lass, I'm lookin' into golf courses. I may be workin' with a developer back in my town of Lahinch."

"That sounds exciting. I bet the land in Ireland is beautiful." The perfect segue. *Okay, here goes.* "Speaking of which, I just found out that I am inheriting some land there. A parcel that my dad owned." I waited and watched for something to happen, anger mostly.

Aidan's eyes widened as if dazed, his mouth dropping open. "If I'm not mistakin', the land was waitin' on your graduation. Congratulations. Hell of a present your da gave ya."

"I agree. I didn't even know about it until now." I swallowed hard, wondering what was coming next.

At least he wasn't denying he knew. *That's something, right?*

He shot one hand up in the air as though he couldn't contain his excitement. "Well, isn't that grand? We'll be neighbors." And then he slapped that same hand down on the table, making me jolt. "You'll have to come visit and see the place."

I let out a huge sigh of relief, my heart almost gleeful. Whatever I was expecting, it wasn't joy. "So you knew about the inheritance?"

"Of course I knew. I lost track of time, is all. You'll love the place. When can ya come visit?" He was beaming over this news.

"Well, it just so happens that we are planning a visit there very soon. And we'd love to come see you. When do you plan to return? *We* leave in a week and a half."

"I head for home the day after tomorrow. You and Scott have to stay with me. I live in my pa's cottage. Not much of a place, but it'll do. I've two bedrooms. You and your fella could take one. I'll show you the land and the sites."

This was going much better than I thought. I almost felt foolish for even thinking otherwise, my untrusting nature working against me. I wanted to hug the man for *not* being the lowdown scoundrel I had imagined he was and even dreamed about. I went from wary and cautious to enamored.

"We wouldn't want to impose. I'm sure we could find a room in ... what is the name of the town again?"

I remembered the name but wanted to hear him pronounce it again.

"Lahinch. On the northwest coast of Ireland."

This time, I memorized the way he said it.

"If ya fly into Shannon, I'll cart ya over there. An hour drive as the crow flies, maybe less. Beautiful countryside for the both of ya to admire."

It sounded amazing, my insides going all fuzzy at the thought. "I'll check our flights. Hopefully, I can make a change before you go so you know my itinerary. I've been meaning to add an international data plan to my phone, but I haven't gotten around to it yet." I thought about that. "Do you have an Instagram account? We could direct message for free?"

"Instawho?" My uncle stared in confusion.

"Instagram. I can help you open an account. And then I can DM you. Direct message, I mean. Do you have good Wi-Fi there?"

Aidan flipped one hand back and forth like a seesaw. "Spotty, but I can go to town if the need arises."

With a squeak of the screen door hinges, Joel emerged with a bottle of whiskey and two cold beers. "Here we are."

Abigail was on Joel's heels, Mel resting on her right hip. She put Mel down, who ran up and jumped into my lap with a plunk, making me grunt a little from the impact.

"Hi, Sawa."

I loved the way she said my name. It would be a sad day for me when she finally mastered her *r*'s.

"Hey, kiddo. Whatcha got there?"

Mel lifted her sippy cup. "Water." She took a drink and smacked her lips. "When is Scott coming back?"

I hugged her cute body, my nose picking up her bubblegum-scented shampoo, which always made me crave a piece. "Soon, why? Are you sick of me already?" I tickled her a bit to make her squirm.

Without answering—probably because she'd already forgotten the question—Mel placed her sippy cup haphazardly on the table and bounced off my lap, then ran for the sandbox. Within seconds, she was making raspberry noises with her adorable lips as she drove a small dump truck through the sand, a story playing out in her imagination.

Abigail raised her shoulders and then let them fall. "I can't get that girl to touch a doll, but you give her a car or a truck of any kind, and she can play for hours. Trains, too."

"A tomboy in the making," I said with a smile. "I was kind of like that, too." I had dolls, but I preferred making forts and exploring. Tiny cars were always fun to play with in the dirt, which I'd been doing all week with my little sis.

Joel put the bottle of whiskey and beers on the table while Abigail placed a sack of three small glasses next to it. She went into the house and returned with a goblet of red wine for herself, coupled with a glass of water.

"I was just telling Aidan about my inheritance." It was great to be able to speak freely about it.

Aidan sat up in his seat, his jaw set with determination. "She sure did, and I plan to show her around the place when she and her fella come to visit."

Abigail's face brightened like sunshine after a cold rain. "That's fantastic. I wish I could go with you now. I'd love to see it."

Joel unstacked each glass and pushed one in front of Aidan, himself, and then me.

I wasn't sure I wanted any whiskey, yet another part of me wanted to embrace the Irish heritage in all its glory.

"Maybe someday we'll take a trip over there, hon. Let's let the kids have this one alone first."

Abigail waved Joel off, making a hmph sound through her lips. "Oh, I wasn't meaning now, silly."

As Joel poured each of us a quarter of a glass, Abigail slid her glass of water in front of me.

"I figured you'd want this for afterward." She winked, her smile telling me how happy she was for me.

I paused as Aidan tapped the table with the bottom of his glass and said, "Sláinte," which sounded like *slancha* before he drank the glass dry.

We all echoed him, doing our best to say it correctly, even Abigail. What came out was something slightly different in various forms.

Not willing to look like a lightweight in front of a real-life Irishman, Joel slammed his entire whiskey and grimaced just as I did the same. Very atypical of us.

The hot, acidy liquid burned my throat and set an immediate fire in my chest, my cheeks flaring like two chimneys. I blew out a breath, half expecting flames to come shooting out. Then I took a quick drink of water, my head immediately lighter than it had been a moment ago. "What does sláinte mean?" I said, trying not to slur my words. *Talk about a lightweight.*

"Health. What better to drink to? And if ya add 'táinte,' it means *health and wealth.*" Uncle Aidan's gaze met mine from across the table.

As I processed this, my stomach wasn't sure what to do with the whiskey I had just dumped into it. It rumbled, contemplating whether or not to hurl or go with the flow. Lucky for me, it chose the latter, which allowed my *instant buzz* to continue.

An experienced drinker, Aidan took the bottle and poured Joel and me a generous second glass, right along with himself. Another "sláinte" and my head was starting to swim, although I sipped the second glass, which staved off Uncle Aidan from pouring me a third.

Joel, still trying to look tough and manly, kept pace with Aidan, glass for glass. By dinner, we were all a bit foolish as we munched on our shepherd's pie and salad, rain pattering against the windows.

"Know any Irish songs?" I said, holding back a hiccup. I shot the rest of my whiskey down, which tasted a lot better than before, my throat not as charred and my stomach enjoying the ride. Then, I lifted a finger. "I know of one. *I'm a rambler, I'm a gambler, I'm a long way from home, and if you don't like me, then leave me alone. I'll eat when I'm hungry, I'll drink when I'm dry, and if moonshine don't kill me, I'll drink 'till I diiiiieeee* ..." I imagined I sounded like a real Irish person as I sang it. I was in love with the world.

A sudden case of giggles overtook me. "My dad used to sing that on Saint Patty's Day."

Uncle Aidan tugged on his ear, his brow rising. "It's 'I'll *live* 'til I die,' and that's Saint *Paddy's* Day, lass, with a d."

He spoke so fast I hardly caught his words. And I was having too much fun to care.

* * *

At nine-thirty in the morning, my phone chimed in a text. I pried my eyes open, the sunlight assaulting my retinas as it streamed through the blinds. So this was how Amy felt after a night of partying? Or Scott, for that matter? A parade of snare drums marched through my brain, my mouth feeling like I'd been chewing on sand.

I sat up and looked at my phone where a text from Scott awaited my attention.

"Are you up yet?"

I took in my surroundings. My bed seemed right. I was wearing my summer pj's. The door was closed. Everything was in its place, the birds singing outside my window, yet, somehow, everything felt different. At least the outer world wasn't as messed up as it was inside of my head. *Am I still drunk?*

Instead of texting, I chose to call.

Scott didn't even wait for me to speak. "Hey, party girl. How ya feelin'?"

"How did you know?"

Scott chuckled. "So I take it you don't remember calling me last night, then?" The humor in his voice was evident.

"I did? No, I don't remember that. I went to bed early." I rubbed my forehead, hoping for clarity.

"*Yeah*, you did. You went to bed early, and then you called me."

Mortification flushed my cheeks. "What did I say?" I kept my head down, avoiding the light.

"After you told me your Uncle Aidan was the best uncle on the planet, you said you were a true Irishwoman because only a true Irishwoman could drink whiskey and sing Irish songs. Then, you started singing some song about gamblers." Scott kept laughing as he spoke. "You told me to take all my clothes off because you wanted phone sex. I think you said Irish phone sex, if I'm not mistaken."

OMG. Was my door closed? Did anyone hear me? I wanted to climb under the covers and stay there. I only knew of one Irish song. *Did I sing that song at the dinner table?* What did Mel think about her drunken older sister?

As though he could sense my inner turmoil, Scott continued. "Don't worry, Babe. You were only horny for about sixty seconds before you passed out. I kept saying your name until I heard snoring and gave up. You had me all excited, too. I haven't had drunk sex with you yet. I guess Uncle Aidan is a bad influence." More sniggering. "How much did you drink, anyway?"

"Two glasses of whiskey ... I think." I rubbed my forehead again, wishing I had a tall glass of water, one that didn't require me to get it for myself. The kitchen seemed so far away. Then I spotted one on my nightstand and grabbed it. *Did I do that, or did someone take pity on me?*

"Two glasses? Man, we gotta get your tolerance up for alcohol. We'll have to practice. I want that nasty girl back from last night. You had all sorts of plans for me that you didn't deliver on."

Nasty girl? "What did I say?"

Judging by his lighthearted tone, Scott was having a blast with this conversation.

If only my stomach didn't feel like it was about to hurl, I might have enjoyed it, too. My lack of memory didn't help matters.

"I'll never tell. You had me hard in about two seconds, though."

Now it was my turn to tease. "Well, when *doesn't* that happen?"

"Ooooooh. Touché, Babe."

Voices and movement in the background told me Scott wasn't at home.

"Hey, listen. I gotta run. Nurse that hangover, and I'll call you later. Love you. Try a greasy burger or a strong tea. Maybe a soda."

"Love you, too." I ended the call and guzzled the entire

glass dry. Man, that was good. Best water I'd ever tasted. Like a mountain spring. Or maybe I was just really, *really* thirsty.

I pulled my depleted carcass up off the mattress, washed my face in the hall bathroom, and then snuck toward the kitchen, where voices and laughter filled the air. When I came around the corner, Mel was in her booster seat, Uncle Aidan, Abigail, and Joel at the breakfast table, eating and carrying on.

"Well, well, well, she lives." My father's lookalike had me ashamed and equally embarrassed.

Abigail rose from her chair as I refilled my water glass at the sink. She brushed my hair over my shoulder. "I knew you were going to need some hydration when you woke up."

Of course, she had taken care of me. That was so her. *Did she dress me in my pj's, too?* I had absolutely no idea.

I cleared my throat and then spoke as though I had been gargling with fireplace ash. "Thank you, Abigail. I'm so sorry. I hope I didn't make too much of an idiot of myself."

Lips pursed, she held back a giggle. "What? Don't be silly."

"What did Mel think?"

Abigail's eyes narrowed but in a compassionate sort of way. "I fed Mel an early dinner—her favorite mac and cheese —and since it was a Friday night, I let her watch *Brave* in her room. She never even saw you." She nudged my arm. "You were a riot. And, no, you didn't make an idiot out of yourself. You were just getting into the mood. Joel was in worse shape. I had to undress him and put him to bed. At least you were able to get *yourself* to bed. It was refreshing to see you let loose a little." She leaned in and rested the side of her head against mine. "You reminded me of your dad in those *rare instances* when he'd relax and loosen up. Before you were born, I remember one time when he took out his guitar and started singing all kinds of Irish songs. You must've been channeling him last night." She pulled away and opened the oven, releasing a flurry of savory smells, garlic being one of them.

Out of the corner of my eye, Mel played with a cup of Cheerios, making shapes with them on the table.

My stomach growled as Abigail loaded a plate with pancakes, sausage, and hash browns, which she handed me as she escorted me to the table as if I was a feeble old woman. Two seconds later, she placed a hot tea in front of me. *God love you, Abigail.*

Chapter Eleven

"So, what was my dad like back when he lived in Ireland?" I had just cast my line into the water and was reeling in the slack, the sound of grasshoppers combing through the grass on the not-so-distant shore.

Since the rain had decided to leave us in the early-morning hours, and the sun chose to provide us with a decent-looking day, pushing those nasty storm clouds out of the sky, Joel had lent Aidan and me his johnboat to use at Crystal Pond, about five miles out of town. We had asked Joel to join us, but his gray complexion told me another few hours of sleep was all his hungover mind could handle.

Even though I had consumed two good-sized glasses of Irish whiskey, Joel and Aidan had downed five, Aidan no worse for wear. Joel was another story. *Thank God I didn't drink more.* A good breakfast, a large cup of tea, and I was almost back to normal, a spacey brain the only remnant of our crazy Friday night of drinking.

"Your da was a kind fellow. He was my kid brother, so I looked out for him." Uncle Aidan had already cast his line, his gaze remaining fixed on the surface of the water, which glittered against the sun like firework sparklers on a stick.

The scent of bacteria floated past my nose every now and then from the algae that lapped the edges of the pond and coated the rocks pushing through the surface. A few mosquitos sprinkled the water, making tiny ripples.

"So, your da never mentioned me, huh?"

Aidan's question lingered in the air for a bit, awaiting my answer. "Well, he died when I was twelve, and he didn't really talk about his family much." *Or not at all.*

Aidan nodded as though he understood. "He was a serious lad most of the time." He looked over at me, his shoulders stiffening, his eyes cautious. "I mean no disrespect. It was just how he was back then. Neither one of us was much for studyin', but Robby liked to tinker."

"Tinker?" And then I remembered the "projects" my dad used to take on: the birdhouse slash feeder that took refuge in our front yard, providing an abundance of food for the feathery friends who lived nearby and even a squirrel who was determined to stick his nose where it didn't belong; the split rail fence that ran along the perimeter of our one-acre lawn; and even the decent-sized shed where he stored his table saw, lawnmower, tools, and a six-pack of beer for whenever his thirst required it.

"Your da was good at buildin' things. He would get into a project and stay focused until he finished it. We had our share of rows, but we were family. Blood." He concentrated on the pond again. "And ya already know your dad loved to fish." He shook his head for emphasis. "Boy, did he."

His words brought forth another memory of my dad and me fishing on a few occasions. Most of the time, we never caught anything. "I remember that. He took me here, in fact." We'd talk about fun shows we were watching on TV, sports, or whatever was going on with me at school. It was a special time with just the two of us. *Burgers and fries.*

"As I told ya, my pa has some prime land off the coast, and Robby would fish in the sea all the time and explore a few caves nearby. The same land ya will soon own." He smiled.

My chest filled with pride. "I love to explore new places." When I was young, my imagination would run wild in the woods behind our property, where stacks of pine needles and branches substituted as small walls for forts. A few neighborhood kids would often join me. Sometimes, we'd spend all day out there, letting our minds guide whatever fairy tale or story we wanted to create.

"I think he liked anythin' that got him away from Pa, to be truthful."

That didn't sound good. Were they at odds? A question loitered at the edge of my tongue. And I hoped it was appropriate to ask. "What are your pa and your mom like?"

Are they still alive?

Uncle Aidan turned slightly toward me. "By pa, ya mean my grandpa?"

"No, your father and mother." I wasn't sure how he referred to everyone. Robby still threw me off, especially since my father's name was Robert.

"My pa is my grandpa. My da and my mum were my parents. They died when I was twenty. Robby was fifteen."

That shook me. Mainly because I just found out that my father and I had both suffered a significant loss when we were way too young to handle it. I stared at Aidan with timid eyes. "Do you mind if I ask how they died?" I had just asked a similar question about JoJo's mom. Too many losses.

If he didn't want to talk about it, I wouldn't press. I understood how difficult these conversations could be. When I had told Scott about *my* parents, I could barely hold myself together. Thinking about Scott made me really miss my man. *Five more days.*

"My da had too much of the drink one night and drove into a ravine. Smashed the car to smithereens. We stayed with my pa for a time after that. I mainly hung around to keep an eye on Robby." He let out a breath, the corners of his mouth crimping downward. "My pa was a hard man to please. Didn't have much patience for us kids. My da was a kinder man. My mum was sweet, too. And they weren't big drinkers, either. They had a pint or two from time to time, but that night, I guess they'd had one too many. My pa was another story. He could drink anyone under the table if he set his mind to it. Couldn't put the jar down."

The hand holding my fishing pole started to tremble, and it wasn't because I had caught something. *A car accident?* I wanted to ask more but realized it wasn't the time. The way Aidan suddenly grew quiet made me realize this. My poor dad. He lost his parents, just like I had. My heart ached for him and for Aidan. I had Abigail, who provided a soft landing for me. Even with that, I still withdrew for years. It didn't sound like they had anyone ... no one who really cared.

"I'm so sorry. I didn't mean to pry." I placed my hand on his arm.

Aidan waved me off. "Sure, look." He shook his head and coughed. "I mean, it is what it is."

There was so much I wanted to know, but I also didn't want to interrogate the man. I wished I had asked my dad more about his family when he was alive.

I thought of another topic and hoped it wouldn't also end with a tragic story. "When did my dad leave Ireland?"

Keeping his eyes distant over the past few seconds, Aidan snapped into focus and straightened his spine. "Robby left when he was eighteen."

Three years later? "Why did he leave?"

Uncle Aidan sighed. "He and my pa didn't see eye to eye on much. Robby wanted another life ... I guess. I don't really know. Without my da around or my mum, Robby wore a more serious hat in the family. He didn't like my pa's drinkin', and the two had several rows about it. Came to fists a few times. Finally, Robby up and left." Aidan reeled his line in and recast it. "Fish ain't bitin' much today, lass. I would've thought with the rain, we'd be getting' a few more caught by now."

Maybe the fish were just as uncomfortable with our conversation as I was becoming. I didn't like knowing that my great-grandfather had treated my father poorly. For the most part, my dad was an even-tempered man. And then I thought of that day when I was ten years old, the one I had remembered when Aidan had first shown up at my graduation.

"So tell me more about when you came to see my dad all those years ago." The question shot out of my mouth like an arrow, determined to find its target.

Just then, my line snagged on something.

Not now.

"Looks like ya got one." Aidan's eyes grew wide. "Reel 'er in." His face brightened, his body angling to assist.

We spent the next several minutes doing just that. The trout I had snagged gasped for air and wiggled about the floor of the boat, helpless and unhappy about its fate. I couldn't help but throw it back once I had detangled the hook from its mouth. My dad understood this remorseful behavior from me, but I wasn't so sure the gesture won any points with my uncle, who raised his brow and stared in disbelief.

"Not much point in fishin', lass, if ya aim to throw them all back."

Ten minutes later, we were on the road home. I drove along Route 7 toward Middlebury, my window halfway down to capture the fresh Vermont air. That was until we passed by a farm that reeked of cow manure. I turned on the AC instead.

The next day, I drove Uncle Aidan to the airport in Burlington, which was about an hour north of us. One never really knew, depending on traffic clogging the one-lane road I had to navigate.

I walked him to the security area where he was about to leave his suitcase, all scuffed and missing pieces of its outer layers, which I had determined was either made of leather or an imitation, when he stopped and placed the aged bag on the floor. "Ya asked about me comin' here over a decade ago?"

I nodded, glad he had brought the topic back up. I had assumed he didn't want to discuss it.

"I did come to see Robby. I was tryin' to sell the land where our parents' house had stood. The house had burned down years ago, and I needed Robby's signature on a few documents. I suggested he take his half of the money and put it in a college fund for ya. That's what I heard American parents did." He rubbed his jaw. "Anyway, that was why I came."

The way Aidan spoke of it sounded so ... normal. What most children of deceased parents would do. Abigail had helped *me* with my parents' estate, which was great since I had *no* idea what to do. I was twelve. I could barely keep track of my allowance.

His face fell into a sorrowful frown. "I'm sorry I didn't come to your da's funeral, lass. I meant to, but my pa had died not three weeks prior, and I had arrangements to make. Heart attack. Probably from all the drinkin'. Although, I expect he had never fully gotten over my da's death." He released a heavy breath, his eyes distant for a second or two. "Your da and I had a nice visit when I was here. I bought him lunch, and he talked a lot about ya and your mum. Showed me pictures. Ya were still in pigtails back then. Your da and I wrote a few letters to each other after that. Kept in touch. We were mendin' our fences, ya could say." The warmth of his hand found its way to my shoulder. "I like to think that Robby and I would have sorted each other out and gotten on. And I guess I came here hopin' maybe we could pick up where he and I had left off." He smiled, the tension in his face melting away like ice on a warm windshield. "Ya have his eyes, ya know? And your ma was a fine-looking woman. You've been blessed with her beauty as well." He picked his suitcase back up, the handle on its last leg. "One thing was certain: Your da loved ya both fiercely."

Hearing those comforting words made me miss my parents so badly it hurt. The grief snagged my heart just as my hook had done to that poor trout. All this talk about my father had me reminiscing more than I had in a long time. They died ten years ago, but in this moment, it felt like yesterday, the ache still very real.

My lower lip quivered just before my eyes spilled with tears, enough that Uncle Aidan lowered his bag to the floor for a second time. "Now, lass. Don't cry." He hugged me, his cotton shirt smelling as if he'd worn it just beyond its wash expiration date. Somehow, that comforted me, too, as I cried in his arms.

When I finally gained the strength to pull away, I wiped my cheeks with my hand. "I'm sorry. I didn't mean to blubber like an idiot."

Aidan's eyes tensed. "Nonsense. Ya miss your da. It's to be expected." He nudged my chin with his fingers. "But you're a Browne, and you'll crack on." He took a step away. "So, I'll be seein' ya next week in Shannon? You'll be my guest, along with your fella?"

I had successfully changed Scott's and my tickets and even helped Uncle Aidan open an Instagram account to communicate. The whole thing blew him away. "World's changing right around my feet," he'd said. I loved the way he spoke. And I loved that he was in my life. He wasn't my father, but Uncle Aidan was the closest thing I was ever going to get to him, and I wasn't about to let him go.

"Yes! I can't tell you how much I'm looking forward to it." I smiled and waved as Aidan turned and entered the security point.

On the drive home, my heart went from sad to floating like a feather inside my chest, each breath lighter than the last. I had been given a gift. The gift of a family, a lineage, really, and I was beyond grateful for it.

Later that Sunday, and after I had gotten all caught up with Scott over the phone, Abigail and I sat on the back deck enjoying a cup of tea as we watched Joel and Mel play in the sandbox.

"No, Daddy, it's my turn to dump the dirt."

Joel abided by whatever game they were playing. Mel was *always* in charge.

Abigail took a sip from her tea and stared at me with that all-knowing, *motherly* wisdom. "I can tell you've been crying. Did you have a nice visit with your uncle?"

The sunlight reflected off her hazel eyes, her auburn hair shiny and soft. My mother was a picture of beauty, inside and out.

"Yeah, we had a nice time." I smirked. "I don't think he was thrilled when I threw the only fish we caught back into the water, though. But aside from that, it was great." I set my mug down and sat forward. "I can't help but wonder why my dad didn't trust Aidan all those years ago. Do you remember me telling you about that?"

Abigail nodded. "I do." And then she pondered. "You

know, I kind of remember your mom telling me something about it. I just can't recall enough to make any sense. So much has happened since then."

She wasn't kidding. My parents' death had thrust poor Abigail—a woman with no kids and no relationship—into a motherly role for me, the lost girl who wanted to stay that way, not to mention everything that happened to me during my freshman year of college. I was surprised she could recall anything at all.

"I wish I knew more about it. My mom did. But like I told you, she just said their relationship was strained, and my dad didn't trust Aidan." I swatted a mosquito that was circling the rim of my tea mug. And then I raised a finger. "Oh yeah. She also said something about Aidan having 'habits,' and I got the impression that those *habits* had caused a lot of tension between them. I'm not even sure I'm remembering the facts right." All at once, I wondered if I had gotten the entire thing wrong. I *was* only ten.

Abigail wrapped her palms around her mug. "Well, he certainly can drink. That's for sure. Do you think he's an alcoholic?"

I thought about that as I slammed my hand down on the table to get that pesky mosquito once and for all. Missed. "I don't think so. He was here for two nights, and we only drank that one time. Plus, he talked about their grandpa having that affliction." I shrugged. "It could be that. Maybe he drank a lot when my dad lived there and made bad choices because of it. He seemed in control of himself here and reasonable. And he spoke highly of my dad, even said they had a nice visit when he was here so many years ago. He seems excited about me coming there." Still, something pressed on my mind like a paperweight that I couldn't quite pinpoint. The skeptic in me said Uncle

Aidan had turned out to be perfect in his own quirky way. *Maybe too perfect.*

"But?"

Like Scott, Abigail had the ability to read me like a book. Honestly, I was sure the government could use them both to interrogate spies.

"Well. If they had such a nice visit, and Uncle Aidan even said they wrote to each other a few times, why didn't my dad ever mention him after that? Why wouldn't he want me to know him?" I swallowed another gulp of tea. "And you want to know what else I learned?" I didn't wait for Abigail's response, even though her eyes held mine. "My dad's parents died when he was fifteen. And guess how they died?" Again, I didn't wait for her answer. "In a car accident."

Abigail's hand went to her mouth, which gaped at the coincidence.

"My dad had to live with his grandpa, who they called *Pa*, for three years until my dad left and traveled here. I guess his grandfather wasn't very nice to him, and they fought a lot." It all made sense to me why he would have left. With his parents gone and the tension between his grandfather and himself, he must've felt like he needed a new start. That was *exactly* how I felt when I finally mustered up the nerve to attend college. It amazed me how close we had come to walking the same paths.

Abigail stared off as though processing everything I had said.

I swatted at that pesky mosquito again. Another miss. *Argh.* "I don't know. Maybe they did have a nice visit, but my dad was just being cautious and wanted to make sure Aidan was continuing on the right path, whatever *that* was." I covered my mug with my hand to keep the bugs out that seemed to be multiplying, the warm liquid making my palm sweat. "And maybe he would have told me if he hadn't died two years later.

You know, maybe he planned on it but just never got around to it."

Abigail met my gaze. "That's certainly possible. We all think we have oodles of time to take care of things, so we put them off for *another day*. We take things for granted. I thought that Aidan seemed like a nice man, and it was really cool of him to come to your graduation like that. I don't see any harm in getting to know him."

She sounded so much like Scott at that moment. That was two people whom I trusted with my life who were giving Aidan the green light. Of course, Scott had said it before we knew about the inheritance.

I drank my tea down quickly, tired of worrying about it getting contaminated. "I don't, either. And I'll be careful. Do you know anything about the other piece of land they sold? I guess it was where my grandparents' house was. Aidan said the house had burned down years ago."

Abigail shook her head. "Not a thing."

I scratched an itch behind my ear, which felt like a bug bite to the touch. "The reason I ask is because, supposedly, my dad received half of the profits."

Abigail's eyes went blank. "Hmm. I'm sure your dad did something with it. Should we ask Mr. Webster about it when he gets back into the office?"

I made a dismissive gesture with my hand. "It's not that important. I'm sure my dad put it to good use." I felt ungrateful even mentioning it. My parents had left me a nest egg that would cover any major expenses for the better part of my life. It was what paid for my college tuition, before the school had refunded it, that was. "I was just curious."

And that was where we let the matter rest until the following day, which was a Monday. When I returned home from Mr. Webster's office just before dinner, Abigail was warming up our leftover shepherd's pie on the stove. I didn't get to meet with my lawyer, who was still dealing with personal issues, but he had at least made copies of the paperwork for me to review. Mrs. Clarke tried to schedule a meeting with me to sign the necessary documents for the following week, but I explained that I would be out of the country. The land wouldn't officially be mine until I returned.

It didn't take long before I had a pretty good understanding of what I was inheriting and why. One piece of information didn't make sense, at least according to what Aidan had told me.

My great-grandfather, Patrik Connor Browne (the man they referred to as Pa), had inherited 180 acres of coastal land from his father, who had inherited from *his* father, and down the ancestral line it had gone. Patrik had only one son, Thomas Robert Browne (my grandfather), who died twenty-nine years ago, which checked out since my dad was fifteen at the time. Before his death, Thomas had two sons: Robert Séamus Browne (my father) and Aidan Thomas Browne (my uncle). Since Patrik's only son (Thomas, my grandfather) had already died, Patrik had included the land in his will to be bequeathed to Aidan and Robert or, according to the paperwork, the next of kin. Here was where things got a little dicey.

The problem was that Patrik had died twelve years ago, yet Aidan said he had died three weeks prior to my dad's death, which was ten years ago. He distinctly said it was the reason he hadn't come to my dad's funeral. *"My pa had died not three weeks prior, and I had arrangements to make."* Those were his exact words, yet the facts stared right at me. Either Aidan had out-and-out lied to me, or something else was amiss. I could see him confusing months with years for a moment, but he actually said it was the *reason* he hadn't come to my dad's funeral. When their pa died, my father was still alive. He knew this.

The paperwork made no mention of my grandparents' house or the land it had occupied before the supposed fire, which I was also starting to question. What it did include, however, was an amendment to the will, which was called a codicil. My father requested this. In a nutshell, it stated that should my father die, the land would go to my mother. In the event that she also passed away, it would entrust to me, but only after I had turned thirty years of age *or* had earned a minimum of a bachelor's degree at any college of my choosing. It also said I had to present proof, which was why Mrs. Clarke had asked me about it.

Why wasn't I notified about this sooner? According to the paperwork, my father didn't want anyone to know about it until *after* I had graduated, which explained why Abigail didn't know, either. A handwritten note tried to explain.

I don't want the land to influence my daughter's educational experience.

Seeing my father's handwriting sent a shiver down my spine. It felt so personal to him, and I understood why.

My father never got the chance to attend college, yet he worked at the prestigious Middlebury College for years as their lead custodian. Being around college students all day, he must've decided back then that my education was of the utmost importance to him. I remember him always being curious about my schooling and how I was doing.

Is this why Uncle Aidan came to my graduation? Did he also need to see proof I had earned my degree?

My lawyer included a small plat of the property that appeared to run along the coastline, or at least a generous section of the land did. There was also a small beach if I was reading the plat correctly. It looked so small on paper, just some lines and measurements, but I knew this land had value.

That night, Abigail and Joel sat across from me at the kitchen table, their eyes attentive while Mel colored a few feet away in her coloring book, the soundtrack for the movie *Frozen* playing in the background. After I explained what I had read, I handed the paperwork over to Abigail and Joel to examine while they sat next to each other. I had already called Scott and explained the whole thing to him. He didn't have much to say about it other than he'd call me later, and we could discuss it further. "My dad's waiting for me in the car," he'd said. "But I want to talk more about this. You're right. Somethings fucked up here."

I released an exasperated breath, rubbed my face, and shook my head. "I don't get it. Aidan told me his pa died three weeks before my dad had died." I pointed with my entire hand at the paperwork they were reading. "It says right there that he died two years prior. Why would he lie about that?"

Both Joel and Abigail kept reading.

"It seems like an odd thing to lie about, don't you think?" My brain was firing up, right along with my chest.

Abigail peered over the paperwork at me. "At least I know I'm not crazy. I was worried I'd forgotten about it. Do you think Aidan could have gotten his timelines confused?"

My kindhearted mother always tried to see the brighter side of things.

"Not really. That's too big a difference in time. My dad was alive when their pa died. You can't confuse that!"

"He and your father didn't get along," Abigail said, trying to understand. "Maybe he didn't have the nerve to tell you that he didn't feel comfortable coming for that reason. Maybe he wanted things to be better between them, but they just weren't."

"Yeah, but why weren't they better? He said they had a nice visit."

Abigail fanned her palms out and sighed. "To be honest, I don't have any idea. Maybe when you go there, you can find out more about it. That is, if you still want to go. I wouldn't blame you if you didn't."

"Oh, I want to go. I'll have Scott with me. It'll be fine. If I find out he's not what he seems, I'll deal with it then."

I rested my elbows on the table and leaned my chin into my hands. "He acted so happy about my inheritance, but now I'm not so sure he was being real. Maybe he's waiting for me to get there, so he can ... I don't know ... show me his true colors?"

Abigail reached across the table and patted my arm. "I'm sorry you have to deal with this right now."

"It's okay. I could be reading too much into it. They could have lost touch, and he regrets that, and now he wants to make amends through me." I wanted to believe that, my heart trying to stay open. Not an easy task for someone with my history.

Finally, I pushed my chair back and stood. "I'm gonna drive over to Middlebury College and go for a run on their jogging path. Anyone want to join?"

Middlebury had gone to great lengths to pave a wide walkway that snaked through the woods and around campus for walkers, joggers, and bikers alike. The entire course ran about seven miles, which was probably how long it would take for my brain to figure out this whole thing or, at least, resign myself to it. Somehow, being near where my dad used to work also helped. Maybe through osmosis, he'd offer me some insight. I could sure use it.

"I have to stay here with Mel." Abigail also rose from the table.

Joel leaned back in his chair and gazed at his cell phone. "I'd love to go, but I've got a meeting at the school with some of the summer program teachers. We're trying to get everything organized now before they go on vacation. In fact, I need to be there in about thirty minutes." He stood. "If you can wait, I'll go with you afterward."

"That's okay. I'll be fine. Maybe it's best I go alone, anyway, I probably wouldn't be much company. I need to think this through."

More than anything, I wished Scott was here. Having him gone this long, which really wasn't long at all, left me feeling as though I had lost a limb. Especially when times were tough, I wasn't complete without him. I knew that wasn't a modern-day concept. This was the twenty-first century, after all, but he and I had been through the trenches and made it out alive. We relied on each other for balance and clarity. I was the yin to his yang, and that was just how it went.

Abigail complimented Mel's coloring and then said, "Are you sure you don't want to wait for Joel? The college term is over, and the summer session doesn't start for another two weeks. Should you go alone?"

I placed my hands on Abigail's upper arms and smiled. "It's light now until eight at least, and I'll be home long before then. I'll keep my cell phone with me and my pepper spray. You know me, Mom, I don't go anywhere I don't feel safe. This is Vermont. I'll be fine."

And with that, I ran off to change into my shorts, sports top, and sneakers. After I braided my hair, which dangled down my back like a blonde rope, I headed out, a water bottle in my hand.

* * *

When I arrived at Middlebury College, I strapped on the jogging belt that Scott had bought for me one Christmas, the one that held my cell phone and keys (and pepper spray, of course), popped in my earbuds, and tried to call Scott. After the fourth ring, I hung up and put on some music, my feet itching to get started.

The Adirondack Mountains rolled off in the distance, complementing the beautiful countryside, the early night air, gentle and satisfying. This was a good idea, and a perfect place to think. And with no people around, I allowed myself to get lost in my own little world.

Once I replayed all the facts about Aidan and my father, even the land I was soon to inherit, I tried to think of another possible angle to this. He and my dad had gone years without speaking. It occurred to me that I had never asked him why my father was angry with him. Did Aidan even know about it? Aidan believed he had looked out for my dad. He was his big brother. I could see in his eyes the need to make that familial connection with me. And it was for the same reason that I was open to it: we needed each other to fill the void that my dad's death had created. But why did he lie? And why did he wait so long to contact me? Was he afraid I'd reject him?

I quickened my pace as I tried to lighten up about the whole thing. My trip to Ireland was coming at the perfect time. I could even see the land. *My land.* How exciting. And I'd have Scott there by my side, the man, who, like Abigail, could spot deception from a mile away.

Ninety acres of coastal land? Was this for real? Amazing didn't even begin to cover it.

As one song ended and before the next one started, footfalls bounded up the pavement from behind me. I hadn't seen anyone hanging around in the parking lot when I arrived, just a few empty cars that probably belonged to staff.

The footfalls drew closer.

My cautious side had me pulling one earbud out, trying to

keep my senses alert, and the other side laughing at myself for doing so. Old habits never died. Not even in Middlebury, Vermont, one of the safest places on earth.

And then I heard it. "Hey."

Hey? I pulled out the other earbud and listened, keeping my pace steady. It was a man. Was he speaking to me? Maybe he wanted me to move over so he could pass? It didn't sound like Joel; otherwise, I would have stopped already.

"Sara. Can you slow down for a sec? I'd like to talk with you."

Oh, no, no, no. This isn't happening. That voice was as unmistakable as his putrid cologne that assaulted my nostrils every time I smelled it. How did he find me? And then I remembered. Back when Scott and I were at odds, Rick had picked me up for a date at Abigail's house. Has he been stalking me all this time?

I grabbed my jogging belt, fumbling with the zipper. I needed my pepper spray, and I needed it fast as I mentally prepared myself for what could be one of the worst attacks of my life. How long had Rick been following me? How did he know I was here? And what did he want? The fact that he'd come to such great lengths said two things: he wasn't going to give up, and he hadn't changed a bit.

Monsters never did.

Chapter Twelve

"Sara, wait! I'm not going to hurt you. I just want to talk."

I ran as though my feet were on fire, my lungs straining to capture every ounce of oxygen my muscles *and* heart needed to keep moving. I hadn't even looked at him yet. I was too busy trying to widen the gap between us. Plus, I wasn't sure what I'd do once I saw those eyes again, dark and imposing, the eyes that had haunted my dreams.

Rick's feet slapped against the pavement staying close. Too close. "Wait. This is not what you think. I'm not a threat. My dad already talked to you. There's no need to run away."

Liar. His being here trumped anything his deceitful mouth had to say. This was an ambush. And people with good intentions didn't need to ambush.

I continued to fumble with the zipper on my jogging belt, and then I yanked on it, trying to liberate my phone. "If you don't leave right now. I'm calling the police. I mean it, Rick."

Finally, the zipper broke free. With my body in full motion, getting my phone out without dropping it was difficult, much less punching the three keys I so desperately needed. And I couldn't slow down, not with Rick on my heels.

"Don't call the police. There's no need. Give me two minutes ... to apologize. That's all I want, and then I'll leave."

I thought about all the lies Rick had told to convince me that he was my friend. All the warnings he *so subtly* told me about Scott. More untruths. *"Do you have any idea how much effort I've put into you,"* he'd said to me once, as though back then I had owed him. As though my rejection had given him the right to take what I refused to give willingly. If I believed him now, I'd be falling for that same exact ploy. It wasn't happening.

One hand found my pepper spray, the other my phone. Sprinting like this without using my arms left me clumsy and awkward, and I needed two hands to dial. Instead, I let go of the pepper spray and focused on my phone. Once I had successfully made the call, I'd go for my pepper spray next. Only I hit #11 instead of 911. *Crap.*

"Sara, don't call the police. You don't need to do that. Please, just listen."

For once, you don't get to call the shots. I'd gone three and a half years without this nightmare in my life. Things had changed. *I* had changed. I wasn't the scared, timid girl I used to be.

Okay, calm down and make the call. With my attention focused on my cell and not the path, my foot hit a rock, one big enough to roll my ankle and plummet my body toward the earth. The pavement carved up my kneecaps which burned as if branded with an iron. What was worse, my cell phone went flying onto the grass.

"Are you alright?" Like a storm front, the thunder of Rick's voice drew closer.

Ignoring my scuffed knees, I rolled onto the grass and

reached for my phone, which Rick kicked away as he approached.

"Sorry. I didn't mean to do that. Here, let me help you up. Are you hurt?" He bent over and reached his hand out to me like anyone would do with a friend.

But we were *not* friends, which he was about to find out.

As I seized my pepper spray, my right foot shot up and collided with Rick's crotch. He grabbed the injury with both hands and toppled over onto the ground next to me.

"Ouch. Son of a bitch, that hurts. I wasn't going to ..." His voice trailed off, groans escaping from his lips.

I pushed myself up on my knees, the grass more forgiving than the paved walkway, and thrust the pepper spray into his face. And then I released the poison, letting it fall where it may.

"Ahhhhhh. What the fuck? You're crazy. I was just trying to—" He covered his watery eyes with his hands, his mouth spewing saliva, and his cheeks flaring fire-engine red.

I firmed my jaw, my nerves never steadier. It was as if someone else had taken over, filling me with superhero confidence. "You don't get to speak right now. But you're going to listen unless you want another dose of pepper spray and the cops arriving." I snatched my phone from the ground and flew to my feet, my mind in complete control. I had envisioned what I would do in an attack situation—if ever I faced one—but no matter how many probable scenarios I had played out in my mind, the reality was always quite different. It wasn't important. I'd achieved my desired goal: Rick incapacitated.

"Alright. Alright." He raised one palm as a flag of surrender. "Just go. I won't follow you. I won't contact you again." He sobbed between words, his face beet red, his hands not sure which injury needed his attention more.

I loomed over him. I had never loomed before. And although one part of me (a tiny part) took pity on his current situation, the rest of my brain was too angry to care. With my pepper spray aimed and ready to release, I leaned in. "Why are you here?"

It took Rick a few breaths to get his words out. "I'm getting married. I'm starting a new life. I'm not the same person I was back then. I've changed." He paused to gather himself then he tried to climb to his feet.

"Stay right where you are. You can talk just fine from the ground. Is that all?" I kept my poison aimed and ready.

"Can I sit up?" He stared at me with terror in his eyes, helpless.

I nodded.

Sitting up, Rick steadied his breathing, his hands shielding his eyes from the light. "I wanted to apologize for what I did to you. I *know* what I did. I'm sorry. Not a day goes by that I don't regret my actions."

I let that sink in for a few seconds. Did I want to believe him? I wasn't sure. "Your father already told me this. And I told *him* that under no circumstances did I want to meet with you. *Ever.* And yet, here you are, chasing after me on a deserted jogging path. Have you been stalking me? Were you trying to scare me?" In that moment, I couldn't have been less scared.

Rick shook his head vehemently, a noticeable scar riding along the edge of his chin.

Did Scott do that?

"No. This is the only time ... I just wanted to ..." He released a distressed breath, his voice defeated. "I don't fucking know what I wanted." He laughed with no humor in his voice. "I guess I was hoping you could forgive me."

I gave my mind another moment to absorb this. "Why? Why does my forgiveness matter to you?"

With squinting eyes, he peered up at me. "Because I was an asshole back then. I didn't care what you wanted. I only cared about what *I* wanted. And at the time, I wanted you. I knew you were innocent. And I guess I hoped that maybe you could change me. I wasn't happy. I knew what I was. I knew the way I treated people. I knew how I used Derek to get to you. And how I manipulated Mindy and Charlene to get them to do what I wanted. And I *hated* Scott for taking you away from me. He didn't deserve you. He never cared about women. He just wanted to get laid."

I thrust my palm up, anger rising in my chest like a chimney fire. "Stop. You have no right to talk trash about Scott. And you have no idea who he is and how much he has been there for me all these years. And for the record, Scott didn't take me away from you, Rick. I was never yours to take. I was your friend, and you betrayed my trust, and you nearly destroyed me in the process." *How close I came to giving up on life.* No one knew how much. My lower lip trembled, but I ordered it to stop. "I can't give you what you are looking for. And you will never know whether or not I forgive you. It wouldn't be right for you to know that. And if you really have changed, then you need to accept that this isn't about you anymore. The only thing you can do for me now is to never ... *never* contact me again or make any attempt to communicate. And tell your father the same." I bent closer, my fangs coming out. "Because if you ever pull something like this again, Rick, I will not hesitate to contact the authorities and have you arrested. Scott's assault on you happened too long ago. It would be hard to make those charges stick, but not the rape. Women come forward all the time who were victimized years and even decades ago."

At least in Virginia, where the crime took place, I knew this to be true. I had checked on it more than once.

"I will press charges, and it will destroy your family. I don't want to do that, but if you leave me no choice, that is *exactly* what I will do." I straightened up and put my pepper spray back in my jogging belt. Rick was no longer a threat to me. Not anymore. I turned and headed back in the direction I had come, my knees throbbing with each step, the palm of my hand suddenly aching as well. In all the confusion, I hadn't noticed that before.

I was about twenty feet away when Rick spoke up. "Sara?"

I stopped short, but I wouldn't face him again.

"For what it's worth. I am sorry for what I did. And I know what happened to you and Amy with Professor Adams afterward. After that, I really started to see how awful I had been. And what that must've been like for you."

"Is that all?" I kept my back to him, my ears waiting for movement in case the threat reemerged.

"I had some shit to work out, and I've done that. And I don't hate Scott for what he did. I deserved what I got. If someone did that to my Angie, I ..." He stopped speaking, emotion taking over, I could hear it.

Before I left for good, I turned my body slightly. "Just stay away from me, Rick, and focus on your own family." That was all the generosity that I had left. It was far from an "I forgive you," even though I had. Somehow, it felt fitting that Rick could not get that confirmation. When you hurt someone on the level he had, you had to deal with the consequences. Just as my internal wounds would never quite heal, he'd always have to deal with the fact that at one point in his irresponsible and entitled life, he had done something so heinous and so cruel. He would have to accept that fact in the same way I had to accept who he had made me. I hoped that haunting memory would keep him on the right path, striving to be a better person, a man his kids could respect, and his wife could love.

When I arrived home, Scott's big truck sat parked behind

Abigail's minivan. A moment later, he burst through the front door.

"I finished up early and wanted to surprise you." His gaze went right to my knees, his eyes wide with concern. "What the hell happened to you?"

And there was no way I could tell him.

* * *

After I took a very careful shower, I sat on the lid of the toilet in the hall bathroom while Scott delicately cleaned the wounds on my knees, checked the palm of my hand (the one that had endured the impact) for abrasions, and moved my left ankle around that seemed a bit stiffer than the right. The one that had rolled.

"Does it hurt if I do this?" he asked after each maneuver.

Clearly, Scott had seen his share of injuries and had learned a great deal about what to check for.

"No, not really. I think I just sprained it."

Scott threw a wad of used cotton pads that Abigail had given him into the trashcan and then applied a couple of small bandages to the spots on my left knee that cut a bit deeper than the right.

The remainder of my injuries were surface and would heal in a few days.

"Okay, now try standing." Scott rose and helped me to do the same. "Does it hurt to put pressure on that ankle?" He watched my face for any cringes or signs of pain.

I shook my head. "Not really. It's a bit stiff, that's all." I wrapped my arms around his strapping waist and leaned into him, his musky scent doing its best to make my nose happy. "Thank you for taking care of me, Handsome." It was so good to see him. He had no idea how much.

Scott exhaled, ruffling the hair on top of my head. "Do you remember the last time I did this?" He pulled back and examined my eyes for confirmation.

"I do. It was the time I saved Gwen from being hit by that car." It happened during freshman year when I was walking with Amy to see Scott play in an impromptu touch-football game on campus. I barely knew Scott at the time, but from the way he took care of me and my injuries, I realized I had found a winner of a boyfriend. I think that was when Amy realized it, too, which she confirmed when she assigned him his very own nickname: *Big Guy*.

Scott ran his strong but gentle hands up and down my back, his dimple telling me he was in a playful mood. "Maybe hold off on going jogging unless I'm with you. I'm happy to catch you whenever you stumble."

I looked up at him. "I know you are, and you've saved me more than once." Twice, over the past few years, he'd caught me at the last minute when we were jogging together. In fact, the first time he'd kissed me—also freshman year—he'd saved me from nearly breaking my neck at the top of a mountain when a turkey buzzard had landed on a tree and startled me. "I'm sorry you are marrying such a klutz."

Scott pulled my chin upward, his lips landing heavily upon mine. The kiss was intense, his tongue exploratory, enough that my injured knees grew wobbly. "I love that you are a klutz, and a hero, and a badass, and a sweetheart ... and hilarious when you want to be. Plus, you're absolutely gorgeous, injured or otherwise. You are the whole package, Babe, and I wouldn't trade you for the world."

I sighed, the guilt from my little secret about what *really* happened climbing up my chest like acid reflux.

My expression must've revealed something because Scott took notice.

"You sore? Do you need to sit down?" He took my hand and led me into my bedroom next door, where we sat on the edge of my bed.

For a moment, guilt kept me from facing him, so I stared at the floor instead.

"You're not *that* much of a klutz. Plus, everybody falls down. You should see all the times I've hurt myself."

He was being so sweet and supportive, and here I was, keeping a very important secret from him. I felt horrible about it.

"Are you still upset about your uncle? If you don't want to meet him, I'm—"

"No, it's fine." I did, however, recognize the coincidence. Uncle Aidan had lied recently, and so had I. But they weren't the same circumstance. For me, I just needed time to figure things out, mainly my approach with Scott. If I handled this wrong, the consequences could be dire. "I think we should go to Ireland and act as though everything is fine. Maybe it *is* fine. It's not a big lie, and he seemed happy about my inheritance."

"Good plan. And that's my point. Why lie about something so inconsequential, at least to you? Why would *you* care when his grandfather died?" Confusion furrowed Scott's brow.

"Who knows? Maybe he needed an excuse for why he never came to my dad's funeral, and that seemed as good as any." I sighed. "I really enjoyed his visit here. What keeps nagging at me is what he told me about him and my dad getting along better."

I'd filled Scott in on all the details as soon as I'd learned about them.

"If that were true, then why wouldn't he want to come to his funeral? And why did he wait ten years to contact me? I hope he's a good man ..." My thoughts trailed off.

"I hope so, too, Babe. I really do. But I'll be there for whatever comes." After a few seconds, Scott nudged me with his shoulder. "I know something that will cheer you up. I've got a surprise for you."

I snapped out of my somber mood, curious. "You do? This is *your* birthday weekend. I'm supposed to be spoiling you. Not the other way around."

Scott exhaled, his hand finding my thigh. "First of all, my birthday isn't until Monday." His smile reached all the way up to his eyes, making them glow like two fireflies on a midsummer night. "And make no mistake, woman, you *will* be spoiling me."

I had to know what he was talking about. "Okay, I'll bite. What's the surprise?"

"I made reservations for us to stay tonight through Thursday night at the Hilton in Burlington. It's right on the waterfront. We can get dinner on Church Street, shop"—Scott's hand slid up my inner thigh—"and I can worship you until the sun comes up." His voice got all throaty.

"Worship me?" I liked the sound of that.

Scott shrugged one shoulder, his lips pursed. "Well, I wanted to say fuck you until the sun comes up, but I was trying *not* to sound crude." He leaned closer. "But that's exactly what I'm gonna do. Any objections?"

My insides were trembling at the thought. "No objections. But Abigail—"

Scott lifted a palm. "I already cleared it with Abigail. She said as long as we're back Friday afternoon to help set up for the graduation party on Saturday, she's okay with it."

I was looking forward to celebrating with Abigail. I also loved that it was nothing fancy, just barbecue chicken on the grill and a few salads and desserts.

The air from Scott's voice tickled my ear as he stayed close. "Want me to get some Irish whiskey for the occasion?"

I flashed him my teasing smile. "Why, am I not spicy enough for you sober?"

A giggle escaped from Scott's luscious lips. "You know better than that. I don't call you my she-beast for nothing. And once I finish licking every inch of your hot body and making you cum multiple times, I know what I want you to give me for my birthday present."

"Okay ... well, if it's a blow job, I'm happy to oblige."

He smirked. "Not a blow job, but I'll take that, too, if you're offering."

Since we'd just covered the sexual stuff, I wondered what else he had in mind. I had already bought him a gold chain I imagined would glimmer against his tanned skin. I also got him a few polos in pastel colors I expected would do the same, a new pair of hiking boots, and a briefcase with his initials engraved on it that I would wait to give him when he started his first job. "I hope it's not something I need to get before the weekend. It sounds like you've got my schedule booked."

The smile Scott had been wearing stretched wider, his teeth bright. The way his eyes twinkled. I wished I had my phone so I could capture it. This man was absolutely beautiful. "It's not something you can buy, and you may need a day or two to plan for it."

"Okay, now you've really got me intrigued. What is it?" I was drawing a blank here.

Before he answered, he kissed me so long and so hard, I practically melted in his arms, his minty breath tantalizing. My nipples were stiff and ready for his attention, the moisture between my legs about to start a flood.

And then he revealed the secret: "Dance for me?"

I loved that he enjoyed my dancing. It made me feel special, like I had a talent for that sort of thing. For a klutz, that was a real boost for my ego. Of course, Scott always made me feel like I was the only woman in the world for him. He'd made it crystal clear on numerous occasions that he only had eyes for me.

I placed my hand over the left side of his powerful chest, the throbbing from his heart, intense and excitable. "I can do that. In fact, I have something in mind. ... "

* * *

That night, after we had checked into one of the biggest suites on the top floor of the Hilton, we unpacked and got ourselves organized. The longer days allowed the sun to stick around for several more hours, giving an illusion that time had slowed.

Outside our enormous picture window, the Adirondack Mountains rose proud and majestic, keeping watch over Lake Champlain in all its splendor, a few sailboats and motorboats out for an early evening cruise.

I stood in awe for several minutes until Scott's voice brought me back to the here and now.

"You realize I've been living on limited phone sex for over a week and pictures of you to get me by, don't you?" He approached me in the center of the room. His fingers ran through my hair like a soft comb, the glint in his eyes telling me this experience was going to be epic.

I nodded but couldn't seem to make my lips move. I was too entranced by the Adonis standing before me. Tall, muscular, and gorgeous, he was putty in my hands. If I told him to get on all fours and bark, I knew he'd do it. Scott was *always* up for anything.

"Oh, yeah? Well, we'll have to do something about that."

"*Yeah*, we will." He slow-walked me backward toward the king-sized bed until I fell over, my head cushioned by the memory foam mattress. And then he hovered his impressive body over mine. His eyes traveled up and down my body, his mouth practically drooling. "Jesus, I don't know where to start. I want all of you. All at once."

I exhaled a shaky breath, anticipating his next move. "Well, Handsome, you can start by undressing me."

"Right."

With our clothes stripped from our bodies, my panties and bra tossed aside, Scott parted my legs and admired the view. "You're the most beautiful thing I've ever seen." He dropped several kisses on my neck that forged a path down my stomach before his tongue made contact with my lady parts, driving me wild.

He kissed my wounded knees, then gently lifted my legs up over his shoulders and feasted like I was his last meal, and he was starving.

"Man, you always taste so fucking sweet, Babe. I could lick your pussy all day."

While my eyes rolled back in my head and my mouth screamed for more, he continued, his hands everywhere, his mouth determined to blow my mind. I ran my fingers through his soft golden curls and let go, my mind floating.

When he finished, and I had lost all sense of time and space, I tried to do the same for him, but he was too focused, too intent on making this all about me.

And he wasn't kidding.

Next came the massage. Full body.

Scott left no muscle untouched as he rubbed and caressed all my areas. From the fall, a few sore muscles lingered that he managed to loosen. If I tensed, he softened his touch.

As I lay on the mattress like a puddle of melted wax, I struggled to keep my eyes open. I'd never been so relaxed. That was until my generous lover ran his massive erection up and down my inner thigh, his eyes burning with desire. "I can't wait much longer. Are you ready for me?"

I opened my legs and reached out to touch and stroke him. "Always."

And so the lovemaking continued. Hips thrusting, our moans filled the air. Since my knees were sore, Scott remained on top, his brilliant blue eyes anchoring me in place. "God, you feel incredible. I missed this," he whispered as he found his rhythm.

I wrapped my legs around his hips and enjoyed the ride.

The way Scott pushed his body into mine, the force of him, filling me with sensations too powerful to describe, he reduced me to a woman who couldn't speak, only groan. Already primed, I climaxed a moment before Scott did, both of us panting and glistening with sweat.

Then we showered together before we fed on each other all over again, Scott letting me devour *him* this time. Although, he insisted I sit on several pillows instead of kneeling to spare my knees, which I was more than happy to do. I loved tasting him as much as he loved tasting me. And I fondled him everywhere I knew he liked.

Hard muscle, soft, tanned skin, hypnotic blue eyes, golden curls, and a smile that could stop traffic, he was perfect, and I couldn't get enough of him. Not to mention the size of his erection, which always impressed and satisfied.

After an hour of rest, we tried a few more knee-friendly positions. This went on until exhaustion flopped me back on the bed, and my limbs felt like rubber.

"Let me give you a sponge bath," Scott said as he darted into the bathroom, returning promptly with a soapy washcloth, an ice bucket of warm water, and a towel.

Lotion came next.

I'd never seen him so attentive, his smile unwavering. Once

he had me smelling like lilacs and my skin soft and supple, he propped some pillows in front of the headboard, helped me get comfortable, and covered me with a sheet, then pulled it back down to appreciate the view.

"Are you hungry?" He searched the magazines, then a leather binder on the coffee table for a menu. "We can go out to eat or order in if you like."

It was too late in the evening for something like that. Plus, there was no way I was venturing out of this room when I wasn't even sure I could walk straight. "Let's order in."

* * *

After the server had delivered a rolling cart with our food, I came out of the bathroom to a table covered in white linen and dishes wearing stainless still domes as hats.

We sat at our small table, completely naked, and enjoyed our juicy cheeseburgers, loaded with toppings, onion rings, and brussels sprouts covered with shaved parmesan and bacon bits. *Yum.* Scott ordered a beer for himself and an unsweetened iced tea for me.

"How's your ankle?"

I had almost forgotten about it. "Good." I popped an onion ring in my mouth, savoring the sweet onion taste on my tongue.

"Did you see what I ordered for dessert?" Scott lifted the last steel dome to reveal strawberries with whipped cream, which we used later for fun and sustenance.

In the wee hours of the night, we toasted our evening with a bottle of champagne, which Scott managed to spill on my breasts and lick off, and then fell asleep in each other's arms. *I love you* escaped from our exhausted lips before our minds fell under.

I wondered how in the world we could ever top this night. But, at the same time, I knew somehow we'd find a way.

* * *

The next day, we strolled through the iconic Church Street Marketplace, known for its open-air pedestrian mall, and past the honeysuckle trees and street performers. We sampled some chocolate goodies, ate turkey clubs at a quaint café, and shopped before we took a stroll holding hands along the bike path neighboring the waterfront. The sky was cluttered with clouds, big puffy ones, and the breeze was stiff.

A female jogger flew past us, headphones on, sweat soaking her sports top.

"Next time you go jogging, I'm gonna surround you in bubble wrap," Scott said with a twinkle in his eyes and a chuckle.

Even though the joke was funny, a pang of guilt jabbed my heart again as his comment reminded me of my encounter with Rick. Since this morning, I hadn't been able to get it out of my head.

What bothered me most about the whole thing was how Scott and I had vowed to always be honest with each other. We'd endured so much deception at the hands of others— mostly from Rick but not entirely. It was the foundation that supported the beams of trust we held for each other. At the same time, what would telling Scott do to help the situation? *Nothing good.* And after the way he had reacted to the very *idea* of me meeting with Rick—with Scott in attendance—I wasn't sure what damage this news would inflict. What kind of burden would it place on his shoulders? Rick had ambushed me. And I was injured as a result. Scott had warned the senator three and a half years ago that if Rick ever came after me again or Scott even heard he was thinking about it, "*All bets are off.*" I would never forget the resolve in Scott's eyes and his voice as he said those words.

Yes, I was injured, but Rick didn't attack me. I sensed Rick was far more fearful of me than I was of him. It was empowering, and although his methods were shady, somehow, the whole experience had left me feeling at peace, with him and with me.

Not only that, we were leaving in just a few days for Europe to take the vacation of a lifetime. This wasn't the time to unlock Pandora's box of torment and misery.

Rick was the past. It was over. Scott was my future. I reminded myself that I would tell him, but only when the time was right.

A breeze pushed off the water, goose bumps riding up my arms and neck. I shivered just before Scott draped his jacket over my shoulders, his arm also doing its best to keep me warm. For a time, we let the birds, a few distant voices and laughter, along with music emanating from a pub on the waterfront, keep us company, water lapping the lake's edge.

* * *

In the spirit of our upcoming trip, we chose an Irish restaurant to dine at, where I ordered a Reuben sandwich with shaved brisket and melted Swiss cheese, and Scott ordered cottage pie, which was much like a shepherd's pie but with prime rib and a cheddar mashed potato crust. Our order came with soda bread and plenty of butter, which we devoured while Scott sipped his beer, and I enjoyed a glass of hard cider.

After we walked off our dinner, I danced for him back at the hotel. Only this time, I made it interactive. "I have something I want you to watch. And then let's see where it takes us."

"I like the sound of that," Scott said, always my willing participant.

From a laptop I had smuggled in without Scott's knowledge, I queued up a scene from *Dirty Dancing*. We watched several scenes before I put on seductive music that carried a beat and guided him to join me in a dance.

"You want me to dance like Patrick Swayze?" he asked, his mouth crimped slightly downward.

I laced my fingers together behind his neck and stared up at him. "Nope. I want you to dance like Scott Williams."

With the help of the music and the memory of the movie fresh in our minds, we let our bodies do what they wanted. We might have gotten a bit more R-rated than the movie had, but we sure had fun doing it.

And that was all I thought about when we returned to Abigail's on Friday to enjoy a weekend of graduation and birthday celebrations.

Chapter Thirteen

Our flight left Burlington, Vermont, at 3:39 p.m. on Tuesday, and with one stop at JFK and no delays, we would arrive in Shannon, Ireland, at 6:00 a.m., factoring in the time change (Ireland was five hours ahead of the East Coast). As a graduation gift, Scott's parents had purchased us first-class tickets, knowing we'd be flying through the night. And what an experience *that* was. We each had our own cabin-type area, equipped with seats that reclined into small beds, our own individual selection of entertainment, and food that looked like it came from a luxury resort.

After Scott insisted we join the *mile-high-club*, because of course he did, I sipped my sparkling water with a wedge of lime. Scott had a couple of beers, and we soaked up the pampering: warm hand towels, privacy from other passengers, and attentive service that got a little *too* attentive with Scott and two of the flight attendants who looked like fashion models. *Didn't they notice us in the bathroom?* Then again, they weren't around when we came out. The blonde with long, silky hair, big breasts, and a tight uniform that conformed to her perfect body kept striking up conversations with Scott and glancing over at him whenever she was near.

Yup, I noticed.

Then she started talking about her layover in Ireland and some fun places to eat and drink if he'd like *her* to show him around.

That was when Scott leaned forward and said across the console between us, "I'll make sure my fiancée and I check them out."

Man, he loved using that word. Almost as much as I loved hearing it.

"Did you hear that, hon? This is Ashley, and she has some good ideas of places we can check out in Ireland."

The blonde shifted her gaze my way, her green eyes turning icy. And then she smiled as if realizing how petty that was. A woman like her probably met men all the time. Why get hung up on one passenger, even one as dreamy as Scott?

From then on, Ashley and her counterpart, Naomi, another picture-perfect woman with dark skin and warm brown eyes, admired Scott from afar. *Were* these women fashion models?

And, yes, I noticed that, too.

Scott kept leaning forward and checking on me. "You okay over there?" he'd say.

"Yes, Handsome. I'm good. You?"

Eventually, he reached his hand out, and when I leaned my body *way* out, I was able to touch his fingertips over the small partition between us. "Just missing you, Babe." He blinked, his eyes going all soft and cuddly.

Did one of the flight attendants just say, "Aw?"

If she did, Scott sure didn't seem to notice. He kept his attention drawn on me, probably making the ladies around him swoon even more.

What did I care? He was mine. And I was his.

Eventually, my eyes grew heavy. White noise lured me to sleep, while the movement of the plane had the opposite effect, and I slept in and out for the remainder of the flight.

* * *

The sun was already up when we arrived in Shannon, Ireland, the sky mostly cloudy, the temperature a whopping forty-five degrees (forecasted to reach sixty by midday). I'd done my research and packed plenty of layers for all the various stops we planned to make around Europe, my cozy sweaters and jeans reserved for the Emerald Isle.

My heart raced at the thought of being in this country. The place where my father was born. I wanted to pinch myself.

As we hustled off the plane, my eyes must've been the size of saucers as my head turned this way and that, taking in the ground floor of the terminal with its lovely artwork, high ceilings, and vibrant colors.

We traveled through the airport to find the luggage area where we retrieved our bags. That was where we also found a trolley at no charge from one of several bays and stacked our bags on it as we continued toward customs.

Three lighted signs illuminated above our heads like marquees, one purple, one red, and one green, all instructing arriving passengers which line for customs they would need. Half walls of the same corresponding color separated each section. Since we had nothing to declare, we took what was called the green channel. Everyone we encountered was friendly and spoke with that fabulous Irish accent I missed hearing when my father was still alive. The same one I had admired so much in Uncle Aidan.

Once we cleared customs, we meandered through the airport lobby while I continued to take in the beautifully constructed building, including one generous seating area where a red, cushioned bench circled around a large tree that stood at its center, an enormous round skylight casting natural light upon its leaves from above. From the skylight, recessed lighting spanned outward in a pie chart fashion that resembled something one might see in an episode of *Star Trek*. It was quite magnificent, enough that Scott and I both stopped for a moment to admire the view, people milling about around us.

"What a beautiful airport," I said, trying to keep my mouth from falling open. Of course, being an inexperienced flier, I was just as impressed with JFK.

From beside me, Scott nodded. "Yup, not bad."

We passed by several pubs, eateries, and gift shops—each one that I wanted to explore—but what we didn't encounter was Uncle Aidan.

"Did you tell him what time we were arriving?" Scott asked just after we had exited through the whooshing automatic doors toward the parking lot.

I pulled out my phone. "Yes. I DM'd him all of our flight details."

As we stood on the sidewalk, a strong breeze pushed through, slapping my hair against my cheeks. Cars came and went, no one familiar, the air mostly fresh with a few bouts of exhaust.

And then it occurred to me: I didn't know what Aidan's car looked like, probably something I should have thought to ask him. My fear of him not being as nice as he seemed grew exponentially.

We waited another ten minutes, my gut starting to clench. "Do you think he forgot?"

Scott raised his eyebrows and then lowered them. "How should I know, Babe? Do you have his address?"

"Not really. I know he lives like an hour away on the

Atlantic coast. I'll try his cell." After several attempts and no contact, I hung up for the last time. "Maybe he used the bathroom inside when we walked through. Do you think he could still be in there looking for us?"

Again, Scott gave me a how-should-I-know expression.

"The airport's not that big. We can go through it again."

Scott yawned. "Okay, but if we can't find him, we're gonna need to come up with another plan. I'm not spending all day here."

His annoyance was understandable. We'd just flown all night across the Atlantic to be here when there were many other places we could have gone to first, Heathrow being one of them, where we had planned to start our vacation before Uncle Aidan had shown up, offering another alternative.

Just as we were pushing our luggage cart back into the airport, a car beeped several times in the distance. *Please be Uncle Aidan.*

Across several lanes of traffic, some parked, some not, Uncle Aidan waved his hands above his head. "Sara, over here, lass."

Phew. We rushed over to the only living soul we knew in this country and greeted my Uncle Aidan, who stood next to his tan sedan that was coated in rust and looked like he hadn't washed it this decade. Even the windows were cloudy from grime. All I could think was *how badly does it smell inside?* My gaze washed over my uncle's baggy trousers and off-white button-down shirt that appeared to be off by one button. With a layer of scruff growing on his chin and his hair a bit of a mess, he personified the crazy-old-uncle stereotype. Not that I minded. Heck, I was just glad to see the man.

"I knew you'd be right along, so I thought the pickup area was the best place to spot ya. Trouble is I can't stay here long, so I timed it just right. I figured thirty minutes to deboard and get your bags. How was your flight?" Aidan didn't wait for our answer before he opened his trunk and started helping us load our stuff inside.

* * *

I wish I could say I admired the lush and iconic Irish countryside as we drove the hour from Shannon to Lahinch. I wish I could say I spotted old castles and rolling pastures, but I couldn't. Why? Because I slept the entire way. *Really? You're in Ireland, for God's sake, and you're sleeping?*

From the backseat (Scott rode shotgun), I pried my eyes open and wiped the corners of my mouth. All at once, my heart stopped, and my breath hitched. I almost screamed, "Uncle Aidan, you're driving on the wrong side of the road," but then stopped myself when I realized how idiotic that would sound.

I tempered my nerves and swallowed hard. Luckily, no one seemed to notice my near heart attack from the back seat.

"You much of a golfer, are ya, lad?"

Scott exhaled. "Uh, yeah, I play every now and then. I bet you've got some impressive courses over here. I'd love to check them out. You a golfer, Aidan?"

"Never used to be. I always thought the sport was a waste of time, hittin' a tiny ball into a little cup. Where's the sport in that? But I'm comin' around the bend on it. Been workin' with a bloke in Shannon to set up a course in Lahinch. Biggest deal of my life." Aidan spoke with such conviction, then he lowered his voice slightly. "If only Da were here to see it." He turned his head when I sat up straighter.

"Welcome back, sleepyhead." Aidan smiled, his gaze finding me in the rearview mirror, which was about as clean as the windows were.

Stacks of newspapers, old shoes, and books cluttered one

side of the backseat and floor while I cluttered the other. A musty odor permeated the air. And don't get me started on the trunk. I suspected our luggage was going to come out looking as though Uncle Aidan had dragged it through the desert. *Man, Uncle Aidan needs a spouse to clean him up.* I sensed a packrat in his element.

For the final leg of our journey, we rode along the coast, more rock than sand—a stone wall separating the narrow road from the terrain below—and approached a small town.

"Is that Lahinch up ahead?" I wasn't sure I was saying it properly.

"It is, in fact." Aidan rested his driving hand at the top of the steering wheel in a casual manner.

"It's beautiful." I kept my eyes glued to the window, letting reality sink in—I was in Ireland. This was amazing. We drove past a few diminutive restaurants, one with bright blue trim, where several people sat outside enjoying an early breakfast, and past a small store with the words "Beer, Wine, Spirits, Champagne, and Groceries" written on the window. I chuckled to myself at the priority list.

A few times when we encountered oncoming traffic, Scott touched the dash, just enough to let me know he was about as uncomfortable with driving on the *wrong* side of the road as I was. *What did Aidan think when he was in America?*

Most of the interconnected two-story buildings in town wore neutral colors like beige or faded yellow while the lower floors, the ones that housed restaurants, shops, and parlors, exploded with pinks, purples, and bright greens, to name a few.

"Wow. What a cool-looking town. I love it."

Aidan chuckled. "*Cool,*" he said in a mocking voice.

In the center of town, cars lined the narrow street in their designated parking spaces while their owners were fast asleep or enjoying breakfast in the apartments above. A few early risers strolled the sidewalks: an elderly man donning a flat cap and a woman of similar age wearing a light-blue scarf as a bonnet that she tied under her chin. Honestly, the two of them could have been poster models for this country since they were exactly who I envisioned would live here. I admired a set of window boxes, abundant with flowers, which complemented a pizzeria as we drove past.

Even though the modest-sized town was quite colorful, the sky hadn't gotten the message, which remained gray and devoid of sunlight. A firm breeze agitated the surf, waves crashing against the rocks below, a narrow stretch of sandy beach off to the side.

Although it was chilly, I cracked my window a few inches to enjoy the fresh sea air, salty and thick with moisture.

I was a Vermonter at heart, which meant I could handle a little cold. And, apparently, so could the people we passed, not one of them wearing a coat or a sweater of any kind. Forty-five degrees (it might have been closer to fifty by now) and sunny was probably balmy to them. If not for the wind, it probably would have felt that way to me, too.

"I'll take ya out for chips and a pint while you're here. I bought sausage and eggs for back at the house. Oh, and some apple tart. I figured you'd want to get settled."

"That sounds great, Uncle Aidan. Thank you."

"I'm down for that," Scott said from the front, his head turned toward the view.

Normally, Scott was a chatterbox with new people. He could strike up a conversation with pretty much anyone he met. Sports was always his go-to. But this morning, he remained rather quiet. I suspected he was taking it all in. Plus, I wasn't sure how much sleep he had gotten on the plane.

"So my dad grew up here? It's perfect."

More beach appeared below where ocean waves pushed

and then receded over the sandy surface, rocks stacked against a concrete wall that reached up to the road.

"Yeah, your da and I grew up here. The town is old. Needs a facelift. And I'm hopin' my new business venture will give it just that. Bring jobs." His tone lifted as he sat up straighter.

"Business venture? Does it have anything to do with your trip to the United States?"

Aidan nodded. "It does, in fact, lass. But we can discuss that later. Just sit back and enjoy the view."

Soon, we left the paved road behind and traveled over gravel and dirt for several miles, dust kicking up a storm behind us. Each new road we took appeared more remote than the last. At one point, I wondered if Uncle Aidan was a serial killer, taking us into no-man's-land, never to be heard from again. I assured myself that my uncle might have been a tad dishonest, but he *wasn't* another Dr. Adams. Plus, Scott was with me.

And then it happened. The trees, bent over by the steady wind and high brush opened up in one big yawn, exposing a very different view: the coast. I felt like Sam Neill in the movie *Jurassic Park* when he first discovered the dinosaurs.

Aidan peered back at me as he slowed the car to a stop as though waiting for my reaction. He must've seen it before from others whom this place entranced.

As the three of us exited the car, the word "Wow" flew from my lips.

"Holy shit." Scott glanced over at Aidan. "Sorry, man, but this is amazing."

Amid the fresh ocean air that fluffed my hair and saturated my lungs, a patchwork of fields spread out, sporting varying shades of green, while a picturesque mountain range reached out like a protective arm to the left, lifting the landscape to new heights.

At the land's rugged edge, where the earth ended and the

possibilities began, the ocean below remained powerful and inspiring. Even the sun came out for a moment to enjoy the view. I'd pulled up lots of images of Ireland online before we came, but this ... this was something else entirely.

"Are ya takin' a likin' to what ya see, lass? This part of the property is yours." Aidan's chin rose higher, his chest out. "Mine is off to the left. Runs all the way to that mountain range." He turned his body in that direction.

"I guess you could say I'm taking a liking." What an understatement. I was going to own this? I couldn't fathom it. In a state of shock, I walked toward the rugged edge like a zombie, trying to remember the plat drawing as best I could. I'd have to check it later when I opened my suitcase.

Scott took my hand, his face wide and awestruck as though he'd just discovered the magic himself. "Not too shabby, huh?"

"It's incredible." I wanted to sprout wings and soar over the coast with all its wonder, my wingtips just touching the surf that pushed like a freight train against the rocks, receded, and then tried again, its strength never waning.

My heart lifted, my stomach feeling like I'd just taken a dip on the largest roller coaster in the world. Exhilarated, I wanted to stand there forever, never tiring of the majestic blue abyss that spread out before me, the one that traveled three thousand miles, reaching the United States. Did my father ever stand here and wonder what was on the other side of the world, the place where he eventually made a family and a home? This was where boundaries fell away, and dreams came to life.

Once I was able to pull my eyes back into their sockets and close my mouth, the three of us strolled to the right, where Aidan pointed toward a set of stone steps carved by nature down a jagged wall. A narrow beach, half sand and half rocks, sat below. Its own private sanctuary.

Rocks dominated all the beaches I had seen in Ireland.

Here, a narrow strip of sand cushioned the shallows and the tides. And this one was no different. It reminded me of the coastline in Maine, where my family and I used to vacation a lot.

"You will also own a good portion of that beach. That's where your da used to fish all the time. There's a cave in the rocks ya can't see from up here. He used to go in there all the time and explore, said somethin' about findin' hidden treasure." He scoffed. "Kid stuff. One time, my pa got firey angry when he couldn't find him. We were about to send out for a search party when Robby came home, shiverin' to beat the band. Said the tide came in and stranded him for a time." Aidan's eyes saddened in a reflective sort of way. "He got the belt that night, I'll tell ya, and Robby wasn't too keen about that, being a teenage boy and all."

The way Aidan described my great-grandfather, he wasn't so great—just an old curmudgeon. I didn't like him much. *Was he also abusive to Aidan?*

A gust of wind picked up, drawing my chin downward, my arms tight against my sides. Scott came around behind me and wrapped his arms around me like a big heated blanket.

"Ya must be hungry. Let's get ya settled and fed." Aidan turned and walked toward his vehicle.

About a quarter of a mile inland, Aidan's cottage awaited our arrival. After standing on the edge of the world just a few moments ago, where time stood still, I expected a home that was traditionally Irish and reeking of style. What I found, as we drove up the short dirt driveway, was a shack or what used to be a cottage, neglected over the years, its roof on the verge of collapse, its paint chipping. If I were to describe the outside of

Aidan's home, I would call it ragged. A three-bay garage-type outbuilding stood off to the side with no doors, revealing even more of Uncle Aidan's clutter. An old rusty tractor that had eroded into a heap of metal and the skeleton of an old car that was missing its hood and its engine were the only lawn ornaments.

Aidan slapped the car into park. "She's not fancy, but she's been keepin' a roof over my head these past years."

Really? Because the roof doesn't look too sound.

Scott glanced back at me, his eyes saying it all. *Are we supposed to sleep in that place?*

I tried to offer a reassuring smile, but I wasn't quite sure what we were walking into. I mean, Aidan owned ninety acres of prime property less than a mile away. He and my father had inherited their parents' house. What did he do with the money? How could he be living in such squalor? Grass, thick from salt air, reached my waist as we lugged our bags into a house that reeked of dust and old tobacco. *Does Uncle Aidan smoke a pipe?*

I walked slowly and carefully into the kitchen, my eyes on full alert for a rodent or a ghost to come flying out.

"I know she doesn't look like much, but she's sound, I promise ya."

I wasn't sure how to respond. The house was owned by a hoarder, one who needed an intervention. Under crumpled newspapers, letters, old jars, dirty dishes and mugs, not to mention a rusty tool or two, an actual kitchen table emerged, and even a set of chairs, albeit different styles and colors. The countertops were no different, cluttered with boxes or cans of food, dishes, and everything else known to man, the sink stacked high with plates, bowls, and mugs. Grease stained the stove from years of cooking, and the wood floor slanted to the left. Old curtains, which looked like they were bought in the

'70s, hung tattered and loosely from the windows, the glass obscured by dirt and grime.

The color of the walls was hard to describe. It looked like someone had mixed all their leftover paint and used it. Peach, maybe, pink, or a funny shade of orange? I couldn't decide.

I didn't dare put my bags down and just stood there, awkward and speechless, Scott doing the same.

Finally, Uncle Aidan exhaled as though the jig was up, and he had to admit what this place actually looked like, not what he wanted to believe it was. "The property taxes on the land are steep and have kept me strapped for many years, lass. I've been livin' hand to mouth."

Who's been paying the property taxes on my half? I never thought to check into that. "How did you afford the trip to the States?" I had to ask.

"The bloke I'm in a deal with funded the trip." His voice dipped lower, shame in his eyes. "I'm sorry it's such a mess here. I meant to tidy up, but I've been burnin' the candle on both ends." He dropped his keys on the counter and leaned against it. "If ya don't want to be stayin' with me, I understand. I can bring ya to a place in town or Dublin, even. I'd like ya to stay for a night if ya would. It's my chance to show ya around the land and get to know ya a bit better."

And then he dismantled me with the same look my dad used to give me whenever he was trying to persuade me to do something, his pale-blue eyes reaching out in a pleading gesture. With my dad, it usually involved a large project he needed help with or a shot I had to get at the doctor's office. I never liked shots. I couldn't say no to my dad, not when he needed me, and I wasn't about to say no to his brother.

I rested my suitcases and my backpack on the floor and placed a supportive hand on his shoulder. "I'm so sorry, Uncle Aidan. I thought with the sale of your parents' house and the work that you do, you had enough to live on. Of course we'll stay the night." My gaze found Scott, his mouth crimped, his eyes tentative, and his two suitcases still clasped in his hands, which he slowly lowered to the floor.

I'd discuss it with him later, and I hoped he caught my offer to stay "the night" and not the week as we had planned.

"The sale of my da's place held me for years, but I had a lot to contend with here on my own. I wish Robby was here to help. The taxes will drain ya." He lowered his gaze to the floor as though it was too heavy to keep upright. "I've been tryin' to keep this property intact, but I fear that that time has come to an end." He lifted his chin and made a dismissive gesture with his hand. "No need to get into that now. Let's get ya settled."

Scott grimaced, which thankfully, Uncle Aidan didn't see as we ventured farther into the house—if you wanted to call it that. We proceeded past the dark-paneled living room with one large recliner, a crocheted afghan draped over its back, several tears allowing yellow foam to poke through, a couch worn to its threads, and a bookcase that stood bursting with papers, knick-knacks, and old books.

We ventured up the stairs, each step creaking under the weight of our feet, and down a short hallway, where Uncle Aidan opened a door to the spare room that smelled like a thrift store. Light filtered in through the broken blinds bringing more clutter into focus on the dresser and floor. The bed stood higher than most, boxes peeking out from underneath, and the blankets and pillows looked old and tarnished by age. *Did he wash the sheets?* I didn't dare ask.

"The bed is clean, I assure ya. I took the linens into town and cleaned them up for ya yesterday. I'll leave ya to it while I go make breakfast."

"Um. Is there a place where I can wash up before breakfast?" Fatigue had me wishing for a shower, but I realized that probably wasn't an option and hoped a few splashes of water on my face would perk me up.

"Straight down the hall, lass." Aidan backed up from the doorway and stared in the direction that he was intending.

I peered around the corner, wondering what other house of horrors the bathroom had to offer. *At least it's indoors.* "Okay, great. I just need to freshen up, and then I'll be down to help you make breakfast." *And to make sure I don't get food poisoning.*

"No problem at all. Glad to have ya, lass. It means a lot." And with that, Aidan disappeared down the creaky stairs, pans clanking and footfalls traveling back and forth a few minutes later.

As I closed the door to our bedroom, Scott unleashed his outrage, albeit in a whisper-shout sort of way. "What the fuck is this place? The man is a hermit. How could he own all that land and live this way?" Scott's body turned as he took in his surroundings. "I thought my Uncle Kenny was bad. He's a packrat, too, but this—" Scott clamped his mouth shut as he ran a hand down his face, his stubble starting to poke through his chin and jawline.

I approached him and threaded my arms between his arms and waist, pulling him close. "I know. It's hard to believe anyone could live like this, but I think it means a lot to Aidan that we came. Obviously, he doesn't have anyone in his life."

Scott rested his chin on the top of my head. "It's fine. We'll stick it out." He chuckled. "At least you don't have to worry about me trying to get you naked. I'll be sleeping with my clothes on."

We pulled back from each other, Scott's eyes a little red from our *red-eye* flight.

"And on top of the sheets, not in them." He stared at the bed.

I shook my head and smiled. "Yeah, no arguments here. Okay, I'm gonna splash some water on my face and get down there to help Uncle Aidan. Do you want to take a nap or a shower—?"

"Nope. I'm waiting right here for you. I'm afraid this house might swallow one of us up if we don't stick together. At least I can hear you scream from here." He gave my butt a light slap. "Now, go do your thing."

Chapter Fourteen

Breakfast was a lot to contend with. Uncle Aidan wanted to fry up the sausage in a pan that wasn't clean until I insisted on washing it. With my sleeves rolled up, I had to wash quite a few pans and then dishes, Scott drying them and putting them away in the handmade cupboards that used to be white and liked to stick as though someone had painted them shut at one point, judging by the way layers of dried paint coated the edges.

As *I* cooked the sausage, and since there wasn't any real organization to the room, I organized. Something I was good at and enjoyed. In fact, Scott relied on me to pack our car whenever we took a short trip together. I liked order, maybe because I'd dealt with so much disorder in my past.

While I pulled the sausage off the stove, Scott found a small dumpster out back, which he filled with several bags of trash Uncle Aidan had neglected to throw out. Of course, he made sure it was actual trash first, and not something Uncle Aidan was saving.

"Ya don't need to fuss. And the sausage is going to get cold.

Want me to fry us some eggs? I got them from a farmer down the lane."

He sounded a tad Mother Goose-ish when he said those words.

I swiped a hand across my brow, my mind already entrenched in this new project. "Let's put the sausage in the oven to keep warm for a few minutes, and then I'll cook us some eggs." I didn't want to appear pushy, but I also couldn't seem to stop myself from getting this house in some sort of shape. "I love cooking breakfast. I hope you don't mind."

Aidan waved me off. "Suits me." He opened the oven, removed two large baking pans (also in need of a wash), which he replaced with the pan of sausage I had just cooked, and then set the oven to warm, which made the air smell of old grease. "It isn't often I have a woman in the house." He went into the living room and came out with a large wad of old newspapers, which he threw into the trash, then disappeared again. It seemed he was getting into cleaning mode as well. Good, because some packrats had trouble with that.

What surprised me most was how bad Aidan had let his house get. He wasn't an old man, not even fifty yet, so why wasn't he dating someone or living in better conditions? He was handsome, in an unkempt sort of way, with beautiful eyes like my dad's, a straight nose, and a strong jawline. He had a bit of a stomach, but nothing a good walk several times a week couldn't fix, maybe a little less sausage and a bit more oatmeal added to his diet.

I also recognized that hoarding was a sickness, a serious one. Maybe he couldn't help himself. Or maybe he had been alone so long he'd forgotten to care. I hoped our being here would help change things. Wishful thinking, I was sure.

A window sat above the sink, looking out at the brambles and brush that had grown wild over the years, trees dwarfed and bent from the weather, and the garage off to the left. I cracked it open to invite some fresh air into the house (and get the old grease smell out) as Scott passed by, holding an old mop and a small bucket in the air like a trophy.

"Look what I found."

Once inside, Scott asked Uncle Aidan if there were any cleaning supplies. "I'll mop the floor before we eat."

Aidan tried to wave him off. "No need. Ya didn't come here to work. This is supposed to be your vacation ..."

Not in the mood to argue, Scott searched the cupboard under the sink where I was standing and found something for cleaning wood floors, the lid caked with dried goo.

Aidan, recognizing that he wasn't getting through to Scott, returned to the living room to unclutter.

While I washed and stacked and organized, Scott mopped until he was at my feet.

"Move it, woman," he said with a grin, his tone light-hearted. And then he leaned in for a kiss.

"Scott, you don't need to do all—"

"Don't even say it. Do you remember the bathroom you had to clean up after me in the frat house?" He stared with intent.

I did remember that bathroom, splattered with Scott's *and* Rick's blood from their altercation at the water tower. The one that had almost taken the love of my life away from me. Permanently.

"I could clean this entire house and paint the exterior, and I'd still owe you for that one. Now, move it." He pushed his mop at my feet, determination in his actions.

I raised both palms in surrender mode—"I'm going. I'm going."—and hopped out of the way.

And then I spent the next half hour helping Aidan stack books in his bookcase and throw out things that he approved could go.

"Most of this stuff was my pa's. I just never got 'round to gettin' rid of it."

When Scott's stomach started growling at us, enough that Aidan could hear, he became insistent.

"That's it. We're stoppin' for breakfast."

No one argued. My stomach was doing the same thing, just a little quieter.

As we sat at his kitchen table, the opened window freshening the house, we munched on our eggs, sausage, and apple tart Aidan had purchased in town while we kept idle chatter, mostly about our flight and the weather. My stomach thanked me with a burp when I finished. The two men seated across from me stopped their conversation and stared me down.

I put a hand to my mouth. "Excuse me." And then my mind went to another subject. "Uncle Aidan, is this new deal you're working on going to help you fix up the place? You have that beautiful piece of land. Can you build a new house on it?" When I had asked him what he did for a living back in the US, his answer was a jack-of-all-trades, which didn't reveal much. "Will it help you with finances?"

Scott didn't speak, but his expression told me all I needed to know. *Don't offer financial help until you know what the situation is.*

How did he know I was considering that?

Scott took a sip from his mug, his taste buds doing their best to acclimate to tea and not coffee, judging by the grimace he was making. "Got any coffee, Aidan?" He stared at his mug as though mud filled it.

"Sorry, lad. Just tea. I can pick some up in town if ya wish."

Scott waved him off. "Nah, I'm good."

Aidan sat back and ran a hand over his now-full belly. "The deal I'm workin' right now is with a developer in Shannon, lass, who would like to turn my fine piece of property into a luxury golf course." He sat forward. "Think of it. What better way to enjoy the land and the scenery? Another bloke tried to get me to sell years ago, said he wanted to put condos out there." Eyes hard, Aidan furrowed his brow. "I told him, nothin' doin'. I wasn't gonna let them ruin my grandpa's land. No siree. But a golf course, with a small meetin' house to enjoy a pint or two, with a few minor adjustments." He waved an optimistic finger in the air. "That would be a good way to enjoy the land and the sea and for me to make a few bob in the process." His face fell into a frown. "I can't maintain this land anymore, lass. As much as I want to. I've gotta let it go." He stared at me with sorrowful eyes. "A lot of the money from my parents' land paid the taxes. It's become a hardship. And I'm not gettin' any younger. Another deal like this one may never come 'round again."

You aren't that old. "I understand, Uncle Aidan. You have to do what you have to do. I hope this new venture will allow you the financial stability you need."

Something registered in my uncle's eyes. "Have ya thought about how ya plan to use *your* half of the land, lass? Those taxes could drain ya, too, doncha know."

That worried me a bit as I shook my head. "No. I haven't had much time to consider what to do with it. It's beautiful, though. I still can't believe it will be mine." I fanned my hands out in a reassuring sort of way. "And about your golf course, I have no problem with you doing whatever you want with your land." I cleared my throat, feeling awkward about it all. *Is that appropriate to say?* I hoped so.

Aidan observed me for a moment, his expression hard to read. "That is kind of ya, lass." He pushed his chair back and stood. "Now go get changed and washed up." He stacked our plates together, grabbed the utensils, and headed for the sink. "Place is so shiny, I don't recognize it anymore. Ya both did some good tidyin' up."

He was being kind. Nothing here shined. All we did was make it a little less messy.

Aidan placed the plates and silverware, plus our glasses that we had filled with water and tea mugs, on the counter and turned the faucet on. "I'll repay your kindness by shufflin' ya around Ireland to explore. I'll take ya anywhere your hearts desire. Ya won't be here long, so we won't waste the daylight. Tomorrow, I'll show ya the land."

"Why don't we walk the land now, Uncle Aidan? We can visit the sites tomorrow, instead." I felt like I'd won the biggest prize of my life, and I wanted to see as much of it as possible.

"The forecast for tomorrow will be better for walkin'. But we could take a short look on our way out. I'll show ya more tomorrow. Does that sit right with ya, lass?"

"Sure." I tried not to sound disappointed. It was fine. There would be plenty of time to explore later, and he certainly knew the weather better than I did.

As he worked away at the dishes, he waved a hand behind his head. "Now away with ya both."

* * *

We had just packed into Uncle Aidan's car once again, my mind still reeling from our short tour of the land. Aidan took us far enough that I could see the border between his property and mine, marked by a line of trees. His side was just as nice, minus the beach. As we strolled back to the car, I wondered *Who inherits something like this?* Until I had the deed in my hands, I wasn't willing to believe it. And I'd have to check into those taxes.

So far, Aidan was behaving just as friendly as he had when he came to the States. No red flags were flying. None that I could see, anyway.

"It's early yet, so I can take ya to either Dublin, Shannon, or Galway. Your choice."

From the backseat, I looked at Scott, who sat in the front. "I'd like to see Dublin, myself, but I'm sure they're all spectacular."

"Dublin works for me." Scott turned his head and smiled, his face freshly shaved, his hair damp from a five-minute shower he allowed for himself. I say shower, but the hose that ran from the spout made you feel more like a car in a car wash. Oh, well, it got the job done. He was clean, and so was I, the bathroom no worse for wear, which I had scoured beforehand. My hands were getting raw from all the cleaning, so I made sure to moisturize and brought some travel-sized lotion with me.

Soon, we'd have a nice hotel room in Dublin with amenities. I just had to break the news to Aidan first. I planned to come back and see him plenty before we left the country. It was nice having an uncle in my life. I was receiving two valuable gifts, and I didn't intend to squander either one of them.

"Dublin it is. Sun's splittin' the stones." Aidan fired up the engine of his car, and off we went, his muffler rattling the floor beneath my feet.

Sun's splitting the stones. I gazed up at the sky, partly cloudy and promising dry weather. Another thing I had read about Ireland involved the rain. It wasn't whether or not it *would* rain; it was when and how much. Vermont could be like that, too, depending on the summer. Today, however, the sun was eager to win that battle. And I had wanted to see Dublin for years now with its castles and rich heritage.

* * *

The city did not disappoint, other than the three-and-a-half-hour drive to get here. Double-decker buses and trains blended with cars, trucks, and bicycles traversing the narrow streets. Taverns abounded, some with Irish music spilling out from their doors, and people were everywhere.

After a lunch of fish and chips, which I insisted on paying for, we walked off our meal in the lush and iconic Phoenix Park where several runners were getting their exercise and even a few deer feasted on the vegetation, not at all uncomfortable with their human neighbors. Everyone was enjoying the now sixty-degree day.

Since Aidan didn't have a lot of money and he was kind enough to deliver us to this fair city, Scott opted to pay for a horse-drawn carriage that carried the three of us. We rode past St. Patrick's Cathedral in all its spires and splendor, a place I planned to revisit and tour before we left Ireland for good, and by a white-picket structure called Ha'Penny Bridge, made specifically for pedestrians. I had seen this bridge in at least one movie and had read about it in a novel or two. And then there was Dublin Castle, a mammoth stone tribute to history that transported you back in time when knights on horseback fought gallantly for their king.

As the day wore on and the carriage ride came to an end, Uncle Aidan took us to Grafton Street, another place designated specifically for pedestrians, who were out in abundance. Aromas ranging from fresh garbage to bath bombs to fried goodies competed with each other in the air, except for one location, abundant with flowers. Caught up in the action, we watched traditional fiddle players entertain streetgoers, their music uplifting and energetic. Several kiosks cluttered the street, offering hats, scarves, and sweaters, as shops displayed clothing and Irish souvenirs from their windows. Honestly, Grafton Street was much like Church Street back home, only bigger and a tad more Celtic, although Burlington had that, too.

As the sun dipped lower in the west and the clouds came rolling in, we headed home, Aidan's noisy car forging the way.

"That was an incredible day, Uncle Aidan. Thank you for taking us." I was still toying with how to bring up the white lie he'd told me. Not an easy topic considering it dealt with his grandfather's death.

"Grand. Glad ya enjoyed yourself, lass. Tomorrow, I'll show ya more of the property, and if there's time, we can visit Galway, which is much closer."

"That would be great." I swallowed. "After that, Scott and I were thinking we'd like to go back to Dublin and take some of those tours. I feel like I only got a glimpse of it today. St. Patrick's and Dublin Castle both have tours, and I got the sense we only saw part of Grafton Street. Scott really wants to check out the Guinness Storehouse Factory, too."

Aidan didn't respond right away. "Well, I suppose I could lend ya my car. Are ya sound with drivin' on the other side of the road?"

"Oh, we couldn't do that. And I'm not quite confident driving just yet." My giggle came out fake and nervous. "If it's too much for you to take us back there, we can get a bus. We'd like to stay there for a couple of days. Maybe get a hotel in the city." My voice weakened with worry. "Is that okay with you? You've been great to host us, and we've really enjoyed ourselves, but it sounds like you have a lot to do with your new business venture, and we'll definitely come back before we go—"

"Lass, this is your holiday. Do with it what ya wish. Of course, I'll cart ya there. And if ya choose to come back, I'll cart ya back."

I swore I heard Scott exhale from the front seat.

* * *

That night, after Scott and Aidan enjoyed several pints of dark beer (I could only stomach a few sips) and a shot of Irish whiskey, we all headed to bed, Scott able to weather the alcohol much better than Joel had back home. After Scott had exhausted the subject of soccer, letting Uncle Aidan know he played as well as spectated, he visited the subject of golf courses. "How big is your course going to be, Aidan? Which section of the property do you plan to develop it on? When is this all gonna happen?"

With each question, Aidan just waved him off. "Enjoy your ale, lad, we can discuss this another time."

He didn't seem to have the need for any bragging rights. Either that, or he worried I'd have a problem with it, even though I said I wouldn't.

* * *

I awoke in the middle of the night, the moon glowing through the water droplets on my window left behind by the rain, and tossed and turned for what felt like an hour.

Deciding I was dehydrated from those few sips of beer, I ventured downstairs to get a glass of water, my feet light, not to wake anyone. I scolded myself for not bringing a glass upstairs with me.

When I reached the landing, Aidan's voice carried past my ears. The one-sided conversation told me he was on his phone, something he hadn't done since we'd arrived.

The few times that *I'd* checked my phone here, the cell service was non-existent, so I hadn't bothered much with mine, other than letting Abigail know when we'd arrived at the airport and that we were doing well as we drew closer to Dublin, where the cell service was stronger.

"I'm tellin' ya, I'm close. Just give me another day to seal the deal." And then he said something that stopped me in my tracks. "I have her ear. I just need a little more time."

I have her *ear?* My ear? What other *her* could there be?

"It's all goin' accordin' to plan. Ya needn't worry yourself, Declan."

My heart raced, and my throat tightened as I crept up the stairs and into the hall bathroom, where I splashed water on my face and used my palms as a cup to drink from. The remainder of the night, I tossed and turned some more, listening to the snoring man next to me. I wanted to wake Scott up but was afraid the noise would alert Aidan, whose room was on the other side of the wall.

The next morning, I packed my things, doing my best to behave normally as though I didn't hear my uncle hatching a scheme with a man named Declan that now involved me. As I hose-showered and Scott brushed his teeth, I tried to convince myself that he could have been talking about someone else, but my inner voice knew better. "*According to your dad, he's not to be trusted,*" my mother warned from the past.

As Scott wiped his mouth dry and ran a comb through his wet hair, he watched me get dressed from the small antique bathroom mirror mounted against the wall. "Are you okay, Babe? Did you not sleep well?" He turned to me, his eyes showing concern.

I made a motion with my hands that I didn't feel comfortable talking just then, and then I moved my lips closer to his ear. "I'll tell you about it when we get to Dublin."

Scott whispered back. "Tell me what? Did you find a rat in our bed or something?"

I shook my head and mouthed the words, *I'll. Tell. You. Later.*

He rattled his head as if confused and then started shaving.

Leaving Scott upstairs to finish grooming, I entered the much-cleaner kitchen downstairs to find Aidan whistling around the room like he'd just won the lottery. Or maybe that was just how my suspicious mind chose to see it.

"Mornin', lass. I thought I'd pop out for some more apple tarts." He touched a pan on the stove. "I was about to start some sausage but hoped ya'd be willin' to cook it for me while I'm away?"

That was exactly what I wanted to hear as I smiled wide and filled my voice with mock enthusiasm. "That would be great. And those tarts were delicious." At least that part was true. The sweet apple filling encased in a golden crust had my mouth watering. It was more like a pie than a tart, really. "How long will you be gone? I can start the eggs before you get back."

"Not long. I'm meetin' a fella for a few minutes in town about the land deal, and then I'll grab the tarts and be back in a flash. I won't be longer than a wee hour at best. Does that work for ya, lass? Ya can start the sausage and keep them warm. And we can do the eggs when I return." Aidan kept his relaxed stature, and his eyes shined with warmth as if things were finally going his way.

I headed for his dented metal teapot on the stove. "That works for me, Uncle Aidan. Take your time. I'll cook the sausage and make us some tea." I opened an upper cupboard, hoping to find a tea less malty flavored, not the stuff he kept out on his counter.

Aidan collected his keys. "And then we'll walk the land before ya leave me. Does that suit ya?"

Keeping my plastic smile in place, I said, "It does. I can't wait."

* * *

The minute Aidan's car rumbled out of earshot, I turned toward Scott, who had just entered the room, and told him the whole story.

He didn't appear as alarmed as I would have thought.

"That doesn't sound too terrible. 'I have her ear?' Maybe he wanted to make sure you were okay with his golf course deal."

I placed a hand on my hip. "Yeah, but I already told him I was okay with it. And why would that matter to this Declan guy?"

"Do you think he wants you to go in on the deal with him?"

"Maybe. He sounded so secretive about it, like he was hiding something. Every time we've brought up his golf course 'deal'"—I made air quotes—"he's brushed us off about it."

Scott leaned against the counter and rubbed his eyes. He yawned. "I really need some coffee when we get to Dublin." And then he shook the cobwebs out of his brain and focused. "One thing I wanted to mention is that if Aidan only owns ninety acres, and if some of it's mountainous, they must be planning on a small course. It's possible, but most golf courses are bigger than that. I'm not saying it couldn't work, though."

I replayed Aidan's phone conversation in my mind. "Why did Aidan tell Declan he needed a little more time, then? Time for what? I had already told him I didn't have a problem with it. Unless he wants *my* land. I don't want to sell my land." Now that I'd seen it, I wasn't willing to part with it so soon—unless the taxes were so high I'd have no choice.

"If he wanted you to sell, seems like he'd have mentioned it to you by now."

Scott was right.

"I get the sense he's waiting for something. Like to convince me of something. But what?" *Am I crazy? Am I looking for problems that don't exist?*

I blew out a breath and filled the teapot before putting it on the stove to boil. Like Scott, I also needed a caffeine boost.

Tired and anxious, I reopened the kitchen window Aidan must've closed, searching for comfort. "Can you watch the teapot? I'm gonna sneak into Aidan's room and look around. Also, see if you can find any other flavors of tea."

I half expected Scott to say, "Are you nuts?" but he didn't. He nodded instead. "Okay, try not to disturb anything." He made a face. "I can't imagine what his room looks like. But I'll watch the driveway from here. If I hear his car, I'll yell up to you. Just be careful, Babe, and if you need me, yell down to me. I'd say stomp your foot, but that might just bring the walls down."

I flung my arms around my gorgeous fiancé. "Thank you so much for not thinking I'm nuts."

Scott draped my hair over my shoulders and ran his hand down my back. "I told you once I would never discount your feelings again. And I meant it. I'm with you ... all the way."

"You're the best. You know that?"

Scott got all smug. "Yeah, and don't you forget it." He pinched my chin.

"I better hurry." I dashed out of the room and up the stairs to Aidan's bedroom door, which sat closed. Not only closed, but it was locked, which was strange considering the only reason Aidan would lock it was because we were here.

My dad used to say that *people who have nothing to hide, hide nothing.* At the time, he was referring to some political scandal, but in this moment, it meant something else. Shaking that thought from my mind like a dog with a bad case of fleas, I searched for a way in.

And then I remembered that my parents used to hide keys for interior rooms all the time and where. I brushed my fingers along the top of Aidan's door casing to find nothing but a thick layer of dust. At the top of *my* bedroom door casing, however, I knocked a skeleton key to the floor.

And it worked. I was in.

Similar to the rest of the house, papers, boxes, old shoes, and heaps of old clothes littered Aidan's room. Clean laundry piled high on one side of his bed. The smell I was getting used to. The man definitely had a hoarding problem. I searched through his dresser and the table next to his bed, coming up with nothing other than regular mail and a few bills.

A tan folder stared up at me from the floor next to his bed. In fact, I was standing on it. Inside, a proposal for the golf course that Uncle Aidan had been talking about confirmed my suspicions. The 180-acre golf course. Scott was right again. Ninety acres must've been too small for them. How arrogant of him to assume I'd sell. Even though he hadn't even asked me to sell yet, they had already drawn up the paperwork. Was he going to try and steal it from me? Or swindle it? *"I have her ear."* The thought of it made me nauseous.

There had to be more, so I kept looking.

Inside his small closet, I found two large shoeboxes on an upper shelf that I pulled down and opened. The receipts in one box appeared to be gambling transactions, and there were a lot of them. So many that when I opened the box, the stack seemed to expand, pieces of paper falling around my feet like snowflakes. Since I'd studied the value of the euro compared to the US dollar before I came on this trip, I was able to determine that some of these bets were rather high, like in the thousands. *Okay, so Aidan has a very bad gambling problem.*

What else? I opened the second box and found several letters from a person who meant the world to me. A person who I had missed with every fiber of my being for the last ten years: my dad. Knowing I didn't have a lot of time, I chose the most recent letter, dated one month before my father had passed away, according to the postmark, and read:

Aidan,

This is the last letter you will ever receive from me, and then I don't want to hear from you anymore. Ever. Once again, you have betrayed my trust and your role as my older brother. When you came to see me here in the States, right after Pa's funeral, you assured me that you would split the money from Ma and Da's land evenly. You even suggested that I use that money for Sara's college fund. All I needed to do was sign on the dotted line. Your words. And I did as you asked. That was nearly two years ago, and I have yet to see a dime, dear brother.

And the story about how Da's house burned down didn't wash with me, either. I suspect you burned the place down for the insurance money (money I also never saw), and when that ran dry, you sold the land. You are a cheat and a fraud, and you will never change.

I gave you one last chance to prove to me that you could do the right thing. Melinda and I could have used that money, but it is pointless for me to say so. You aren't listening. All you have ever thought about and all you will ever continue to think about is yourself. After our parents died, you did nothing but complain about how you never got that big break.

You think I left Ireland because of Pa, the nasty old bastard that he was, and I did. But I also left because of you. I knew you would never stop trying to take advantage of me. How many times did you steal from me? How many jobs did I get for you, only to have you steal from our employer? I almost went to jail because of you.

I have a family now, and by God, you better stay away from them. I mean it, Aidan. Melinda and Sara are all I have left in this world. They are everything to me, and you will not destroy the only thing that has ever truly made me happy.

And don't even consider asking me to sign over the coastal property. You would be wasting your breath. It is the only thing left of our legacy. I've been paying the taxes on it, and someday, I will hand it down to my daughter for her to decide what to do with it.

I'm not asking you to pay me back for the thousands of dollars you have pissed away for nothing but a high at the track or a prostitute. Keep it. It's yours. I don't want any part of it.

As far as I'm concerned, I don't have a brother. You are lost to me. Don't bother responding to this letter because I will burn anything you send to me.

Goodbye, Aidan. I hope you find whatever it is that you are looking for. Something tells me you won't, but that is not my problem anymore.

Robert

Chapter Fifteen

I stumbled into the kitchen, feeling faint and unsteady, and my eyes spilling tears.

With two cups of tea brewing on the counter, Scott stood peering out the kitchen window as my lookout. He turned, his head jerking back, his face wide with worry. "What's wrong? What the hell did you find out?" He grabbed me and held me in his arms. "You're scaring me, Babe. What's happened?" He held me back and shook me as if to rattle an answer free.

But I couldn't speak. This was so much worse than I had anticipated. What I *could* do was hand him the letter, which I did a moment later.

Scott read, his brow bearing down as he pored over my father's words. Finally, he placed the letter on the table and looked up at me. "I'm so sorry, Sara. We never should have come here. We need to go ... right now." He snatched his cell phone from the table. "There has to be some sort of ride service here, don't you think? Shit." His nostrils flared. "I've got no service. Didn't you say Aidan was on the phone last night?"

I nodded, my mind swimming with too many thoughts and feelings.

"How does *he* have service, then? Does he have a house phone or something? What room was he in?"

"The kitchen, I think." I stood there like an inanimate object, trying to get my bearings.

"Yeah, but we cleaned the kitchen. Did you see a landline? Maybe he had a cordless, and the base is in the living room. We didn't spend much time in there." He was rambling, trying his best to figure out a solution. "We paid the international fee for our wireless. It should work." He sounded as frustrated as *I* felt.

Just as Scott was bolting out of the room to search the house for a phone, I clutched his arm to stop him, my mind starting to process the situation as best I could.

"Forget the phone! Maybe he has a different cell service here than we do. We're in a pretty remote area. I think we should pack our bags. I want to have them down here and ready to go when he arrives. And then, I will confront him. He doesn't strike me as the violent type, but if he gets that way, I'm not worried with *you* around." I was projecting who I wanted Uncle Aidan to be against who I feared he was. I realized this, but part of me refused to accept anything else. *He was dishonest. He was broken, but was he violent or dangerous?*

"After that, he's going to drive us to the nearest bus station, or we're taking his car there ourselves, and then I am never going to speak to him again. We've paid thousands of dollars for this vacation, and I won't let him ruin it. He can't have my parcel of land, no matter how much he begs. And I know you will hold me to that." I paused, allowing Scott to grasp what I was asking of him.

"You got it, boss," he said with conviction in his voice.

Another tear ran down my cheek, bumping into Scott's warm hand.

I put my hand over his. "I'm so glad you're here with me. I feel so much stronger with you by my side." I sighed and stood back, wiping my cheeks and pulling myself together. "Okay, let's get packed."

My plan would have worked out perfectly if Aidan hadn't come back so soon. We'd barely reached the top of the stairs when his muffler rumbled up the driveway.

I'd wasted too much time searching his room.

"You go pack us up. And I'll deal with him." I started down the stairs when Scott stopped me.

"Sorry, but no. I'm coming with you. If he gets out of line, I want to be there. We can throw our shit together in a couple of minutes afterward. We've barely unpacked as it is."

I agreed, knowing he was probably right. This wasn't a time for heroics. It was a time to set the record straight. And it was about to get real for my *so-called* uncle.

I wanted him to explain things in a way that I could understand. *Is that possible?* The possibility that this wasn't as bad as it seemed was becoming a pipe dream. My dad knew who Aidan was, and now, so did I.

We reached the kitchen at the same time Aidan came floating through the door, a box of sweet treats in his hand, a smile stretching his lips. "Breakfast ready?" He practically sang the words like he was channeling an Irish version of *Mary Poppins.*

I approached the kitchen table, where I lifted the letter from my father. "No. And it appears you've been lying to us."

It was as if someone had run a squeegee down Aidan's face, replacing a bright smile with a frown. "Where did ya get that?"

His tone accusatory, he placed the pastries on the counter with a plunk. "Did ya break into my room?"

Scott came to my side, his muscled arms crossed, and his stance wide and intimidating.

I let out a huff and shook my head. "Is that really all you have to say?"

Aidan stood there dumbfounded, his gaze bouncing between Scott and me.

"Okay, then let me start. First of all, you said you didn't come to my dad's funeral because your grandpa had died just before that. *Three weeks before.* I already knew that wasn't true when I came here. Your Pa died two years prior. I saw it on the paperwork from my lawyer back home when I learned I'd be inheriting the land. But what I didn't know was the real reason you didn't come to pay your respects to your *only* little brother —the one who you looked out for and protected—the one who you *said* you were 'mending fences' with"—I used air quotes— "and the one who you regretted losing touch with. Did I get all the facts straight?" I went into sarcasm mode, big time. "You remember ... that visit you had with him in the States? The one where you caught up with each other and my dad told you all about our family?"

I swore Uncle Aidan gulped, his Adam's apple bobbing up and down.

I waved the letter in the air. "All lies. You never looked out for my dad. He left Ireland because of you. You stole every-thing you could from your family, and now it appears you are trying to do the same thing with me."

Aidan shook his head. He took a step forward but stopped when Scott thrust a palm up.

"Stay where you are, dude." My fiancé stood there like a monument, his tone unyielding.

Aidan's cheeks fired up, and his forehead shined with

perspiration. He wiped his brow. "I know ya think ill of me, lass, but I've never gotten—"

"What? Your big break? Poor you. From the sounds of it, you've had many chances to turn your life around, but you've squandered every opportunity. My father even gave you a chance to prove yourself, and you let him down. Again. Let me ask you something, Aidan. Do you care about anybody? Besides yourself? You even had me fooled." I huffed and shook my head, exasperated.

He didn't answer right away. He just stood there, the gravity of the situation bending his spine and slumping his shoulders.

"I'm not giving you my parcel of land."

Aidan propped his shoulders up and lifted his chin, defiant. "Why not? Ya don't care about it. Ya didn't even know ya had it until recently. Why not let me have it and then never see me again?"

"So, you *do* want it for free? You weren't even going to make me an offer?"

He exhaled and waved a hand out, averting my attention to the shack he lived in. "Ya see how I live. I would have no way to pay ya, lass. I deserve this land. I've been watchin' over it all these years. This is a once-in-a-lifetime deal." His voice shook in an imploring sort of way.

"What about your partner? It sounds like he has plenty of money."

He hesitated to answer.

"I said, 'What about your partner?'"

And then he mumbled the words, "When I got him to agree to this deal, I told him that ya would sign it over to me."

That was the phone call from last night. If I weren't so angry, I would have laughed at his audacity. Instead, I took a stabilizing breath. "You're right. I don't care about it, not now, anyway. And you're also right that I hope I never have to see you again. It would be just as easy for me to sign it over to you. That's what you want. That's why you invited us here. I heard you on the phone last night. I already knew what you were planning. I just hoped I was wrong. You brought us here to witness the squalor you live in. You wanted to gain my pity for all the years you've spent trying to hold onto this property. My father paid the taxes on our half. Not you! Everything about you from the moment you showed up at my graduation until now was all a ruse. You wanted me to sign over the land, and then you'd be done with me, right?"

Aidan rubbed a heavy coat of stubble growing rampant on his chin.

I screamed at him. "Right?!"

"Answer her, asshole," Scott piped in, ready to fight my battles to the end. He placed his hands on his hips, staring my uncle down.

Man, I could have used Scott at Dr. Adams's house.

"No, lass. But even if that were to be true. Why not sign it over to me and be done with me? Ya never have to hear from me again. Ya have my word."

Oh, like that means anything.

I held my dad's letter even higher. "Because he wouldn't want me to. And although you never cared about what my father thought of you, *I* do care what he thinks of me. And I will honor his wishes. You can do whatever you want with your parcel, but you can't have mine."

Aidan's eyes started to moisten in a pleading sort of way.

I wasn't falling for it.

"But my half isn't the prime real estate ya find yourself with, lass. The deal won't work without your half. I implore ya to listen to reason."

I set my jaw. "Don't bother. You know, I was so happy to

meet you, Aidan. You reminded me so much of my dad. And your voice." I swallowed, trying to keep a grip on my emotions. "It was like I was spending time with him again. But you are *nothing* like him." My words shook as they stumbled out of my mouth. "I would give anything to have him back, and my mom, too. He was a good man. He taught me a lot. We weren't rich, but we were happy. And from what I've read in his last letter to you, he was willing to give you another chance, even after you had almost gotten him arrested from jobs that he had helped you get."

Breathe.

"You stood in that airport and told me how much you wanted to have a relationship with me and how you missed that with my father. You said all of this *knowing* at the same time you were hatching this new deal." I approached him, my hand finding his shoulder, Scott watching like a hawk the entire time. "Let me break something to you, Aidan. You will never be happy when your success stands on the necks of the people you have betrayed to get there. I don't know what your father was like, and it sounds like your grandpa was a hard man to love. Life is about choices. I've had to make some hard choices over the years. I could have let excuses turn me into someone ugly, but I refused to do that. Because if I did, then all those terrible people who hurt me would win. Right now, you are letting a bad legacy govern your life. All you have to do is choose the right path, and your life will be better."

Aidan's chin sunk, my words chipping away at his resolve; I could see it. And then a tear fell from his cheek, making a tiny splash on the floor.

"Money comes and goes, but integrity is something that no one can take away from you."

Looking like he was about to topple over like a tower of bricks, Aidan shook his head. "It's too late for me, lass. I've done too much harm. I already know the hell that's waitin' for me." More tears fell from his eyes.

It was the first time I sensed he was being brutally honest. *With himself.*

My uncle transformed into a weaker version of the man I thought I knew. He had no love in his life. Isolated and alone, his future was bleak. I could relate to him on a level that most couldn't.

"That's not true. You're a young man. You have a lot of living yet to do. You could even have a family. It's not too late." Why was I saying this? Why was I bothering? *Because, for better or worse, he's your dad's brother, and he is the closest thing you will ever have to him.* I wanted to be tough. I wanted to be angry. But, at the same time, I couldn't ignore my true feelings any longer. Deep down, I wanted to save this flawed uncle of mine, just like I wanted to save my parents when our truck careened over that embankment. And just like I wanted to save my best friend, Amy, from a deranged psychopath.

Uncle Aidan had a choice. We both did. So I *chose* my words carefully. "And you still have me, unless you betray me again. How do you want to spend the second half of your life, Aidan? There are people out there who have done far worse things than you have and turned their lives around, and so can you. In fact, I know some of those people. You just have to decide. No one controls you but you." I stood back and let that sink in.

Please listen. Please try.

At first, Aidan didn't speak. He just remained there like one of those trees outside, bent over by the wind, his face drawn, making him look older than his years.

"Right now, Scott and I are going upstairs to pack our bags, and then we'd like you to drive us to the nearest bus station. Can you do that?"

He nodded, his eyes remaining somber and distant.

I peered back at Scott, who gave me his nod of approval. He reached his hand out to me as I passed by him, and together, the two of us climbed the stairs and got busy gathering our stuff together.

I felt so empowered, so righteous. If I could turn Aidan's life around, I was sure my dad would approve. Everything felt intentional. I was supposed to be here.

"From here on out, this vacation is going to be about us," I said, only to have my optimism plummet like a lead balloon when Aidan's car sputtered to life, his muffler rattling down the drive, away from the house and away from us.

I should have known.

Feeling like the biggest idiot on the planet, I flew down the stairs, half expecting my feet to break through each step. How in the world did I think my words were going to get through to this man? He'd gone his whole life cheating people. Was I really that naive?

But when I reached the kitchen table, a handwritten note sat waiting for me, the words jumping off the back of a recycled envelope.

I will fix this.

* * *

With our bags packed and waiting by the front door, I paced the kitchen while Scott watched me with wary eyes. "Do you think he's being honest? Why wouldn't he wait and bring us with him? Do you think he's stranded us here? How long do you think he plans to be gone?"

Finally, Scott met me in the middle of the room, his hands bracing my shoulders. "Look, there's nothing we can do about it right now. He'll be back. He said he'll fix things. I'm guessing he's gone to tell Declan the deal is off." He ran his hands up and down my upper arms in a comforting rhythm. "Unless he's a really good actor, I think you got to him. I saw it on his face. Give him a chance to prove himself."

I stared deep into Scott's eyes. "But what if you're wrong?" The heaviness of my words made my heart feel as though it was being pulled down a drain—one with no bottom.

Scott let his arms fall by his side. "If you believe that, then why did you offer him a chance to redeem himself? I know you, Babe, and you wouldn't do that unless you thought he was worth it." His gaze washed over me like a warm shower. "You know I don't have the same capacity for forgiveness that you do. And I probably never will, but I think you were right this time. I sense Aidan wants to change. Those weren't fake tears I saw."

"But what if—"

"If he's full of shit, then we take his car and get the hell out of here. Let's just give him a couple of hours to prove himself."

This was my last chance to find a blood relative who I could actually call family. We shared the same ancestry. I wanted so much to embrace every bit of it, but I also didn't want to risk our safety or be delusional about how this could go.

"That's Plan A. Let's get something to eat in case we have to hoof it for several miles to find a phone, which is Plan B," Scott said. "He's got food, and I'm hungry. You must be, too."

My stomach rumbled, demanding food.

And so we ate.

Chapter Sixteen

I took my last bite of eggs then finished the meal with some of that apple tart, which cleansed my pallet with its sugary sweetness.

Scott devoured four eggs, a bunch of sausages, and some soda bread Uncle Aidan had also picked up at the same bakery.

It appeared we both needed the boost. I made us another cup of tea, and we sat at the table pondering our situation.

Still no sign of Aidan.

"How long do you think he'll be gone?" Since we couldn't locate any other flavors, I took a sip of that same tea that tasted like dirty dishwater. Even the tea was old and dusty in this house.

Scott put three teabags in his cup, hoping for a zing.

"You can keep asking me that, and all I can give you is the same answer: I have no idea." He sighed deeply, his expression sympathetic. "It hasn't been that long. I understand your worry. It's a shame he was such a dick to your dad when they were younger. Let's hope he's trying to change."

I contemplated that as we carried our plates to the sink.

"I hope you're right." I plugged the drain in the large farmhouse sink, a few chips in its porcelain, and filled it a quarter of the way with water, a few squirts of dish soap, which I used to wash our dishes and forks.

Why was I bothering to clean the dishes? Because my anxious hands needed something to do.

Scott dried and placed the dishes in the cupboard, the forks in the drawer to his left that he had to yank to open and shove with his hip to close.

"You don't think he'd bring that guy back here, do you?"

Scott narrowed his eyes. "Who?"

"Declan." I started to worry about a whole gang of men showing up to bully us, bats in their hands.

My pulse ramped.

"I doubt it. Why would he?"

I pulled the drain and rinsed the sink down. "To get me to change my mind."

Scott's tone was decisive. "I don't think he'd do that. Aidan knows you mean business. Plus, the land isn't even yours until you sign the paperwork, right? There's nothing you can really do about it now. I don't know the law here, but I would think you have to own it before you can give it away." Scott pulled me into his arms and held me, his hands soft against my back. He kissed the top of my head. "I think ole' Aidan is probably shitting a few bricks trying to get out of this deal." The hug turned into a swaying hug, which I loved. "I'm so proud of you. You never stop surprising me. Your father would be proud, too." He unlaced his arms as though an idea had come to him. "It's been what, an hour? I say we give him one more hour to return, which means we've got nothing to do but wait. That's not enough time to check all the property lines, but let's take a walk down there, anyway. You got that plat drawing, right?"

I nodded.

"Bring it. We can stay within eyesight of the driveway, although Aidan's car is so loud, I don't think we'll have any trouble knowing when he returns. Our bags are ready to go. We've eaten, so what else have we got to do?"

"We could try to find a house that may let us use their phone?" I thought about the two times we'd driven to and from here: once from the airport and once from Dublin. On both occasions, Aidan had driven on the same roads. "I don't remember seeing any other houses, although, once we got off the main road coming here, I did see a dirt road that turned off. But it was really narrow, and the grass growing up the middle of it makes me think it's probably not used much." Aidan's driveway wasn't anything great, either, full of rivets and washboards.

Scott seemed to think about that as he placed his hands on his hips. "Huh. I don't remember seeing a road, but we've gotta be four or five miles off the main drag. We can't be lugging those bags around, not knowing how far we have to go." He took my hand and kissed it. "I really don't think we have anything to worry about. He'll be back soon. And that view down by the coast was pretty amazing. I'd like to check it out one more time before we leave." The edges of his eyes crinkled as a smile crept up his face. "You're gonna own it, Babe, and it's pretty great."

I agreed. In all the confusion and disappointment, that message had gotten lost on me, as did the fact that I was in Europe on vacation with my soulmate.

I filled my lungs and then released a stabilizing breath. "Sounds good." After I found my plat drawing in my backpack, I grabbed my jacket, gave Scott his, and the two of us ventured outside.

We strolled the quarter of a mile until the dwarfed trees, brush, and brambles gave way to the coast and that incredible view that had nearly knocked me over the first time I'd seen it. Although it had rained the night before, the sun had been up since six, warming the air, opening the flowers, and brightening the lush greenery. The wind picked up as we ventured closer to the edge, but it wasn't as gusty as it had been before. Today felt much warmer than it had since we'd arrived. We might just get a summer day out of dear old Ireland, after all, which lifted my spirits even more.

Scott kept his hand laced in mine, swinging back and forth as we strolled along, the plat folded in the back pocket of my white capri jeans. "Aidan said that you own the better part of this property, so I'm guessing this entire area will be yours." He swept an arm out.

I took out the plat, and we examined it, the breeze ruffling its edges. Unfortunately, the drawing didn't include the property surrounding it, just mine. "See, it says the ocean is here." I pointed forward. "And I think that's the beach down there, which Aidan said I will also own. That appears to be true from what I can see here."

Scott agreed.

That was really all it said. For more details, we'd have to walk the perimeter.

I folded the paper and returned it to my back pocket.

And then we stood near the edge, side by side, letting the salty air brush against our skin, the sun warming our cheeks. Somehow, the situation with Aidan felt less bothersome than it had just a moment ago. Had I gotten better at handling deception? Or was I just sick of people bringing me down? I wanted to cherish this trip, not stumble through it with my gut clenched. Plus, if Aidan came through, there was still hope for him and me. Scott believed that to be true, and I trusted Scott with my life. I wondered if Scott thought about the times I had doubted *him* as well. Different circumstances, for sure, but still ...

"We talked about going to Dublin and a few other places. Do you think we'd have time to see the Cliffs of Moher while we're here? I've heard it's breathtaking." I tried to imagine it as I enjoyed the view in front of me. "How high would you say these cliffs are?"

"Maybe fifty feet or so, why?" Scott asked, burying his hands in the front pockets of his jeans. He turned his body as he took in the view, distracting me from my thoughts.

During our years at school, Scott hadn't worn jeans as much as he'd sported workout pants and shorts. But when he did slip on a pair of those Levi's, just faded enough to look worn, his butt filled them out as though they were designed specifically for him. It was probably those jeans that kept the flight attendants swooning, not that everything about Scott wasn't dreamy. When he threw on a cashmere sweater or a T-shirt (depending on the season) just tight enough to outline his abs and pecs, I had a hard time keeping my hands to myself. Add in his windbreaker jacket and leather boat shoes, and today Scott was ready for a photo for J. Crew.

What were we talking about? Oh, yeah.

"I think the Cliffs of Moher are like over seven hundred feet high. Not that I'm knocking *this* view."

"I'd be down for the Cliffs of Moher. Depending on what happens with Aidan, we can rent a car and go anywhere you want." Scott quirked an eyebrow. "I'll drive."

I tugged on the arm of his jacket. "Why? Don't you trust me?"

Scott pulled one hand out of his front pocket and scratched his chin. "Uh."

"Thanks a lot, bucko." I tried to sound indignant, but I wasn't. Amy hated my driving, too. Said pedestrians could walk faster than I could drive, and given the opposite-side-of-the-road conditions, I was happy to be a passenger.

That prompted another hug from my man. "Bucko, huh? Is that becoming my new nickname? Has Big Guy been worn out?"

With my arms securely around him, I let my hands drift south to grab those irresistible butt cheeks of his. "No way. You could *never* lose that nickname. Not with what you've got packing." Feeling free and uninhibited, and since no one was around, I nudged my hips into his lower half, which brought an immediate reaction from the protrusion in his pants.

"Yeah? You like what I'm packing? Do you?" He dropped his lips on mine, his tongue searching for fun. "Want me to make you scream?"

As the sun beat down upon us and the salty air refreshed my mind and spirit, I lost myself in Scott's delicious mouth, a hint of breakfast on his breath. The deeper the kiss, the more we got into it, our bodies mashed together, my insides craving more.

When we finally detached lips, Scott's eyes darkened with dirty intentions. He turned his head to the right. "Didn't Aidan say there was a cave down there? Do you want to check it out?" He brought his mouth to my ear, not that anyone could hear us. "I've never had cave sex. You want to give it a shot?"

By now, the bulge in his pants had grown to the point I worried he'd break his zipper.

"Do you think it's safe?" I was *always* the cautious one, but with a fiancé like Scott, someone had to be. Plus, were we really considering this?

Scott pulled his arms away from my waist and took a few backward steps, pulling me along with him. "Only one way to find out, right?"

Feeling amorous, I said, "Sure." Together we traipsed to the edge and down the stone steps to a swath of rocks I had to step over gingerly to avoid breaking my neck, my tennis shoes doing their best to stabilize my legs. A black-and-white bird with a long bright-orange beak darted off as we approached, several other species of birds either flying overhead or pecking for morsels in the rocks farther down the modest-sized beach.

Once we reached the sand, which was limited, we stood there and watched the surf, my lungs taking in the mist, my mind shifting from cave sex to my father. I adored that man, and after reading his letter to Aidan, my feelings toward him had only amplified.

He grew up here. I wanted to soak up every experience he had, see what he saw, and feel what he felt. Given the abuse he endured at the hands of his grandpa *and* his brother, I could relate to him so much more now than I ever could before. He moved on from this place, which must've been difficult given its beauty, and he found a better life.

He found my mom, and then they made me.

Scott's voice broke through the crash of the waves. "Aidan said your dad used to fish here all the time."

In my mind's eye, I watched as my dad cast his line out, his pants rolled up to the knees, a flannel shirt over one of his old T-shirts like the ones he used to wear back home to prepare for any cold or warmth the day might bring, a can of bait and a bucket of beer, sitting next to him.

"My dad loved to fish with me when I was younger." *Burgers and fries.* "This looks like a perfect spot for it."

Scott's face softened. "You know, for what it's worth, I could really relate to your dad when I read that letter. He was a good man. I can see why you admire him the way you do. He was very protective of you and your mom, and I respect that. I can also see where you get your bravery from ... and your honesty. And I'm sure your mom was the same way."

I let the sentimental moment absorb my thoughts for a few more minutes until Scott's hand slid across my lower back.

"Do you still want to check out the cave? It's okay if you don't."

I gazed up and down the coast, not a soul in sight. And then my eyes found my gorgeous hunk of a man. Yes, it was crazy to consider this. My inner voice fought back with *why not?*

"Okay, Handsome. If I'm going to own some portion of this property soon, there's no reason why we can't make our mark." After joining the mile-high club, I was becoming more daring in my sexcapades. "But only if it's safe and there aren't any bats flying around our heads. I don't want to take too long, either."

That made Scott laugh. "Roger that. And *you know* I can be quick." He reached his hand out for me to take, which I did as we navigated over the rocks again toward the mouth of the cave I hadn't been able to see from above, its entrance dark and mysterious. Much larger than I had expected, this natural wonder stood there waiting for visitors. Over the centuries, I imagined it had provided shelter from the elements or a home for wayward travelers, its walls thick and protective.

The idea of exploring a cave in Ireland was exhilarating. I felt like an anthropologist when opening a new passageway in a pyramid. Plus, my dad had done this, which meant I had to do it, too.

Water fanned out just inside the entrance like a small lake, the temperature dropping ten degrees, I was sure. A small hole in the rock ceiling cast a beam of sunlight onto the water in an almost celestial way.

"Before we go in, do you think we should check to see if Aidan is back? Plus, I can roll up my capris, but you may have trouble with those jeans."

"Yeah, I was thinking the same thing. I didn't realize there was water in here. Tell you what. I'll take a run up to the house and check for Aidan. If he's back, I'll come and get you. Wait by the steps and watch for me." Without hesitating, Scott ran off.

I sensed he enjoyed a bit of exercise, something he hadn't had a lot of since we'd arrived. Scott liked to run most days, and he also liked to weight train. The hotels we planned to stay in from here on out would suit all of his needs, with a few bed-and-breakfasts staggered in between. I'd made sure of it. No more sleeping in a bed that crawled with unpleasant possibilities under the covers. No more relying on unreliable people to do the right thing. Although, there was still hope there. Either way, from now on, this trip was about us.

After I rolled up the cuffs of my white capri jeans, I stood at the base of the steps watching the clouds float by until Scott appeared above me.

Wearing gym shorts, flip-flops, and the same T-shirt he'd had on before, no jacket, he carried what appeared to be towels down the stairs with him.

"What's that?"

Scott hopped off the bottom step. "Aidan isn't back yet, and I grabbed a couple of towels I had brought with me. I figured we'd need something between us and whatever we planned to lay on in there. How are your knees?"

I shook my head. This man had a one-track mind. "Fine. All healed, just a few scrapes left over. Why?"

I don't know why I asked him that since I knew the answer.

"Because if we *can* find a ledge or a safe place to get naked, I'll take the bottom, and I'll put these"—he lifted the towels in the air—"under each of your knees."

"As usual, you've thought of everything."

Scott walked by me. "How often do we get to make love in a cave in Ireland? Let's go, woman. We don't have all day."

My eyes glued to his backside as he led me to the mouth of the cave, where I removed my sneakers, and he removed his sandals.

We placed both pairs on a rock that jutted out about four feet off the ground.

"Does the beach look smaller to you? Is the tide coming in?"

Scott watched the water and what seemed to be its flow patterns. "I don't have a tide schedule, but don't worry, I can work fast. And if there aren't any good spots, we'll just bag it. I'm horny, but I'm not insane."

The wind rustled the flap of my navy windbreaker against my wrist. "Should I leave my jacket out here?"

"I would." Scott reached a hand out. "Give it to me, and I'll hook it on that rock."

He was referring to the same rock that held our shoes.

We hadn't even started our cave sex yet, and already our layers were coming off.

A few steps into the shallow water and the temperature dropped again. "Brrrr," I said. "It's cold in here."

From right next to me, Scott said with a lift in his voice. "Perfect. Are my ladies nice and hard for me?"

"Your ladies?" And then I got the message. *Duh.*

He pointed, the excitement in his voice rising. "See that ledge over there?"

I squinted until a small ledge appeared about thirty feet ahead, that same beam of light from the natural skylight diving into the water right in front of it. Honestly, it looked like something out of a movie set.

"I'll go first to make sure the water doesn't get deep." Scott took a slow step forward and peered back at me. "I only want one part of your anatomy wet in here. Besides your feet." His left dimple teased.

He was such a brat. A gorgeous brat, but a brat nonetheless.

"Be careful." I tipped my head this way and that, my eyes taking in the rock formations, the small stalactites, and the rough ceiling, an earthly smell coating the walls. No animals or bats in sight.

Just past the ledge that Scott was wading toward, the area became dark, whatever lay beyond it, hidden.

A wave came pushing through the entrance and around my ankles, making me turn toward what used to be a small patch of sand on the beach that was now underwater. *The tide.*

The water was cold—like Maine cold—or maybe even colder if that were possible. My toes screamed as blood struggled to circulate through my feet.

Up ahead, Scott made a noticeable shiver.

"Do you think it's too chilly for this?"

He shook his head. "Nah, I'm almost there. And then I'll come back and get you."

I flirted with my voice. "You mean, you expect *me* to walk all the way over *there*? You're not going to carry me to our love nest? Humph." I crossed my arms in mock annoyance.

Scott turned his head and made a face. "It's a little too slippery for that, Babe. Just hold on."

I pursed my lips. "I was only kidding."

Another wave approached, circling my calves, before it backed away like a car in reverse.

"Tide's coming in. I don't think we have much time. Have you seen any creatures over there?"

That earned me a headshake. "What do you think is in here? A croc? This water must be fifty degrees. The only thing I might find is a leprechaun. Or an ice cube." He flashed me a smart-aleck grin.

In a lot of ways, Scott reminded me of a little boy inside, always looking for his next adventure. It was one of many things I loved about him. Nothing much scared the man, which made me braver being near him. Whatever else happened from here on out on this trip, I'd never forget making love to my fiancé within the confines of an underground chamber.

I was thinking about that as Scott was closing in on the ledge. But then he stumbled and then slipped, his entire body going under the freezing water.

What?

How was this possible? I was only ankle-deep.

When he didn't come up, my heart froze right along with my toes. How could anyone withstand this cold?

"Scott? Oh my God. Scott?"

Chapter Seventeen

Scott crested through the surface, thank God, flipping his hair back, water droplets flying through the air.

He ran a hand down his face and shivered.

While my heart skipped about ten beats, I yelled, "Are you okay?" I took a step closer when Scott flung his palm out of the water and cringed. "Ouch! Son of a bitch, that hurts." What was even more alarming was how deep the water was around him, like shoulder deep.

I rolled my pant legs higher and rushed over, my toes screaming for mercy.

Hair soaking wet and making a tense face and a few grunts, Scott appeared to be trying to break free of something. The towels he was carrying floated on the surface and then below it.

"Babe. Don't come over here. It's too deep. And it's colder than shit." He tried to move again, yelling, "*Ouch*," but his body remained submerged, his shoulders barely reaching through the water. He placed his hand on the nearby ledge to steady himself, the same ledge we were planning our *fun* on.

"I'm coming. Don't move." I waded cautiously closer, the

rocks slippery and cold beneath my feet. It was like walking on a wet ice-skating rink with no shoes. How Scott got that far was beyond me.

Now I understood why my joke about him carrying me went so unappreciated.

"It's okay." He made another halting motion with his hands. "Stay where you are. I can't move my right foot. It's stuck between something. This was a bad idea." He kept trying to move, short guttural sounds escaping from his mouth.

I ignored his orders and kept going until I was five feet away.

"Stop! Goddamnit, Sara, you need to listen. You're about a foot from where the bottom drops off sharply, and it's too slippery to avoid if you get any closer. Stay. Where. You. Are." Scott worked on his restrained foot, disturbing the water around him, but he didn't seem to be making any progress.

"What happened?"

"I just told you. I slipped when the bottom dropped off like a water slide, and my right foot got wedged between two rocks." His lips started to shake. "I've gotta go under and try to wiggle it free. It hurts like a motherfucker." And down he went.

A few moments later, he came up again, cold water sliding off him like sheets of ice.

I was shivering with him, my mind trying to fathom this situation, my stomach lurching into my throat. "Do you think you injured your ankle?"

Scott nodded, his voice low. "I think I may have either sprained or broken it. Every time I try to move, the pain is intense." He forced a smile, but it was weak. "At least the water feels like an ice pack. Sort of."

Jokes? You're making jokes?

He plunged down again, his movement causing ripples and waves in front of me as though two sea monsters were battling it out underwater. A few seconds later, his shoulders burst through the surface again.

Every time he shook the excess water from his hair, droplets landed on my arms, which froze against my skin. "Scott, this is serious. We have to get your foot out. The tide's coming in."

Scott laughed in an exasperated sort of way. "I know that, *Sara*." He flung both hands up. "What do you think I'm trying to do?" Even though his voice shot at me like a baseball at a batting cage, I ignored it.

He was scared. So was I.

My mind searched for solutions. "I'm going to dive down and see what you're stuck on." I took several short breaths, trying to prepare myself.

Scott firmed his jaw. "No, you're not. This water is fucking cold."

"Stop it. You can't see well from where you are. I might be able to figure out how bad your foot is stuck. I'll only go down for a second. Trust me." On my last breath, I filled my lungs with as much air as they would allow and tried not to think about how cold my world was about to get. Then I plunged underwater and opened my eyes, which stung immediately from the salt. The cold weighed on my limbs, and the lack of light and the murkiness compromised my vision. Algae and seaweed waved up at me from below as if mocking my efforts.

With the help of the natural skylight above, I pushed forward until I could just make out two human pillars that were more greenish-yellow than skin tone. When I was close enough, I held onto one of Scott's calves to steady myself and did my best to focus. His left ankle was fine. But two flat rocks had swallowed his right, both running lengthwise like plates around his foot.

I tried to pull his leg out, and it did shift, but not enough to free his foot. A muffled sound came from the surface, and I sensed I was hurting him.

Without much lung capacity remaining, I swam back the way I had come, using my hands to guide me. Where the cave floor evened out, I stood, soaking wet, the water taking its sweet time to roll off me. I trembled, my teeth chattering, my muscles cramping.

"Are you okay?" Scott watched me, the wells of his beautiful blue eyes emitting something I hadn't seen in a very long time: fear. "You shouldn't have done that." He kept trying to move toward me, the rocks below forbidding it.

"I'm-m o-ok-kay." I wrapped my arms around my torso and then started frantically rubbing my arms, trying to generate friction.

Scott was beyond shivering, his lips turning blue, and his jaw unable to keep still.

"Your foot is wedged between two big rocks. Flat ones. And you're right, there seems to be a ledge between where you are and where I am. Now that I know where to go, I'm going to try one more time to move one of those rocks." I plunged under just before the words "Sara, no" bounced off the water above my head.

The second dive wasn't as bad as the first, or maybe my body was numb from the cold. Either way, I was able to reach Scott much quicker. I kicked my feet upward, forcing my head down until I had a firm grip on the edge of one of those rocks. And then I tugged as best I could, my hands trying not to slip from the filmy stone. When that attempt failed, I pulled on the adjacent rock in the opposite direction. That one didn't budge, either. Or not that I could see. The way the two rocks angled downward made it easy to see how this had happened and how gravity was now working against us.

Almost out of oxygen, I did my best to swim back to my

starting point. My limbs felt like someone stuffed them with fifty pounds of sand.

I pushed my shoulders out of the water and shivered, my skin starting to burn. I had turned into a human-sized icicle.

"Don't do that again, Sara. You're really pissing me off r-right n-now." Scott stopped short. He clamped his mouth shut.

It was too late. I'd heard the tremor in his voice.

More water came into the cave, making this bad situation worse.

"Scott, the water is rising!"

His shoulders were now just meeting the uppermost layer, his chin, inches above life and death.

"How much higher can it get?" My heart pounded like a hammer despite the cold working so hard to slow it down. "Scott, how high does the tide get here?"

Once again, he didn't answer me. Instead, he looked away for a moment as if to gather himself. "I d-don't know. Sara, you need to g-get help." He slammed his mouth shut again as though trying to stop the shivering that crawled over his beautiful body like a slithering sea monster trying to knock something loose.

"I will." Tears stung my eyes. "I don't want to leave you, though. What if the water keeps rising?" My heart whimpered, begging for a miracle.

Scott raised his arms and planted both palms on the top of his head like a soldier would do when trudging through an unfamiliar swamp. "I'll be okay. It w-won't come in that q-quickly. Now. Go."

Not wasting another second, I waded through the water, which was now reaching my upper calves, almost landing on my butt twice along the way. I could feel Scott's eyes on me, and I could sense his worry. I was petrified to leave him. I was petrified to stay. My mind refused to accept what could happen here.

Outside the mouth of the cave, the entire beach had surrendered to the surf. I snatched my shoes off the rock where I had placed them and splashed through the tide toward the path that brought us down here. My jacket dropped into the water, so I left it there.

At the rock steps, I flung a tennis shoe onto each foot and ran up the steep incline toward the top.

My lungs heaved. And then I thought of Scott alone in that awful cave freezing to death, and adrenaline pushed me faster, my thighs burning as I reached the top. I was sweating and cold at the same time, the sun trying its best to help, the breeze doing the opposite.

At the summit, I ran like the wind toward Aidan's cottage and his empty driveway. *Crap, he's not back yet.* I slammed through the door, nearly knocking it off its hinges, and searched for my cell phone, which I found in my backpack, my hands trembling.

Expecting to find no reception, I powered it up anyway, praying something had changed. Zero bars tormented me from the tiny screen. *A house phone?* I dashed out of the kitchen.

On the living room floor sat a landline all covered in dust, a cordless, one with no dial tone. My pulse thrummed in my ears. I checked the plug in the wall. I checked everything. The phone just didn't work.

"Damn it."

Scott had calculated that the main road was four or five miles away. How long would it take me to run there ... and back? What about beyond that point? Were there any houses nearby? I couldn't remember.

The dirt road. It was less than a mile away.

I set off running, my legs eager to reach my destination, my heart ten steps ahead. The salt water made my hair course and ragged, my skin like chalk.

A trivet in the road sent me stumbling forward, my legs out of control. When I hit the ground, I jumped back up and continued on. Scott had always protected me when I fell. Now it was my turn to protect him.

Keep your feet up, don't trip, I coached myself, eyeing the ground.

My heart pumped like a jackhammer, my lungs feeling like a balloon ready to burst. I pushed myself harder, my feet faster, until the turnoff appeared.

I sprinted down the road, tall grass brushing against my legs until a farmhouse came into view. *Yes!*

And then I saw it: a large tree growing tall and wide up through the center of the roof, the windows broken or missing, and no front door. No cars, no people, only overgrown vegetation, and a dilapidated structure that cried for attention.

Abandoned.

With no time to squander, I turned and rushed back to Aidan's house, where I dashed into the old garage-looking structure with three wide openings. Trash, old tools, and an old engine were just a few items that cluttered the space, most of which looked like they belonged in another time. Off to the left, a cluster of garden equipment leaned against the wall: a rake, a hoe, and a broom. I grabbed the hoe since it had the thickest handle and bolted into the house, where I snatched one of many sheets of paper on the counter along with a pen and wrote Uncle Aidan a short note in case he decided to return this century.

Uncle Aidan, Scott is in trouble. He's in the cave on the beach. His foot is wedged between two rocks. He can't get out. The water is rising. Please, help us. It's life or death.

My knees weakened as I wrote this, the possibilities too unbearable to accept.

I stormed out of the house, my hoe in hand, and ran like I'd never run before. How long had I been gone? How quickly was the water rising? *Please be okay.* Panic coiled around my heart like a viper. My breath hitched, my muscles weak and uncertain. I'd had dreams where I couldn't get to where I needed to be. Frustration dreams, where nothing was going right. But *this.* This was the mother of all nightmares.

I hurried down the stone steps as fast as I could. When I reached the cave opening, I dreaded what I would find. *Is he okay?* My mind wouldn't swallow any other alternative.

Just a short time ago, we were flirting about cave sex. How could life be so cruel?

"Scott, I'm here. Are you okay?" I waited, wishing with all of my heart that he'd answer.

And then, like a canary in a mine, his voice came to me. "Yeah, can you hurry? I'm f-freezing."

The distress in his voice bounced off the stone walls, amplifying the danger before me.

With my shoes still on, I waded forward, alarmed that the water had swelled to knee-deep. And then my sweet man came into view. My eyes were drenched with tears at the sight, my heart begging for his safety.

Not only had the water climbed up to my knees, relentless, but it had also reached Scott's chin. Trapped, my beautiful fiancé was pale, his lips bluer, the light in his eyes fading.

"Aidan's phone doesn't work. I ran to that turnoff about a mile away and found a farmhouse, but it's abandoned. All I could find was this hoe in Aidan's garage. We can use it as a wedge and pry those rocks apart. I'll slip it between the outer side of your foot and the rock first, okay?"

Scott nodded but didn't answer. Instead, he focused on doing the one thing he needed to do right now: breathe.

Keeping a firm grip on the hoe, I dove into the water and pushed my body closer to Scott. Then I wedged the metal end between his foot and the rock, the way I had just described, hoping I wasn't hurting him, and pulled with all my might. Nothing happened, so I switched sides and tried the inside of his foot, Scott's body becoming a barrier from this angle. He tried to move out of the way, but the rocks refused to let him.

When I couldn't stay under any longer, I surfaced, took another lungful of oxygen, and dove back down to try again. The water was freezing, but my mind refused to care.

Not once did Scott argue. He even tried to help, but his strength was leaving him, and it was killing me to watch it happen.

Together, we pushed, we pulled. And then, *crack.*

What happened? I came out of the water holding a long wooden pole, the metal piece broken off and missing.

Nooooo.

Without the hoe's narrow metal edge to use as a wedge, the pole couldn't get deep enough to make a difference. Scott's ankle was in the way. And now the shape wasn't right.

I tried, anyway, over and over again, but it was no use.

My muscles were tiring, my stamina dwindling.

"Can you move it at all?" I asked after my last attempt.

Scott wiggled his body, his motion slow. And then he stopped. "I'm still stuck." He exhaled a frigid breath. "I think I broke my ankle."

"I'll try again." I wished I was stronger. I wished I was smarter and could figure a way out of this. More than anything, I wished *I* was the one stuck and not Scott.

The bitter water played tricks on me, urging me to give up and rest. I was tired beyond belief, my body unable to stop quivering. I knew the danger presented before me, yet my mind grew foggy and sluggish.

Snap out of it. I was ready to dive back under when Scott reached out and snagged my arm. "Stop. It's n-no use."

"But I think I felt it move the last time." I was lying, of course, or maybe I was delusional.

Scott shook his head. "I would've f-felt something, Babe. It's n-not moving." Water licked his cheeks with its evil tongue. "How l-long d-do y-you think y-your uncle w-will be g-gone?"

I stared at him, wishing I knew. "I l-left a note." I turned toward the mouth of the cave. "I can r-run out and see if t-there are any people d-down the beach."

"Did you see a-anyone b-before?" The cold had Scott's teeth chattering, his skin as gray as wet cement.

"No, but—"

"Sara. Melinda. Browne."

His words, serious and determined, cut through me like a buzz saw. He had never used my full name before.

"You n-need to l-look at me."

I did as he asked, hating the water for swallowing up the love of my life, hating this cave, and hating Ireland. I knew it wasn't logical, but I didn't care.

"There is n-nothing m-more you can d-do."

"But."

"Sara. You n-need to listen to m-me. The w-water is s-still rising. It's inches f-from my m-mouth and nose. Soon, I w-won't be able to b-breathe. My b-blood is t-thickening. I c-can't take m-much more of this c-cold. I've had enough t-training to know w-what's going to h-happen."

What are you saying?

"Nothing is g-going to h-happen. We're going t-to g-get you out!" My body trembled, my lips right along with it. My eyes gushed tears. "Please d-don't s-say these things. P-please don't g-give up." The air, filled with algae and distress, made my stomach turn and my brain unable to process.

Scott's eyes filled with tears that he rarely shed. "I n-need y-you t-to go away f-from here."

I shook my head so hard that the muscles in my neck revolted, sending pain everywhere. "NO! I'm *not* leaving y-you."

Scott exhaled, his breath so precious I wanted to capture it in a bottle and feed it back to him.

"I'll k-keep you w-warm." I swam over to him and wrapped my arms around his waist, doing my best to send my heat into his cold body, my head buried in his neck.

The water tried to hide it, but it couldn't wash away his musky scent. It was still very much alive, just like he was, and I wasn't letting go.

Soon, Scott leaned his head against my shoulder. He felt frail against my body, so unlike himself.

"It's going to b-be ok-kay." I kissed him. I held him. I prayed for something to happen to get us out of this nightmare.

"C-can you l-look at me again?" He kissed my cheek, his lips as hard as marble.

Once again, I did as he asked. How could I not?

"I h-have an idea."

Chapter Eighteen

I stared into those eyes I had trusted with all of my heart—those eyes that had called to me the moment we met, those eyes that steered me through turmoil and pain—hoping Scott had a plan. And then I kissed his trembling lips. "W-what is y-your idea?"

"W-when I knew we w-were c-coming to Ireland, I did some r-research about w-weddings here." He paused as I watched him gather mental strength. "I k-know we planned to g-get married at home, b-but I w-was curious about it a-anyway." The water was closing in on his mouth, trying to muzzle him.

With my body plastered against his, I rubbed his back, my bones aching down to my marrow. "Oh, y-yeah? T-tell me m-more." *Tell me anything you want, just stay with me.*

"Y-yeah. There is t-this tradition called h-handfasting." Scott slowly closed his eyes, his head starting to droop.

I jiggled his body. "Stay with m-me. W-what is handfasting?"

His eyelids fluttered. "W-what?"

My voice quivered and shook. "W-what is handfasting? You were t-talking about h-handfasting." I was practically yelling at him as I continued to jolt his body with my own.

Scott lifted his head. "Yeah, it's a C-celtic ritual w-when a man and a w-woman t-tie their hands t-together. It s-sort of m-marries them." He kissed me, his lips so weak and devoid of color. "L-let's h-have our o-own c-ceremony."

"Why? We c-can do t-that when we g-get home." I wasn't liking this at all.

"Of c-course. B-but, w-we c-can practice, r-right?"

For a moment, I thought his eyes were rolling up in his head, but they weren't. He was looking at something up on the ledge next to us.

"G-grab t-that vine."

Vine? I turned my head toward a lengthy piece of seaweed that sat on the ledge, long and green. Seaweed left over from the last tide, I guessed. Seaweed that told me how high the water planned to rise.

I let go of Scott's body, which was as stiff as a board, and grabbed it before I regained my hold on him. "G-got it. N-now what do we d-do?" The tremors in my body grew so strong I feared I would shatter like glass.

Very slowly, Scott lifted one arm and placed it on the lip of the ledge. "Put your a-arm over m-mine and wrap the v-vine around our w-wrists."

I hated letting go of him again, but I did as he asked. I'd only been in this water a short time compared to Scott. What-ever discomfort I felt, it was far worse for him. I moved to the ledge, placed my arm over his, and draped the seaweed over our wrists. I made sure to stay close to him, but with my arm up on the ledge, I wasn't able to hold him like I wanted to.

Keep him talking.

"Now w-what?" I asked.

Scott lifted his head eerily slow, his eyes unfocused. He took a moment to come back to me. I could see the confusion in his eyes. Disorientation was probably one of the stages of hypothermia.

I wanted to scream. I wanted to cry. But my mind was starting to drift right along with his.

"Now, w-we say our v-vows."

"You g-go first," I said, hoping to wake up his brain.

Scott looked at me, his eyes fighting to stay open.

I went into pretend mode. It was just him and me. Our whole future was ahead of us, Scott in a white dress shirt and tan trousers and me in a sundress with flowers in my hair, a soft breeze dancing around our shoulders.

As he spoke, I filtered out his stuttering and chattering teeth and listened as though we were standing under a beautiful sky, the birds chirping from the trees, the flowers fragrant and colorful.

"I was asleep before I met you, Sara. I just didn't know it. I had no idea what I wanted for my future or who I wanted to spend it with. You woke me up, and you showed me a different path in life that I never dared to want for myself. You changed me, and from the moment I met you, I knew you and I had something special. I can't say you are everything I wanted in a woman because you are more than that. I have to pinch myself to realize how lucky I am. My heart belongs to you and no one else. However long we have together, six minutes or sixty years, I will do my very best to be the man you deserve. Thank you for saving my heart and for bringing so much joy into my life. I can honestly say I am the luckiest son of a bitch on the planet. You gave me peace, and you showed me selflessness and what true love feels like."

Tears forged rivulets down my salty cheeks. I tried to stay

strong, but I couldn't. As I moved closer to embrace him, he raised his palm.

"Your t-turn. K-keep your h-hand up there for your v-vows."

Can I do this? I hadn't written my vows yet, but something told me neither had Scott. If this was our end, my heart would know what to say. And so I began. "You were asleep before you met me? Well, I was alone and very, very sad. I'd lost my family, and I never thought I'd ever find anyone who could make me feel whole again. Someone who I could build a life with. I didn't even dare ask. I was surviving. I wasn't living. And then I met you, Scott Williams."

The ghost of a smile floated across his face.

"You showed me what it was like to live again. You found places in my heart that I had abandoned, and you brought them back to life. It took me so long to accept that you were real. How could you be? You were everything I had dreamed about and more. I am the woman I am today because of you and your faith in me. I know I deserve the best life has to offer because you gave it to me. I love you, Scott Williams, from the bottom of my heart, and that will never change. Six minutes or sixty years, I am yours for eternity."

"O-okay, now g-get over h-here and k-kiss your h-husband."

I removed my hand from the ledge while Scott let his own drop into the water like an anchor, the cold liquid swallowing it whole, the chain of his body soon to follow.

I took hold of him with all the strength I had left in me, and then I kissed him, my heart overflowing with love and despera-tion. "Please, S-scott, you have t-to stay with m-me. I c-can't lose you. Aidan w-will come." My voice changed, weak and uncer-tain. What was happening to me?

Scott leaned his forehead against mine. "I w-want you t-to go now, S-sara."

I pulled my head back as though he'd slapped me. "No! I w-won't d-do it. I w-won't leave y-you, and you c-can't make me."

Scott inhaled a shuddering breath. "You h-have t-to. I w-won't let you w-watch me d-die."

How could he say this to me? The admission was too much for my heart to bear. "No! If y-you're going to d-die here, I'm g-going to die w-with you." I clamped my arms around him, refusing to let go.

Using strength I was sure he barely had left, Scott pried my arms away. "You've s-seen enough d-death to last you a l-life-time. Please, B-Babe, d-do this for m-me. Go find A-aidan. Maybe h-he'll get here in t-time."

He was lying, and we both knew it. "NO!" How could this be happening? How could God do this to me? Again? It was too much like …. I wailed. "Please, don't m-make me l-leave y-you. I c-can't." Tears, mixed in with saliva, spewed from my mouth. "I'm not s-strong enough t-to leave y-you." I bawled. My heart severed from my soul. My wails filled every inch of that cave with my sorrow. *Nooooo.*

Scott sighed, the light in his eyes nearly extinguished, his eyelids closing. "I k-know, B-Babe. I'm so s-sorry. You are my heart, Sara. Forever." He started to sink, and I watched my whole world sink with him.

Chapter Nineteen

I walked on unsteady legs, Abigail on one side of me and Joel on the other. Without their support, I was sure I'd be doing a face-plant on the ground right now. The sound of sniffling floated past my right ear and then my left, shadows of voices out there, somewhere, but I couldn't see them.

I pushed one foot in front of the other, Abigail coaching me the entire way. "We're almost there."

A stiff breeze rushed at my face, and I welcomed it. My body was boiling over, my mind too clouded to keep a single thought straight. I hadn't slept, barely able to get breakfast down, yet I continued forward, hoping to avoid tripping over my own feet.

For that, I needed Scott here to catch me. *Scott.*

Joel let go of my hand as Abigail stood in front of me. This was it; she was leaving me now. And my life was never going to be the same. She lifted my veil as a strong and very familiar hand came down to take mine. I stared up at the most beautiful blue eyes I had ever seen in my life.

"You're absolutely stunning, Babe," Scott said with a tear in his eyes and a hitch in his voice. Cheeks ruddy, he stared at me as though he had never seen me before—as though his heart had opened for the first time.

Abigail kissed me on the cheek and placed my hand into the palm of my soon-to-be husband. As far as Scott and I were concerned, we were already married.

As an early wedding gift, Scott's parents deeded that twenty-five acres of land to us. The same land where, within a cluster of tall pines that overlooked a pristine meadow and rolling hills, we had made love on several occasions. In fact, that was where we constructed our altar, everyone unaware that we were standing on sacred ground, already christened by its new owners.

"You look pretty good yourself." I smiled with glossy lips, my hair pulled up in a bun, a few thin ringlets framing my face, and my makeup as perfect as it was going to get, thanks to my maid of honor, Amy, who stood right behind me. Jason stood behind Scott.

Under a white arch abundant with flowers and greenery, one I designed specifically from a vision I'd had when held captive inside of Dr. Adams's house, Scott wore the same crisp, white shirt I had also imagined, cotton khakis and casual loafers on his feet, his hair combed and wavy, and his cologne just the right scent of perfect.

Before our wedding officiant spoke, Scott's gaze traced over my simple white satin dress with a low neckline, a plunging back, and a short skirt (all at Scott's request), which did little to hide my thighs, and a white pair of heels that brought me closer to his eye level.

My diamond stud earrings complemented my necklace, the one with two white gold hearts intertwined he had given me during my freshman year. He'd spoiled me with lots of jewelry over the years, but this was his first gift to me, aside from his heart, so it was extra special.

Finally, his eyes returned to my face, where he smiled with such contentment it filled me with light.

Three months we waited to get here but, really, we'd waited our whole lives.

"Welcome guests on this very special occasion ..."

* * *

After the nuptials, the photos, and the quick congratulations from our guests, we headed over to the country club where Scott's parents were members and where dinner awaited, followed by several toasts, yummy desserts, and plenty of dancing.

With the party in full swing, I stood back and admired my friends, my family, and my life. Abigail was holding Mel on one hip while chatting it up with Amy, Luke by her side, a modest ring glistening on Amy's finger, a sign that another wedding was coming soon, despite Amy's ramblings that "she was in no hurry." Joel was dancing with Scott's mother and Scott's sister with her dad.

But that wasn't what caught my eye in that moment. It was my Uncle Aidan and Scott who remained off to the side, Aidan's hand on Scott's shoulder.

And then it all came back ...

Three months ago, I was lying on my stomach on the ledge in that awful cave, holding Scott's face upright as water continued to rush toward his nose and mouth. I kept shaking his head or slapping his cheek. "Wake up!" Scott's eyes were closed, and I wasn't even sure he was breathing. I told him how much I loved him. I told him about Rick. I told him anything that would generate a response, but nothing had.

I cried, oh, how I cried, unable to do anything but hold him. I didn't want to live. I didn't want anyone to rescue me. It was over for me.

And then, out of nowhere, the sound of feet splashing through the water slammed into my eardrums. I looked up as Uncle Aidan came rushing over with the longest crowbar I had ever seen. Only Aidan's version didn't have a curved end, just a pinched one, perfect for digging down deep.

"Scott, wake up! Aidan's here! We're going to get you out!" I shook Scott's head some more. "Uncle Aidan. Please hurry. I don't know if he's breathing." I didn't dare hope.

"I'm almost to ya, lass. We'll get him out."

I explained the situation as best I could, not sure if I was making sense.

"Calm yourself, lass. It'll all work out." When he arrived, he plunged the metal bar down deep, and his body went right behind it. More thrashing came from the water until something remarkable happened; Scott's body shifted, his feet floating upward.

I pulled Scott close until Aidan crested the surface. He threw the metal bar off to the side and helped me guide Scott's robust body to the shallows. Given the size of Scott and the size of Uncle Aidan and me, we were at a disadvantage. But, interestingly enough, we had one thing working in our favor—the very thing that had caused the problem in the first place—the water, which acted like wheels, allowing us to guide his body out of the cave and over the flooded beach.

Soon we were at the base of the stone steps that would elevate us out of danger.

"We have to get him up on land before we can check his pulse, lass."

I nodded, ready to do anything required of me to make that happen. Every second we had to wait was agony. What hope I had left was scarce. I knew how long Scott had been down there.

"I'm sorry to say, lass, but your fella is just too big for me to carry. But I have an idea. I'm gonna lie on the steps. I want ya to pull his body up over my back. If ya hand me his arms, I can pull, too. I won't be able to stand, but I can crawl up these rocky steps with ya keepin' him steady on my back. I think it will work. And my car is topside, so we can rush him to the hospital straight away. I brought your suitcases so ya can change him into dry clothes and a blanket to keep him warm."

I nodded and did exactly what Aidan asked of me.

With all the effort we both could muster, Uncle Aidan and I pulled my mountain of a man up each step until we were finally at the top.

Uncle Aidan knelt down as I helped roll Scott off his back and onto solid ground. I checked his vitals, not entirely sure I wanted to.

On my knees and with my ear on his chest, I listened, my hand on his neck, checking for a pulse. When I felt one, I didn't dare believe it. I hugged him while kissing his face and chest, thanking his heart for still beating.

"He's got a pulse. It's slow, but I felt it. I felt it, Uncle Aidan. He's alive. I know he's alive."

Uncle Aidan put a hand on my back. "Let me check, lass." He gave me a sorrowful blink. "Just to be sure."

While he examined Scott's body for signs of life, I leaned back on my calves and clutched my body, wishing I was right. I prayed to both God *and* the Devil, whoever was listening. *You want my soul? You can have it. Just please let him be—*

"You're right, lass. Now let's load him in the car."

On the ride to the hospital, I ripped Scott's T-shirt from his body, his skin more zombie-colored than human, and redressed his upper half in dry clothes. Given our confined space, the shorts were too difficult to maneuver. I covered him with a blanket and lay beside him, fearing that his lungs would stop functioning if I put too much weight on his chest. I rubbed his arms and legs as I spoke to him continuously.

"We're on our way to the hospital. Just hold on a little while longer. Don't leave me, Scott. I can't live without you. Just hold on." And then I thought of something. "You promised you'd tell me what you said to my parents at the cemetery. You can't go without telling me."

Time lost all meaning as we traveled along one road and then another, trees, houses, and buildings blending together outside my window like a time-warp video. Then Uncle Aidan pulled his clunky old sedan to a screeching halt in front of a pair of emergency room doors.

Everything was a blur after that. Attendants rushed out to us, a stretcher coming at me, then away with Scott's body loaded on top of it. Uncle Aidan answered questions. A man with short brown hair then turned to me. "How long had he been under? Did ya have to perform CPR?" I answered what I could, my arms wrapped around my waist.

When they carted Scott away, I tried to go with him, but they wouldn't let me.

Not sure what to do with myself, I waited as Uncle Aidan parked his car. When he returned, he guided me inside. "Do ya want to put on dry clothes yourself, lass? There are plenty of jacks ... toilets, I mean. And I've got your bag in the car as well."

I shook my head. "No, I'm fine." I must've looked like a monster from the black lagoon, not that Uncle Aidan looked any better, but my appearance held no importance. I could have been naked and not cared. All I cared about was Scott and how he was doing. Were they pounding on his chest right now? Or giving him the paddles? I shuddered to think about it.

"Please take me to him, Uncle Aidan," I begged.

He inhaled deeply and then stared at me like my father used to do when he was trying to be gentle with my feelings. Back then, it was mostly about Santa Claus not being real or the time our cat got hit by a car. "I can't take ya inside the room where they are workin' on him, but I can get ya close. Come on, lass." He wrapped a comforting arm around my shoulders and guided me to our final destination: a small, empty waiting room where the two of us sat anxiously.

At one point, an administrator came by who couldn't have been much older than I was. She knocked on the doorframe. "Have ya got a moment?" She then asked me to fill out some paperwork. "It will only take a minute to get ya sorted out. From what I can gather, ya have to pay out of pocket," she said since we didn't have insurance covering our stay in Ireland. The nice woman with blue highlights and a friendly smile explained how costs were much lower here than in the States. No ambulance was required, which also helped. She patted my arm. "Don't worry about it now. We'll get ya settled before ya leave us."

I nodded, barely registering anything she said. *Money? Take it. Take everything I have; just bring Scott back to me.*

The more time passed, the worse it got for me, the ache in my chest unbearable. If Scott were okay, they'd be back by now. I was spiraling. My mind lost inside a torrent of emotion.

When the doctor appeared in the doorway, I rose, terrified of what he might say. This man with the red hair and freckled skin— this man who had educated himself on saving lives—this man who was the difference between my life being over and it just beginning. He held the power. With Uncle Aidan by my side, the saint, who introduced himself as Dr. Walsh, informed us that Scott was going to be okay. "The lad has broken the lower portion of his right fibula, but his ankle appears to be sound, just sprained a wee bit and swollen, and his breathin' is steady. His body temperature is returnin' to normal. We'd like to keep him another night for—"

And then everything went black.

I awoke lying on a bed, my uncle hovering over me like a hummingbird over a flower. An elderly woman in a nurse's uniform checked my pulse on the other side of me.

"Jesus, Mary, and Joseph, ya scared the livin' daylights out of me, lass." With messy hair and scarlet cheeks, Aidan's gaze darted between me and the nurse.

I sat up, a few lingering white spots clearing from my vision. "What happened? Where's Scott?"

Before panic could take over, Uncle Aidan patted the air in a calming manner. "He's fine. And ya can even see him, once you've regained your strength, that is. Ya fainted, lass. Right after the doctor had told us your fella was gonna be okay. Went down like a sack of potatoes. I caught ya just before your head hit the floor."

Dr. Walsh appeared in the doorway. "Grand. You're awake. Are ya feelin' a fair bit better?"

I nodded, embarrassed that I had collapsed like that. I'd never fainted in my life. "I'm sorry."

The nurse let go of my hand. "Her pulse is back to normal, Doctor."

"Try drinkin' some of this." Uncle Aidan handed me a bottled water. "It's got electrolytes. Doc said you're dehydrated."

"And probably dealin' with a bit of shock as well. The cold water and the trauma can do that to ya." Dr. Walsh examined me for a few minutes, surveying my eyes and my heart rate, listening to my lungs. "No real damage done. But I'd take it easy for the next twenty-four hours. And make sure ya drink all of that." He regarded the bottle in my hand.

"I will. And thank you, Dr. ..." *What is his name?*

"Walsh. And you're most welcome. Take your time gettin' up. It's been a slow day." And with that, he was gone, his nurse, right along with him.

I swung my feet over the edge of the bed. "I'll pay for everything, Uncle Aidan. I know you don't have money." I guzzled the bottle dry, the liquid thicker than water, but refreshing nonetheless.

"Now, lass, don't ya be worryin' yourself about trivial things. Doc said they won't be chargin' for *your* short stint, and I'll leave Scott's bills for the both of ya to sort out. Fair enough? Are ya feelin' up to scratch?"

"Yes, much better."

Instead of leading me out the door, Aidan sat in a chair next to the bed. "Before we go, there're a few things I'd like to say." He stared down at his hands and then up at me. "I should have sent Robby the money I'd promised him. It was wrong of me not to. Back then, I owed a lot of bob to some bad people for gamblin' debts. I was over a barrel, ya see. If I didn't sort what I owed, I wasn't sure I'd be walkin' for much longer." He swallowed, his eyes resigned to what he was about to say. "But I promise ya, as sure as I'm sittin' here, I don't gamble no more. Been ten years now." His voice shook. "It was the day I discovered my little brother had left this world. And I keep the receipts and the letters from Robby to remind me never to follow that dark road again."

Anxious to find Scott, I stared deep into my uncle's eyes, trying my best to listen. I could feel his regret, and I could sense his desire to change. "Uncle Aidan, you just saved Scott's *and* my life. Nothing else matters to me. You can have the land. I don't want it." At that moment, I never wanted to see the land or that despicable cave again.

Aidan raised a definitive palm. "No, lass. I won't have it. I already told my business partner, no deal. It's off. And I *will* make somethin' of myself, you'll see."

"How did Declan take the news?" This wasn't exactly a small deal he was working on.

"Don't concern yourself with that." He cleared his throat. "Ya said I still have ya in my life, and I want ya to have the land." He tried to smile, his lips uncertain. "I may have exaggerated the taxes just a wee bit. Maybe you'll come back. Build a place where ya can go on holiday. Whatever ya do with it, it's yours. Your da wanted ya to have it. But we can discuss that later." His eyes gleamed with pride for a moment as he stood and placed a warm hand on my arm. "I want ya to know what a good job your mum and da have made of ya. I know they'd be proud."

His words cradled my heart and brought me closer to my dad once again. I was grateful for Aidan coming into my life. For all his flaws and his mistakes of the past, he *was* my uncle, and I loved him. "I love you, Uncle Aidan."

"Love ya, too, lass. And I'll make ya proud, you'll see." Aidan sighed. "Now let's go find your fella."

* * *

Three months later, Scott and I wed. Why three months? Scott wanted his leg fully healed. "I'm not limping down the aisle with my bride," he'd said.

After what Scott and I had been through, a justice of the peace would have suited just fine, but my two mothers weren't having it. Abigail and Beth had to plan.

A hand came sliding around my lower back, Scott leaning in for a kiss. "Come with me. I need to tell you something."

I stepped out of my memory bubble and smiled. "Where's Uncle Aidan?"

Scott tipped his chin toward the dance floor, his hand remaining on the base of my back. "He's dancing with Tazzie."

My uncle had my little sister laughing as he spun her around like a little ballerina.

Scott took my hand and led me away from the fun. We traveled down two long hallways until we came upon a private bathroom, large and luxurious, the scent of clean linen wafting from the air freshener plugged into the outlet.

"Where are we going?"

"Perks of being a member at this place for years. I know where all the private bathrooms are, and this one's the best." He winked. "I just need a moment alone with you."

Once inside and with the door locked, he parted his lips and landed them against mine, his tongue going wild. I laced my fingers through his hair and matched his passion with my own, his breath champagne sweet from our last toast.

Scott's lips danced down my neck, his hands riding up my inner thighs. "You look so hot in that dress, Babe. I could barely contain myself out there." His voice hummed with passion. "All I want to do is get inside you as quickly as I can."

"Sounds good to me, Handsome." I unlatched his belt and opened his fly, his erection ready and waiting for my stroking hands. As I worked on pleasing my man, Scott moaned, his eyes closed, his breathing heavy.

He stood back and pulled a wrapper out of the front pocket of his trousers.

He tore the package open.

"Why a condom?" I asked. "You know I'm on birth control."

"I'm well aware, Babe. I know everything about you, including how you sometimes talk in your sleep; how you love lasagna, but breakfast is your favorite meal of the day. I know what types of movies make you cry and how you love to watch horror around Halloween, also your favorite holiday. You like all music, but classic rock is your go-to, mostly because that's what you used to listen to with your parents. And you have a soft spot for anyone with a disability. I know *all* your sexual wants and when to avoid you when you're dealing with some major PMS. You name it." He tapped his temple. "I got it stored right up here."

The PMS comment was funny. *And true.* When little things like how Scott pushed a cart down a grocery store aisle ran up the back of my neck, I knew hormones were in control.

With his forefinger and his thumb, he took hold of my chin, his lips finding mine again. "To answer your question, you look like a princess in that dress, and I don't want to soil it with what I'm about to do. You got a problem with that, Mrs. Williams?"

I stepped out of my heels, shimmied out of my lace panties, and lifted my skirt. "No problem at all, Mr. Williams." I tapped the end of his nose with my finger. "And don't forget, I know just as much about you."

Scott let his pants fall, his boxers puddled around his ankles, and then he lifted me onto the white-marble counter as I opened my legs for him.

His fingers found their way inside me, gentle and skilled at knowing a woman's anatomy. "Man, you're so wet already. If I had more time, I'd have to taste your sweet nectar."

I closed my eyes, enjoying the internal massage. *Do whatever you want.*

"I've never had sex with a married woman before," he said, a note of derision in his voice. "That I know of."

"Oh, yeah?" I opened my eyes as he winked.

"This will be a first for me. And before I put a baby in that gorgeous belly of yours, I hope you don't mind if I spend the next few years spoiling the shit out of you. Or, as your uncle would say, shite." He grinned, his lips peppering mine with kisses, his fingers diving deeper.

I gripped the edge of the counter, my knuckles turning white. *Oh, God.* As my breathing labored, my insides went haywire. I spoke through pants. "I think I can handle that, Mr. Williams. Just no more cave sex, if you don't mind." I meant it as a joke, but Scott didn't receive it that way.

Scott removed his fingers.

No. Don't stop.

He jerked his head back, his eyes narrow and feigning outrage.

I think he was feigning.

"What do you mean? When we go back to Ireland, we *have* to try it again. We know the layout now. That would never happen again. You can't deny me, your man, this one simple pleasure, can you? I've got it all planned out."

Since we cut our original trip short for obvious reasons, we were planning a belated honeymoon next spring that would take us back to Europe, and Ireland, a definite stop on our itinerary. I realized the cave-sex idea was *not* an idle threat.

Once I caught my breath, I gave him a look. *Are you crazy?*

Scott cupped the side of my jaw and spoke with such tenderness, my defenses evaporated like a fine mist. "You can't possibly be afraid. Not you. And not after everything you've been through. Whatever challenges or adventures await us in Ireland or wherever else we go, I know you can handle them. And one thing I've come to realize about you, Babe, is that life with you will never be dull. I wouldn't want it any other way." He tilted his head, the warmth from his words sprinkling down on me like magic from Tinker Bell's wand. "So, cave sex is a go, then?"

The look in his eyes told me he was serious. Of course he was.

I shook my head, not willing to give in to this idea. I mean, Aidan had just saved his life *and mine* from our reckless behavior. What was he thinking? "No way. No cave sex. No cave anything. I'll do anything but that."

He bent closer, his lips brushing against my ear. "Not even if I tell you what I say to your parents every time we go to the cemetery?"

Crap. He always managed to find my weak spot. As he said, he knew me well. "You are such a brat." I pursed my lips, knowing he had now gained the upper hand. "Fine. What did you say, then?"

He took a breath. "I thanked them for creating such an incredible woman"—he kissed me—"and I promised them that I would protect you and make you happy for the rest of my life." His smile melted away, a more resolute expression taking its place. "And I meant every word. I will always be here to protect and love you."

My heart melted. His words touched me so deeply. And I was sure my parents understood. What a man I had chosen. My soulmate.

And then his smile returned, a zing sparking in his eyes. "Trouble is, you keep saving everyone else's life." He looked upward and tapped his index finger against his chin. "Come to think of it, maybe I should have said *you* were the one who was going to protect *me*." He lowered his gaze to meet mine. "And, just so you know, I remember what you told me about Rick. Good thing *you* kicked his sorry ass because you saved me the trouble." He fanned his hands out. "See. Not freaking out on you." And then he tickled me for comedic impact, making me squeal. "Can I assume cave sex is back on the table, then? Or should I say the ledge? A deal's a deal."

"You are unbelievable. Is there anywhere you *don't* want to have sex?"

Scott leaned in, his voice husky. "Not where you're concerned." He tapped a few more kisses on my lips, his tongue brushing the edge of my mouth. "The question is, Mrs. Williams, are you ready to take a leap with me."

It was a silly question, considering I had just married the man, but I understood his meaning. Was my mind open to new possibilities?

I thought about that. Nothing about my past had ever been *normal*. At times, I wondered if I had been cursed. But I also had to remind myself that in spite of all the ugliness that had transpired, I still managed to find a bonus mom, one who came with a little sister and a kindhearted stepfather, a best friend who could go head-to-head with any foe, and an actual blood relative in my Uncle Aidan. Best of all, I found the love of my life, a man who continued to make me swoon every time he looked at me.

I sighed. "I sure am." And then I thought about something my Uncle Aidan had said to me when we were at the hospital in Ireland. "You know, Uncle Aidan mentioned me using the land in Ireland for vacations or holidays. Wouldn't that be cool? We could build a small place there to visit. Our friends and family could use it, too." I still had a hefty savings, and I knew Scott, who had also inherited money from his grandfather, did as well, not to mention the land *his* parents had just given us. With no college loan payments, we were doing quite well for ourselves.

Scott smirked. "That's fine, Babe, just don't let Uncle Aidan design it."

We both chuckled for a moment at the thought.

"No one gets to design our place but my sexy architect."

That brought another smile to Scott's lips, a glimmer to his eyes. He regarded me for a moment before he seemed to shift his mind to something else. "We've got guests waiting, woman. Now, move those hips closer. I've got a job to do. You see, I have this insatiable wife who can't get enough of me."

I laughed as I wrapped my legs around my husband's waist, thinking *no truer statement had ever been made.*

Tell me what you think.

I am eager to hear what you think of *Handfast*. If you feel inspired to do so, I'd appreciate a review on Amazon, Goodreads, and/or Bookbub (no spoilers, please).

I see more adventures for Sara and Scott down the road, not all of them on American soil.

Stay tuned for future updates.

Also by Tricia T. LaRochelle

FLICKERING HEART and *REVIVE*, books 1 and 2 in the *SARA BROWNE SERIES*

Acknowledgments

It was a dream come true to publish *Flickering Heart* last year and then *Revive* just a few months later. It is exciting to work with these great characters and see them evolve through their good times and bad. I'm proud of whom Sara and Scott have become. They have taken on a life of their own. Most of the time, they tell me what *they* want to say. I am just their vessel.

I want to thank a few people who stuck with me, not just for my first book but for all three.

To 17 Studio Book Design, thank you again for creating a cover that blends well with the *SARA BROWNE SERIES*. You did well.

Thank you to Rottie Books and Indie Penn for taking on this project to promote and distribute and to those wonderful book bloggers who get the word out and support authors in any way they can.

My website designer, Zuni.com, has always responded quickly and creatively whenever a new book emerges. I am grateful to you.

I am so thankful to my talented writer, friend, and editor, Kim Catanzarite, for her sharp editing advice, proofing, and anything else that lands on the literary spectrum. Her knowledge and wisdom blow me away every time. I value her opinion immensely. Her contributions to *Handfast* were immeasurable. Knowing Kim is on the other end of my emails, I feel less alone in this vast publishing world.

Melissa S. Harrison was my first writing partner, and although we've not always been in constant contact over the years, we have managed to stay current in each other's lives. Melissa's expert advice, impeccable proofing, and attention to detail on *Handfast* were beyond helpful. Her kind and encouraging words guided me through more than a few tricky patches.

My daughter-in-law, Hattie Firebaugh, is a natural at proofreading and a gem for any other input I may need. Her advice is always sound, and her support is unyielding. I am proud of her and all of her accomplishments. She is an incredible young woman. Welcome to the family!

My son, Ryan, is the perfect man to keep Scott from sounding inauthentic. His proofing skills still manage to amaze me. Ryan is supportive, kind, and brilliant, making me proud every day of my life.

My husband, Bob, has always been my rock. He's outstanding regarding book advice and my sounding board whenever I have a new idea I want to explore. I couldn't do this without his constant encouragement. I've lost count of the walks we've taken where we discussed a new scene in the book or a possible marketing opportunity. This journey is as much for him as it is for me.

Finally, thank you, readers, for taking the time to read my books. A time commitment of this magnitude should not be taken lightly. I hope my stories have entertained you and made it worth the effort.

About the Author

Since she was a little girl, award-winning author, Tricia T. LaRochelle, has been obsessed with tragic love stories. No beach reads for her. Bring on the grit with a double side of turmoil. She likes to feel the character's anguish as they fight to overcome obstacles to be together.

Growing up in central Vermont, she has seen her share of tragedy but remains a hopeful romantic. She now lives in Virginia where she continues to foster the possibilities of how love can conquer all.

Her book *Flickering Heart* won first place in the 2022 Incipere Awards for romance, and her sequel, *Revive,* received an honorable mention in the same category.

Stay tuned for updates and announcements on Facebook, Instagram, and Twitter, or sign up for her newsletter at Tricia-LaRochelle.com.